THE GIRL VANISHED

JESSICA ANN

SOMEDAY LADY
PUBLISHING LLC.

THE GIRL VANISHED

Published by Someday Lady Publishing LLC

ISBN-13: 979-8-9992879-7-7

The story of Della started a long, long time ago around a crackling campfire on the shores of the real Bear Lake with the stars hanging above like celestial spiderwebs in the night sky and the echoes of the past drifting over the water from the abandoned girls camp across the lake.

This book is dedicated to the little girl who sat at that campfire and dreamed of one day writing a story like this.

Little Jessie Annie, you did it.

Note to Reader

Note to reader:

This story mentions traumatic pregnancy loss. If you'd rather not read that part, skip Chapter Eighteen. You'll still get the story if you do.

And know this – nothing will ever happen to the dog. I make it my solemn vow.

ONE

The most difficult part of my job is convincing Dottie Uttin she needs to wear underwear.

"I don't care if it's period authentic, Dottie. This is a family production, and you must be wearing underwear," I tell her for the seventh time.

Allie Kim glances up at me, eyes woeful, pins pinched between her lips as she kneels at Dottie's feet, once more fixing the hem of a period-appropriate nineteenth-century walking dress in gray muslin after Dottie tore it going to the bathroom for the third time during her fitting.

Dottie is eighty-two. She's allowed to pee as many times as she'd like. That's not why I'm here.

As director of programs for the Bellegrave Historical Society, the Founder's Day reenactment is Allie's rodeo, and she only calls me in for the big stuff. Like getting Dottie Uttin to wear underwear.

The three of us are crammed into Allie's small office in the recesses of the second floor of the Bellegrave Public Library. The room once stored the archive for the *Bellegrave Bulletin*, but I'd luckily had that digitized before the Great Plumbing

Explosion of 2015. The room had flooded along with a good portion of the children's section of the library below it, destroying a complete collection of Nancy Drew books, which I personally remedied because a library without Nancy Drew books is no library at all.

At the time of the plumbing mishap, this room had only been used for moderate storage, and all that was damaged were a few linens that were quickly repaired by the miracle of dry cleaning. When the library board offered us these second-floor rooms as our winter offices, I'd given Allie this space because small as it was, it was the largest of the rooms here. I knew she would need the space for costumes that were part of the living history performed at the historical society's great camp, Lady Josephine Lodge, during the summer season and for the annual reenactment of Founder's Day, the official start to the summer season in the small Adirondack lake town that celebrates the day when Peter Bellegrave arrived at Bear Lake to build a manor to bring tourists to the wilderness.

The reenactment is followed by a gala that serves as the Bellegrave Historical Society's biggest fundraiser of the year. And as the historical society's executive director, that's my rodeo. As a small Adirondack town, so many people's livelihoods depend on tourist dollars that start to flow after the official kickoff to summer, and my *entire* job relies on the gala being a success.

This is why Dottie Uttin must wear underpants.

"But a woman of my class wouldn't be caught dead wearing drawers, Della. You know as much. How am I to get into character if all of my bits are clogged up like that?" Dottie raises her eyebrows one after the other, and I can't help but think the bushy white lines are like caterpillars inching across her face.

"No," I say, not bothering to elaborate. "Underwear goes on or you don't."

Dottie sticks her tongue out at me, and I stick mine back out at her. Later she'll stop by the cottage with thumbprint cookies and a jar of her homemade elderberry wine and try to convince me once again to plant rhubarb because it's good for the ovaries.

I'm back to sorting stockings for the actors playing the townswomen when a flurry of red, white, and blue sails through the door, the head of David Knolls peeking out above the mass of bunting.

"This simply will not do," he proclaims and holds the fabric out for my inspection.

I see nothing of concern and merely raise my eyes to his.

"This bunting has *faded*," he adds, giving the fabric a good shake as if this will make his point clear. "The red has turned to *maroon*."

I'm not sure which is worse, faded or maroon. He says both with such disdain.

David Knolls, Bellegrave's premier real estate agent, is only a few years older than my forty, but he's prematurely gray, which makes him appear a great deal older than he is. He favors pressed khakis with button-down shirts often printed in patterns of aquatic creatures. Today he's wearing periwinkle blue decorated in narwhals. He has a broom mustache from the eighties, and while on someone else it would look dated and out of place, on him, it gives definite Tom Selleck vibes, which the single people (and married ones) of Bellegrave lament because he's taken.

He's also British, a fact that continues to surprise everyone because if time travel is ever invented, David Knolls will be the first person to use it to travel back to 1776 and join them Yankee rebels.

"I'm going to ask Quinn if there's anything we can do to save it," he says, referring to his husband who has kept the costumes at the Bellegrave Stock Theater for the past fifteen years. "Lord knows there isn't money in the budget for it."

I bite my lip to keep from smiling as David repeats a phrase I use so ubiquitously my secretary, Frances Blum, had it printed on a mug she gave me a few Christmases ago.

"What's not in the budget?" The historical society's facilities director, Steve Fitzpatrick, appears behind David in the doorway.

David shows him the bunting, but Steve just shrugs, nearly sloshing the coffee out of his Buffalo Bills coffee mug.

"It's bunting."

"It's faded," David reiterates with the same disgust before stomping out the door.

"We're lucky to have volunteers like David," I remind Steve who is already turning toward the space we had converted to a break room at the end of the hall.

He shrugs again. "I just don't see what the fuss is about. Peter Bellegrave came tramping into the middle of nowhere. Set up a hotel, disrupted indigenous hunting parties, instigated the near extinction of forests in the Adirondacks, and died of tuberculosis leaving a heap of debt his estate could never cover. I don't see why we celebrate him."

"Because of him, you and many people have jobs. With dental," I remind him, knowing he left early the previous day to take his youngest son to the orthodontist to have his braces tightened.

Steve raises his coffee mug. "All Hail, Peter Bellegrave!" he calls and saunters off in the direction of coffee.

I start when Steve is immediately replaced by someone else. The offices are busy this time of year as we prepare for both Founder's Day and the opening of Lady Josephine Lodge after the spring thaw, but the person before me is neither a volunteer nor one of the very few members of my staff.

It's my best friend and detective at the Bellegrave Police

Department, Carmen Neil, and she's carrying a telltale mauve rectangular bakery box.

"No," I say before she has a chance to say anything.

Her brilliant smile of perfectly straight teeth vanishes. "C'mon," she whines with a heavy dose of guilt directed at me. Her earrings, the size of frisbees, bob as she taps the mauve box with one hot pink manicured hand. "They're still hot."

She doesn't need to say what because I know what's in that box. I know because Carmen Neil has been my best friend since second grade when her family moved to Bellegrave from Manhattan for a better life for their children, a yard for their dog, and fresh air.

Carmen would have selected several chocolate croissants and a single black and white cookie from Cake & Cookie, the bakery on Water Street, knowing full well I'd eat a croissant now and the cookie during my two p.m. slump.

Both Allie and Dottie snicker behind me, and I glance down to where Allie's tying off her stitches.

"We all know you're going to listen to her just for the croissant," she says around her mouthful of pins.

I can only give her a frown before Frances steps in front of the door, blocking out Carmen as Frances's sharp eyes zero in on me over the rimless glasses perched at the very tip of her pointed nose.

"Your husband called," she says in her no-nonsense, atonal yet slightly husky voice.

Frances started working here after her first son was born. Her sixth grandson got his driver's license last week. I imagine she'll never quit working, and one day she'll disappear into the archives with the rest of Bellegrave's history. She likes sweater sets, and today she's wearing the plum one that sets off her long white hair that she wears parted in the middle and swept back in a bun pinned low at the nape of her neck.

"He said he's been trying to reach you, but he thinks you've lost your phone again."

My hand goes to the back pocket of my jeans, but my fingers find only emptiness. I bite my lower lip. Logan has been on me to get a smartwatch for months if only to alleviate some of the annoyance for others trying to reach me when I've misplaced my phone, which happens with stunning regularity.

I force a chagrined smile. "And what did Mr. James want?" I ask.

"He said he has to head into Albany this afternoon. Some emergency about an easement."

Albany. Again.

"Emergency, huh?" Carmen mutters.

I meet her gaze, and she gives me the same look she and every member of my family has been giving me since Logan started making these unusually frequent trips to Albany.

Instead of pressing me though, Carmen holds up the box. "I brought sugar."

"The last time you brought sugar to the office I got bedbugs from that sleazy motel the state put me up in at Monticello."

Carmen smiles a smile more suited to a second-grade teacher and not a decorated detective with the Bellegrave Police. "We treat our expert witnesses with the utmost care."

I frown. "I'd hate to see what you do to your suspects."

Carmen's smile doesn't waver. "Chinese finger traps."

"I knew it." I nod in the direction of my office down the hall. "Let's get this over with."

Frances lowers her chin, her eyes locking on mine, and it's like upping the power on a laser beam set to annihilate. "And what about Mr. James?"

"I'll text him," I say. I turn back to Allie. "You got this?"

She waves a hand, the pin cushion strapped to her wrist sparkling in the weak watery April light from the single window at the back of the room. "I've got this, I've got this," she mutters.

"You think I shouldn't be wearing drawers, don't you, Allie dear?" I hear Dottie probe as I leave the room, and I know that conversation isn't over yet.

Carmen is already in my office when I get there, pouring water into the single-serve espresso maker she got me at Christmas because she enjoys enabling my caffeine addiction.

My office is small, but as I'm only in it for the few short winter months when the lodge is closed, it suits me fine. I've made it cozy with stacks of musty boxes caring and thoughtful, if misguided, villagers have dropped off, filled with their family heirlooms they are just so sure the historical society would want. Sometimes I'll find a rare gem in one of the boxes, so I keep taking them in even if they're mostly filled with water-stained insurance calendars and receipts for fast food.

I've covered the uneven wooden floorboards with a rug I bought on clearance from Maeve's Home Furnishings on Water Street, and the bookcase underneath the swarm of dog-eared reference books came out of my parents' basement.

My desk is an old dining room table from my college apartment I could never bring myself to part with, and it holds my laptop surrounded by unfinished grant applications, academic journals, and this morning's *Bellegrave Bulletin*.

"Logan's going into Albany again, huh?" Carmen asks as she starts the milk frother and bends to retrieve the milk from the mini fridge under the espresso machine.

I shake my laptop awake to check my calendar for my next appointment time that afternoon and see I'm free the rest of the day. I can only hope Frances will interrupt us with some emergency, so I don't have to tell my best friend *no* to her face. I like to save those kinds of loving messages for text.

I minimize my calendar, and the dopey, drooly face of my

chocolate lab grins back at me. I can't help but smile and shut my laptop as Carmen hands me a cup, steaming and fragrant.

"If only you looked at humans the way you look at your dog," she mutters.

"If only humans knew unconditional love," I reply, taking a blistering sip of my espresso. It burns all the way down just as I like it.

It's a second before I realize Carmen is blinking at me.

"Do I need to tell you again it's been thirteen years?"

"Nope." I take another sip, savor the bitterness of it as it fills my cheeks. I swallow. "My mother reminds me every Sunday night at dinner."

"Then how about the fact that he chose you?" She pauses, and I know this is for emphasis. "To. Live." There it is.

"Nope, I know that as well. And I still have your therapist's card from the last time you gave it to me." I place my mug on my Nancy Drew coaster and poke at the Cake & Cookie box, selecting an exquisitely puffy croissant. "Now tell me why you're here, darling." I toss her a sarcastic smile and take an overlarge bite of my croissant as I begin the hunt for my phone somewhere in the detritus on my desk.

"Bob Reynolds," she says without preamble.

The croissant turns to ash in my mouth.

"Nope," I mumble around the buttery remnants on my tongue.

"You said you would listen," Carmen protests, getting her own coffee and settling in the chair across the table from me.

I plop into my chair and wash down the now undesirable croissant with more coffee. "I said let's get this over with. I didn't say I'd listen."

My fingers latch on to my phone under last month's copy of *Museum Curator*, and I tilt the screen so I can see it.

Three missed calls, and I'm not sure how many texts. I swipe up and scan Logan's messages. Albany. He'll let the dog out when he goes back to the cottage to pack a bag. He'll try to be back by Friday. Today is Tuesday. I type a quick reply and shove the phone back under the magazine.

When I look up, Carmen's face is a maze of disappointed lines.

"Bob Reynolds once told me to go into the Navy because I wasn't going to amount to anything else," I say.

Carmen peels off a layer of croissant with her hot pink nails. "He said that to everyone at least once. You know he only became superintendent of schools because of Marty's connections." She pauses, her face scrunching into a grimace. "He never really was good with kids." She pops the croissant into her mouth and chews thoughtfully.

"You know I don't like doing this stuff, and now you're asking me to do it for the Reynoldses?" I look around my cramped office. "Maybe next I'll pop over the pond and ask King Charles if he has any ghosts he'd like me to evict from Buckingham Palace."

Carmen shakes her head. "Bob is dying, Del. Martha says the doctors told him he has months if not weeks. She just wants him to know what happened to his daughter before he dies."

"Lisa Reynolds disappeared like twenty-five years ago."

"Twenty-seven," Carmen clarifies.

I wave a hand as if swatting away a fly. "Same thing. If there was anything left to find, it's probably gone by now."

Carmen makes a face that sends her earrings bobbing. "Is that how it works?"

I shrug. "I don't know how any of this works."

You know that part in the movie *Sixth Sense* when the kid tells Bruce Willis he can see ghosts? I didn't know that was the twist. I thought everyone could see ghosts.

I didn't know anything at all was strange about me until my first-grade teacher, Mrs. Nickelson, asked to speak to my mother after school. Mrs. Nickelson was huge, giant of hip and shoulder, and not at all what you would think of when you might conjure an image of a first-grade teacher. She wore her hair clipped shorter than she should have and hair-sprayed into a puff of right angles on her head. She only wore big, swinging skirts of military-grade material, and I often wondered if she were really a troll. I still wonder actually.

Mrs. Nickelson told my mother she was concerned about how frequently I was talking to myself and wanted to recommend me for mental health testing. My mother only smiled and led me away. I spent the remainder of first grade at the Catholic school in Saranac, and my mother told me not to speak to the ghosts in school.

Carmen purses her lips and plucks another layer from her croissant. "Lisa Reynolds disappeared on the night of April 25th, 1997. She was driving her red 1989 Oldsmobile Cutlass home from the high school after Key Club, but she never made it. The car was recovered the next day on Route 3. Blood found in the trunk of the car matched Lisa's. That's it. No ransom note, no more clues, dead end after dead end for twenty-five years."

"Twenty-seven," I correct around a mouthful of croissant.

Carmen gives me the second-grade-teacher look again.

I swallow the bite of croissant. "What exactly do you want from me?"

"Come with me to the Reynolds house. Marty says she's kept Lisa's room just as it was since the day she disappeared. Just stand in the room and tell me if you feel anything."

"That's it?"

Carmen leans back, hands spread. "That's it. I promise. If you don't feel anything, we let it go."

I let my gaze drift out the single-pane window of my office. It's the original nine over nine glazed window, and the image of downtown Bellegrave beyond it is blurry, but I feel the tug of affection for it anyway.

Settled around Bear Lake in a valley just south of Saranac in the Adirondacks, the village center of Bellegrave is made up of most of the original brick and stone buildings that now serve as a home to the shops and businesses along Main Street where the public library sits, and their facades proclaim names of long forgotten outfits like Providence Vine Bank and Otis and Son Haberdashery.

My favorite is the building almost to the end of town on the right side of Main Street, overlooking the lake at the bottom of the valley, the single word Water spelled out in pink granite along its top. I don't know what or who Water is. It was one of the first things I tried to find when I became director of the Bellegrave Historical Society when I returned to the village after grad school, but even in my years of searching the archives, I never found reference to it. I like to think it's just a founder of the village reminding everyone of the important part water has played in the life of Bellegrave. Maybe in the life of everyone.

"Remember Lisa Reynolds?" Carmen says now with a slight disbelieving tone interrupting my reverie. "What a girl. She could have been so mean as popular as she was, but she wasn't. Remember?"

I nod, my mind drifting back to 1997 and the horrible awkwardness that is seventh grade. Is there anything crueler than a combined middle/high school? Forcing awkward middle schoolers to mingle with blossoming teenagers?

Lisa Reynolds had a curtain of red-gold hair that undulated as if it were alive. She would turn her head, a musical laugh trilling from her lips, and you could just make out the pert tip of her nose. I'd never felt the grubbiness of my thrift store jeans and bangs I'd cut myself more than when I saw Lisa Reynolds walking down the hall in front of me.

"She had everything. Beauty, brains, talent, drive." Carmen sounds like she's writing Lisa's dating profile. She leans forward suddenly. "Remember how she started donating blood right when she turned sixteen? Wanted to donate ten times before she graduated and went off to—" She stops, her hand stretched toward the window, the muted morning light reflecting off her glossy nails. "Where was she going?"

"Berklee in Boston," I supply.

Carmen drops her hand. "Lord, the pipes that girl had." She shakes her head. "She had everything, Del, and she was still the nicest person I ever met."

"You hardly knew her. She was a senior, and we were ogres."

Carmen ignores this. "Something terrible happened to her, Del, and you can help us find out what."

I pick at my croissant. "You know I don't like doing this, Carmen."

She leans forward again and nearly knocks me out of my chair with her earnestness. "I know. I know, and I'm only asking this one time."

"You've asked like a hundred times since you made detective."

Carmen lets her eyes drift innocently upward. "A hundred? Really?" Her voice goes up an octave.

"You're right. Probably closer to two hundred."

Carmen leans back and crosses her arms over her stomach. "Della James, you know you're coming with me to the Reynolds house."

It's at that moment Frances pokes her head into my office.

"The bags for the gala party favors just came in," she says, her voice brusquer in the confined space. "They're leopard print."

I blink, my croissant and espresso turning in my stomach

before looking back at Carmen. "Why don't we go now? It looks like my morning just opened up."

Two

The Reynolds home sits on a small peninsula at the west end of the lake. While the east end was built up by weekenders looking to escape work in Albany or Utica in a modest fisherman's cabin, the west end was made of homes built in the very last years of the nineteenth century by industrialists and financial tycoons from New York. Sprawling, magnificent homes with towers and wraparound porches often referred to as Adirondack great camps like the historical society's Lady Josephine Lodge.

The Reynolds home is one of those, a late-nineteenth-century camp that sits on several acres stretching from the county highway out to where the main house sits on the peninsula surrounded by the dark waters of Bear Lake.

Like Lady Josephine Lodge, there is a lengthy drive to the main house, and we pass several outbuildings that show signs of neglect, which unfortunately, is common for great camps as the expense of keeping them up is prohibitive even for a family like the Pruitts, who come from plastics money out of Plattsburgh and who purchased the camp from the original owners probably in the latter half of the last century. Any resources are usually dedicated to the camp's main lodge and focal piece of the camp, which means the outbuildings fall into disrepair.

Great camps were designed to be self-sufficient. Many still contain the remnants of the farms and service buildings that had supported them and the cottages that once served as guest quarters and private bedrooms. It's not unusual to see multiple buildings occupying the site of a great camp. While at Lady Josephine Lodge, the outbuildings have been restored to their original purpose to allow us to conduct an outdoor living history museum on the grounds, private owners use outbuildings for storing their boats and snowmobiles, and some even rent the cottages to tourists.

When we pass a small track off the main drive that cuts through the forest, I imagine more outbuildings lingering in the forests and worry they may be in worse condition.

But even now in early April, the lawns are well-kept, and the main drive shows signs of having been recently graded. I'm not surprised as such attention to detail fits with the image I have of Martha Reynolds from my school days.

My anticipation builds as the drive curves toward the peninsula. I've only seen the camp from the lake, its beauty obscured by trees, and despite my reluctance to be there, the historian in me is eager to see the camp from its land entrance.

Except when the main house comes into view, my anticipation evaporates. At some point the camp had been updated, and while I had been expecting peeled logs and notched corners, a roofline dissected by dormers, I am met with planked logs covered in clapboard stained a greenish gray and faux corners that are nothing more than square blocks of wood designed to appear as though they were interlocking logs.

The main house perches at the end of the drive where a cluster of boulders peek up from the ground, crowding the rear entrance of the main structure. The original builder likely situated the structure with those boulders in mind to allow the camp to blend with the nature around it. From the left of the main structure is a walkway that at some point was likely open to the air but is now closed off to form a hallway leading to a circular room that might be a dining room or library.

The main entrance would have been on the water side as camps were built to be approached via water, and I wasn't expecting much, but even this is disappointing.

"This is it?" I say to Carmen as she puts the car in park. "I thought Martha Reynolds came from money."

"Pruitt," she says. "She kept her maiden name."

"For real?" I look at her in disbelief. "I've always called her Mrs. Reynolds. All through school."

"I think a lot of people do, but you know Marty. She wouldn't say anything. She wouldn't want to be rude."

I shrug. "I get it," I say. "I only changed my name so I would have the same last name as our kids."

Carmen looks at me swiftly. "What?"

Ignoring the question, I nod at the house where the door on the porch has just opened. "Ms. Pruitt is waiting," I say and get out of the car.

Martha Pruitt stands on the small porch, her hands folded in front of her. I can't make out her expression as she is still in shadow, and I wonder if she's pleased I've come or nervous. I can never tell which way it's going to go with people, but I'm usually only called in when someone is desperate, and desperate people can do strange things.

"Marty," Carmen says, climbing the wooden steps to greet the older woman.

Marty Pruitt has always reminded me of a bird both in appearance and behavior. I haven't seen her much since graduating high school, and I find she hasn't really changed. She's too thin, so her birdlike features are more distinct than they might be if she carried more weight. Her nose has a slight beakish quality to it that accentuates her eyes. She wears her hair short, and it's gone entirely white now. She favors gold jewelry, and she's wearing a pair of gold pear earrings with a slight sparkle where the stem would be.

I remember from school functions when she would address someone directly, she would lay a soft hand on their shoulder as gentle as the wing of a bird, and it's a gesture I've come to associate with the upper class.

She does it now as she greets us. "Carmen, thank you for coming." Her hand falls softly on Carmen's shoulder. Her voice is careful, polished, and I picture a young Marty Pruitt pressed into elocution lessons, and I'm immediately flooded with pity for her. "I know this is a lot to ask."

"Marty, this is Dr. Della James," Carmen says as I step up beside her. "You probably remember her from school."

I smile and reach out a hand, but Ms. Pruitt doesn't take it. She studies me with those protruding eyes.

"So it's true. You're a psychic."

In a place as small as Bellegrave, it's hard to avoid the rumors about you, especially ones that involve talking to the dead.

"I'm a historian," I answer, which makes her lips pinch. "I just feel things any human is capable of feeling but which we sometimes forget how to feel as we get older."

Ms. Pruitt holds her hands in front of her, one folded over the other delicately like the wings of a bird. "Any human?"

I nod. "You know the feeling of unease you get when you peer into a dark basement?"

Ms. Pruitt's gaze shifts to Carmen and back to me. "That's hardly the same thing."

"It's exactly the same thing. It's your sixth sense warning you to be careful. It's just over time we've evolved, our lives have become easier, and the need for survival less urgent." I shrug again. "Some people lost that sense all together."

Ms. Pruitt doesn't look as though she believes me.

Carmen steps forward and places a hand on the woman's shoulder while indicating the house with the other. "Why don't we go inside, and you can tell Della about your daughter. About Lisa."

Ms. Pruitt gives me one more assessing glance before turning back to the house. We step into an entryway the walls of which are constructed of planked logs still in their original color, I'm relieved to see. A staircase winds its way up to the right, its railing made of twig and branch design. Ms. Pruitt beckons us down a long and narrow hallway at the end of which is a rectangle of light.

I can't stop myself from peering around me, studying the white chinking between the log planks and the peeled saplings used as trim around the doors. There are two picture frames hanging on the wall to the right. They stand out as the rest of the space is empty of decor, and I take a second to look at them.

One is the original architectural plans for the camp, its original name in small capital letters at the bottom right edge. *Camp Wildmere*. I thought I remembered the Pruitts changing the name of the camp when Walter Pruitt, likely Ms. Pruitt's father, purchased the camp, and I make a note to search the property records for the original owner.

The other frame contains a print of a black-and-white photograph featuring a group of young men in uncomfortable-looking uniforms blazoned with a big B. They're standing on a riverbank beside a small wooden craft I take to be a rowing skull. The name of the boat is clear in white letters along its bow. *Caledonia*.

Carmen's and Ms. Pruitt's voices have faded, and I walk as quickly as possible down the hall to catch up. I find myself in a great room lit from the weak sunshine coming through the windows at the opposite end that overlook the lake. The windows are plate glass bordered in diamond panes, which break up the light as it comes through. The view is obscured by tree growth, but I can just make out the roof of the boathouse at the water's edge.

The great room itself is a double-story space decorated in what looks to be custom twig and branch furniture with a fireplace made of dressed granite at the base and rubble rock at the top, taking up the entire wall to my right. The second-floor gallery spills out from either side of the chimney, disappearing into shadow, but I can just make out the maple and cherry alternating beadboard in the hallway above.

"We'll be most comfortable in the library," Ms. Pruitt says as she fades into the next room.

I follow, but something makes me stop. I look around, my senses prickling, but there's nothing there. There's no *one* there. I wait a moment longer, sure something has caught my awareness, but my conscious mind can't figure out what it is. I follow Ms. Pruitt and Carmen into the next room.

The library is a single-story structure at one end that branches into a double-story at the far end with eyebrow dormers and clerestory diamond windows allowing sunlight to penetrate the gloom of an April afternoon. The walls on each side contain built-in bookcases and even a custom desk fitted into the wall under a diamond-paned window. The room ends in a semicircle where a small seating arrangement sits before a bank of windows, and this is where Ms. Pruitt leads us.

"Please sit," she says.

I take one of the chairs nearest the windows, so I have a good view of the room. I don't like sitting with my back to the room, not since my dead grandfather snuck up on me in 1989. It's quiet in this room, unusually so, but the carpet beneath my feet is squishy and the walls are draped with tapestries where there are no bookcases, and I imagine it's a strategy to muffle the sound in such a space.

Carmen takes the seat beside me as Ms. Pruitt perches on a chair opposite, her back to the windows like me so it's hard to read her expression as her face is once more in shadow.

"Bob doesn't need to know about this," Ms. Pruitt says in a rushed voice that's unusual for her, and I realize suddenly how this is taxing her. I wonder just how desperate she is for answers. "It's just—" I look back to see her worrying her hands, a gesture I can't recall her ever making. "It's just I don't want to get his hopes up. Not now with everything he's going through."

It hadn't taken long for news of Bob Reynolds's diagnosis of pancreatic cancer to spread through Bellegrave, nor for the dire determination that he was dying to follow swiftly behind it. It's one of the things about a small town that sometimes grates. While the members of a small town want to smother you in pity and concern, they can also hurry you to imminent tragedy.

I don't like to see people who are actively dying, a morbid phrase, and I'm fine with never having to encounter Bob himself.

Carmen lays a calming hand on Ms. Pruitt's agitated ones. "It's all right, Marty. What happens today stays between us. Now tell us about Lisa."

"What is there to say that hasn't already been in the papers? Or gossiped about at Shelly's counter?" she asks, referring to the lunch counter at Shelly's Diner in the village. She gestures toward me. "You knew Lisa in school. What else can I say?"

Carmen answers before I can remind Marty that her daughter was a good deal older than me. "Perhaps tell us what Lisa meant to you. What were the things you remember most about her. How was she acting the day she disappeared?"

Marty shifts in her seat, not in an uncomfortable way but as though she's settling in to give her answer. How many times has she been asked this question? How many opportunities has she been given to solidify her answer into something other than the truth? These are questions I'm forced to ask in order to find and latch on to the right energy in a situation such as this.

"You know what Lisa was like," she says, keeping to the same tone of her story. "She was the light of every room, the laughter that filled empty spaces, the heart of this family."

Marty has had years to perfect what she says about her missing daughter, and she *has* perfected her speech. I recall those few times when she would attend school functions with her husband, and though the memories are vague, I remember this about her. She always knew what to say and how to say it perfectly.

She might not be hiding anything, and she might not be trying to present a certain image of her family. She might just be being herself. This won't help me connect with Lisa though as it's far too circumspect. I need something personal if I'm to find her.

"Why don't you tell us a story about when she was young, Ms. Pruitt?" I say.

It's easier to capture youth. Young people have had less time to build those defenses that will allow them to blend in, and I can more easily attach to youthful energy that's unbidden.

"Please call me Marty," she says with a twitch of her nose. She takes a deep breath. "Well, when Lisa was small, about three years old, she spotted a caterpillar on the sidewalk. She started yelling. I remember because we were on our way to the square for the start of Old Home Days along with everyone else, and Lisa's screeching drew everyone's attention." Marty's hand floats up to her cheek, pressing there dramatically. "I was so ashamed, but Lisa wouldn't quit until I unbuckled her from her stroller and let her get down. She marched right over to that caterpillar and picked him up with her little hands. Set him aside on the grass. I couldn't quite believe it. Bob couldn't even believe it." She says this with a forward lean as if to emphasize her point. "She just had to save that caterpillar. I knew right then Lisa was going to be someone special." Her voice hitches now, but her eyes remain dry. "She was someone special," she finishes, her voice softer.

"Did Lisa's habits change in the weeks leading up to her disappearance?" Carmen asks. "Did she make any new friends? Stop hanging out with old ones?"

Marty's lips pinch again, her eyes narrowing in thought. "No, no. Lisa wasn't really like that. Once she made up her mind about something she really stuck to it. She had the same friends from kindergarten to senior year, and from the first time she heard Whitney Houston sing, she knew that's what she wanted to do." She pauses, her head tilting. "She did mention some people she met at the Gale Center. You remember that goal she made about donating blood? That's where a collection center was set up once a month. I took her there initially for her appointments, but once she started driving, she took herself after school, and I lost track of the volunteers who were there every month." For the first time, I hear real sorrow in Marty's voice. "She only had two more donations to make to meet her goal."

"What about her singing?" Carmen asks.

Marty looks up as though she's forgotten we're there. She smiles now, a real smile full of warmth. "Oh, she did love singing. She would sing the hymns on Sunday so loudly Pastor Jon put her in the choir. She was only twelve." Marty's hand flutters to the arm of her chair as if the thought fills her with restless joy. "Couldn't stop that girl's voice. No, sir." Again, Marty's voice fades away.

"And she was still intent on attending school?" Carmen asks.

"Berklee," Marty says automatically, but then her face folds. "That was something different before she disappeared. She started talking about music helping troubled teens." She shakes her head, presses a finger to her lips. "No, that's not it. But it's something like that. She always wanted to be a singer, but right before the end of her senior year, she started talking about this therapy thing. Thought she might look into it at Berklee."

It's then that the prickle returns to the back of my neck. This time I know I'm missing something, but I can't say what because the thing is missing. I let my gaze travel about the room again and try to figure out what it is I'm not seeing.

Carmen and Marty discuss Lisa's affinity for mini golf as I let my eyes drift through the room. The furnishings are sparse but tasteful, the rug and fabrics cozy but refined. I look back to our little circle, and in the corner of my eye, see a small table I'd missed before because it aligns so perfectly with the frames of the windows behind it.

It's a wooden console table, the kind one might use to display family photographs, but this one is empty. It's not only empty, but a layer of dust has settled on its surface. I glance at Marty who is now talking about one of the phlebotomists Lisa befriended at the blood donation drives, and I note the starched crease of her slacks, the single pearl on a gold chain at her throat, before looking back at that layer of dust that doesn't quite belong.

I start searching the room with purpose now, but it's all the same. There's no evidence of the living spread across the house. No newspapers lingering on the couch in a scattered mess, no shoes forgotten under a sofa waiting to be taken up to a closet. Even the air lacks evidence of the family who resides here. No cloying oily scent from cooking, no vibrant aroma of fresh laundry. Nothing.

I don't feel a ghost, but I don't feel the living either.

"Della?" I jolt when Carmen touches my shoulder. "Want to see Lisa's room now?"

"Yeah, sure," I say, pushing to my feet with a reassuring smile toward Marty. She only watches me quietly before leading us to the stairs we passed on our way in.

"I haven't touched a thing just as I told you, Carmen," she says as we round the half landing. "It's all as she left it." She looks over her shoulder at us as we make our way down a hallway with a thick maroon-and-green carpet running down its center. "She was always a neat little thing, my Lisa. I can't imagine where she got that from." Marty's laugh is birdlike too, trilling and harsh.

I glance behind me, another habit ingrained in me, thanks to dear old Pappy, but the hallway is empty, all the doors along it closed. I wonder which one is Marty and Bob's bedroom or if they even share a room, and a weird feeling falls over me. It's strange being here, in the superintendent's home even if I've been out of school for nearly twenty-five years.

Ahead of me, Marty opens a four-panel wooden door at the end of the hall, pushing it wide with one splayed hand before stepping back to allow us to enter.

It's like stepping back into my childhood. The bedroom is bigger than I expected it to be. There's a bed to one side fitted with a rounded metal frame painted in white. A wicker nightstand sits to the left of it, and a tall slim white bookcase sits to the right. The bookcase is filled with a few crinkled copies of *The Babysitters Club* and *Anne of Green Gables*, but most of the shelves are taken up by knickknacks. A faded and stained plush rabbit, a stuffed rocking horse that looks handmade from a navy-and-hunter-green fabric, a globe night-light.

The wall above the bed is plastered in posters of Ani DiFranco and Lisa Loeb and a Magic Eye.

There's a window seat directly across from the door, and I guess by its orientation it overlooks the lake. I go to it and peer out, seeing the water far below, still and deep. I picture Lisa sitting there, daydreaming out her window.

On the window seat at my knees is a boombox, the kind with a CD player in the middle of the top. A Hanson CD sits next to it, its artwork and lyrics pulled from the jewel case as if Lisa just set it down on her way out of her room. I wonder if she was late for school. It's the only thing not put away in the entire room, and I touch the lyrics for "MMMBop" with one finger.

"Would you like a moment?" Marty's voice startles me out of the image I had created.

"Yes, that would be great. Thank you," I manage.

Marty looks to Carmen as if for confirmation.

"We'll meet you back downstairs when Dr. James is through," Carmen says.

Marty gives me one more assessing look before backing out of the door. I notice she doesn't quite close it all the way as she leaves.

"Do you call me Dr. James during these outings of ours to give me more credibility? Or do you just enjoy it?"

"Would you rather I call you Scooby-Doo?"

I wrinkle my nose as I walk over to a desk pushed against the opposite wall from the bed. "Daphne was always my favorite." There's a neat stack of college brochures on its surface, Berklee's sitting on the top, next to a Bellegrave High School coffee mug filled with broken pencils and blue pens. "I have an affinity for purple."

"You wouldn't look good as a redhead," Carmen comments.

The rest of the desk is neat and tidy like much of the room. I push aside the college brochures just enough to place my hand flat against its surface. I can feel the heat of the wood through my palm but nothing else.

I retrace my steps to the window seat and sit down, careful not to disturb Hanson. I cross my legs and wait.

I can remember my first ghost. It was a young woman. I had thought her a grown-up at the time, but now I realize she couldn't have been more than eighteen or nineteen. She wore a yellow terry cloth romper, her huge brown curls tamed in a polka-dotted scarf that matched her romper.

She took me to the beach. It wasn't like any beach I'd ever seen before. The sand stretched on for miles, bordered by a rocky cliff that towered above me. It was wholly unlike any beach I'd seen at Bear Lake, and this confused me because I didn't remember getting in a car.

We spent the day building sandcastles and eating peanut butter sandwiches that stuck to the roof of my mouth. The woman made me laugh with her stories and confided in me about her secret love, a boy who worked at the ice cream stand down by the docks. I thought her so grown-up and sophisticated. I wanted to be just like her one day. Night fell, and she took me up to her cabin in the woods at the edge of the cliff. We played Old Maid and drank root beer. It's one of my favorite memories.

When I woke the next morning, she was gone, and I asked my mom when she would be back and if we could go to that beach again. My mom didn't even ask questions as my dad slowly lowered his newspaper to the table next to his oatmeal, his eyes focused so intently on me through his tortoiseshell glasses. I can remember how carefully my mom pushed herself away from the breakfast table, my little brother on her hip, and went to the green rotary phone on the wall by the refrigerator in the kitchen. She called my great-aunt Janine, and suddenly I wasn't going to school that day.

Great-Aunt Janine got there before lunch and spent the rest of the day telling me about my special talent, the one we apparently both had inherited from Great-Grandma Theresa. I was so sad to learn that the woman in the yellow romper wasn't real. That she was just a ghost telling me about her last day of life, immersing me in her memories as a way of telling me what she needed to say until they felt like real life to me.

Her yellow romper had been so pretty.

Carmen doesn't say anything as I sit there, and finally I stand. "I'll tell you in the car," I say and head for the stairs.

Marty is waiting for us in the foyer by the front door. Her eyes dart up expectantly as I descend the stairs.

I smile again and step down into the foyer. "I'm still gathering my senses, and I will let Detective Neil know what comes through. Thank you so much for your time today, Ms. Pruitt." I touch her shoulder softly, copying one of her own habits, and it's startling enough to keep her from speaking.

I escape out the front door and down the front steps. Glancing back, I see my gesture has upset Marty enough that she's speaking rapidly to poor Carmen whom I've left in my wake. Carmen will want retribution for this, but I'll worry about that later.

I've bought myself some time, and I use it to take a deep breath of fresh air, heavy with coming rain, and let it wash out my strained senses.

Carmen is as annoyed as I expect her to be when she reaches the car. She drops into the driver's seat of her late model station wagon, not wasting any time. "What in the Lord's name was that about?"

I watch Ms. Pruitt in the doorway of the great camp, her fingers curled around the door as she carefully shuts it.

"Lisa Reynolds isn't dead," I say. I wait a minute. There's an entire crime scene of evidence that refutes what I've just said, and when I turn to meet Carmen's gaze, her mouth is hanging open. "And if she's not dead, where is she?"

THREE

"But how do you know she's not dead?" Carmen asks for the tenth time as we enter the library through the main door.

The artificial odor of conditioned air in an old building and the faint scent of vanilla hits me, and my heart thuds as it always does in recognition. I wave to Sarah at the front desk. She lifts a hand in greeting in between scanning in a pile of children's picture books.

Sarah Ramirez is the children's librarian and always alerts me first when old editions of Nancy Drew books pop up in the library book sale donations. She also makes the best peanut butter cookies and can name every actor who has played Dr. Who. In alphabetical order.

I head up the marble staircase that leads to the nonfiction stacks on the second floor and our offices beyond. I wave to a few patrons I recognize who have fled to the second floor for the quiet that can often be found here, and I envy them their peace.

Peace is not what I find when I step back into my gratingly messy office that appears exactly as I left it except for a single leopard-print party favor bag sitting on the stack of invoices I still haven't approved.

I pick it up gingerly, afraid the print might spread to the other gala decor if I'm not careful when I inspect it. Frances failed to mention the leopard motif is hot yellow and magenta. I drop the bag back onto the desk and make my way to the espresso maker. I'm determined to clear that desk before I leave for the day, and I'll need coffee to do it.

Carmen sails in behind me before I can get the espresso grounds pressed.

"What do you mean she's not dead? Her blood was found in the trunk of her car."

Carmen had been largely silent on the car ride back from the Pruitt Camp. I think the shock had silenced her, and only now she's roused herself to ask questions.

"Just because blood was found does not mean you have a dead body. It just means blood was found."

Carmen shakes her head when I hold up a cup in her direction. "It was a lot of blood."

I shrug. "It didn't come from Lisa then."

"It was her blood type. DNA testing later confirmed—"

I turn around. "Lisa is not dead. You're wasting your breath and your energy, and that's not like you."

Carmen's arms are extended at her sides as if she can hold this whole thing together through her own might. I walk over to her, the espresso machine whirring behind me, and forcibly lower her arms.

I gently cup her elbows. "A mistake was made. I know that's hard for you. Mistakes mean bad guys don't get punished, and innocent people aren't avenged, but mistakes do happen. Lisa is alive. I could feel it."

I've retrieved my cup and made it to my chair before Carmen pulls herself from what I know is a litany of curses she's sounding in her head about making mistakes.

"Feel it?"

I pick up the first invoice. "We leave an echo on the things we touch. I don't know how it works, don't ask me. But when I touch items strongly connected to a deceased person, I can feel them." I shake my laptop to life and call up the budget folder from the server. "Lisa's belongings were cold. There was nothing in them. She hasn't left an echo, which means some-where she's still alive with all her energy still in her." I take a sip of my latte. "But more than that, did you notice the house? There were no personal effects anywhere but in Lisa's room. No signs of life. Didn't you find that odd?"

Carmen sinks slowly into the chair across from me, ignoring my last comment to address the first. "This is that weird e equals $m\,c$ squared nonsense you're always talking about."

I purse my lips and let the invoice sink to my desk. "It's only a theory, and I have no way of proving it. I can only tell you what I feel. Ghosts are simply energy. Energy I believe that comes from our souls leaving behind the mass of our bodies. It's like burning wood for a fire. The wood disappears, but..." I trail off because I know Carmen knows the rest of the theory.

"There's still heat in the room," she mumbles. She shakes her head and leans forward, resting her head in her hands, elbows to knees. "You're telling me Lisa Reynolds is alive because her energy wasn't with her stuff."

"Pretty much," I say.

She leans back in her chair. "Now what?"

I pick up the invoice again. "I don't know. It's not like you have the resources to turn this into a missing persons case when everything points to a possible homicide, and it's been cold for twenty-five years."

"Twenty-seven," Carmen says.

"Exactly." I go back to my laptop.

Carmen lets her head fall back against the chair. "Now

what am I supposed to do? Tell Marty her daughter is alive somewhere?"

Without warning, I picture that console table, so out of place in front of the big windows, the dust still coating its surface.

"You said Marty hadn't told Mr. Reynolds that you were going to ask me to help find Lisa, right?" I try to remember Bob Reynolds, but he only comes back to me in bits and pieces. Mostly tweed suits, a ridiculous combover he sported until no one was fooled and he shaved it all off, a lot of hand shaking and soft words. I recall being ambivalent to him as a kid, but as an adult, I wonder if he was truly effective as a superintendent. And in a small, rural town, would anyone have noticed if he was or not?

Carmen shakes her head, her black curls rustling against the chair. "No, you heard what she said. She didn't want to get his hopes up."

"Do you think he mourns Lisa more than Marty?"

Carmen picks up her head at this, lifting a single eyebrow, her expression disbelieving. "Raymond is a good father," she says, referring to her husband of fifteen years. "But when Ella's prom date shows up and dares to honk his horn from the street like my baby girl is some kind of cheap fare, it's not Raymond who will be running across that lawn barefoot and wild. That boy better hope he's driving a fast car to get away from me."

"What about Anna?" I ask about her younger daughter.

Carmen dismisses this with a flick of her hand. "I'll be running in the opposite direction if a boy dares to disrespect her. Somebody else can arrest her if she kills him."

I smile and shake my head. "Didn't the Reynolds house feel empty to you?" I try again.

Again, that eyebrow goes up. "I thought you said there wasn't any energy there?"

I shake my head again. "No, not the ghosts. I mean the living. It was so…"

"Stale," Carmen finishes for me.

"Yeah." I drop the invoice and lean back in my chair, crossing my arms over my chest. "It just makes me wonder…" Again my voice trails off because I can't quite bring myself to say the words.

"If she ran?" Carmen says them for me.

I let my gaze drift out the single window. "Why would she run? She had everything. She was out of here in a matter of months. Off to the big city. Berklee. Her every dream come true."

Carmen makes a tsking noise. "Nah uh. Every dream these good people of Bellegrave painted for her. Did you ever ask Lisa what her dreams were?"

"I didn't even ask Lisa Reynolds for the time."

"Exactly. We don't know what kind of life she was living." Carmen looks at the floor briefly. "I hate to say it, but statistics and data and all that stuff I love to hate suggests she was taken."

I narrow my eyes. "From Bellegrave? We only got drugs here like fifteen years ago."

"Marijuana is not hard drugs no matter what your mother says." Carmen's expression blanks, and I can't stop a smile. I sober when Carmen says, "Girls have been taken from more remote places. Especially girls like Lisa."

She means pretty, young, white girls.

I glance back out the window. "So are you going to try to find her?"

Carmen shakes her head as she pushes to her feet. "How can I? Like you said it's a cold case with what little evidence we have pointing to a homicide. What am I supposed to do? Tell Chief Tom a medium told me Lisa's not dead so can I please have the entire year's budget to look for a person who's been missing for twenty-five years?" she says.

"Twenty-seven," I amend.

She gives me a look I'm sure Anna and Ella are familiar with.

"Thank you for your help, Dr. James," she says, heading for the door. She stops, and I watch her hesitate, knowing the battle she's waging in her head and which side will ultimately win. She turns back. "You know Raymond has state testing this week." Raymond Neil is an eighth-grade math teacher, and my mother keeps him on her regular prayer list. "He's going out with the boys tonight to decompress. You could come over and—"

"I'm not a pity case," I interject.

Carmen holds up a hand. "I didn't say you were. It's just that Ella was telling me how much she wanted to hear about Bellegrave's strategic position in the Adirondacks during the Revolutionary War, and she knows there's no one better than you to school her on the subject."

"The Adirondacks were nothing but wilderness during the Revolutionary War, and she knows that. Besides, Ella only wants to be schooled on makeup."

"Does that mean you won't come? Friday is a long way away."

I wave her off. "No, I'm good. I'll probably finish up here and take Henry out salsa dancing. Should be a nice night for it."

Carmen doesn't respond right away, and when she does it's to ask, "Did you ever think we'd end up here?" She holds up a hand to indicate my office or maybe the library or maybe Bellegrave itself.

"It's where we started. Why shouldn't we end up here?"

Carmen purses her lips. "I married a man whiter than a snowman's butt and adopted two girls. Adopted. Me." She presses a hand to her black denim jacket, and it sets off her hot pink nails like fireworks. "Adoption trauma is real. What the heck was I thinking?"

"That you had to save those two girls and live a beautiful life?"

Carmen's eyes close briefly, and I see the brackets at the corners of her mouth tighten as she tries to hold back a smile. When she opens her eyes again, they're soft with sadness.

"And what are you doing, Della James?"

I know she's trying to trap me, but I smile the biggest smile I can muster and say, "The same thing I always do, Carmen Neil. Anything I want."

She glances around my office. "Just make sure what you want has more to do with the living than the dead."

I'm still thinking about what she said, the invoices unchecked on my desk, long after her footfalls recede down the corridor, and I'm left with only the distant chatter of library patrons and the creaks and moans of an old building settling.

———

It's late when I finally lock my office to head home for the night. Frances left hours earlier with a stern reminder to feed myself and to not be influenced by this idea of girl dinner her granddaughter keeps going on about. Allie left at four to attend a seminar in Plattsburgh with a promise to be in early the next morning. The rest of the staff have been in and out all afternoon, and with my head down, determined to clear my desk, I can't really say where everyone has been.

It's a Tuesday night, which means I hear both the hushed whispers of the Stamp Collecting Sisters and Misters from the main floor meeting room of the library and the click clack of the gossiping knitters from the open balcony of the second floor as I leave. I wave to Sarah who is still behind the desk. She closes on Tuesday, and I know she still has a couple of hours to go. I mime coffee, but she just shakes her head, pulling an energy drink from under the front desk counter. She makes her eyes go crazy wide and rattles her head like she's being electrocuted, and I wave good night with a laugh.

I stop at Matt's Meats on Water Street before leaving the village, and I haven't stepped two feet in when from behind the counter, Matt holds up a wrapped package.

"Thought you might be coming in," he says, handing it to me. "Your dad called earlier."

My hand freezes in mid-reach, and I remember just in time to find my smile. "Thanks, Matt."

I gather a couple more things I need, pay, and head back out to my car, reminding myself homicide is illegal, and Carmen is my best friend even if she's the most likely suspect to have texted my mom to tell her about Logan's absence.

It's not the summer season yet, but the weather's been unusually nice for early April, and the village is busy with families getting ice cream at the Cow Patty Parlor and patrons dashing into the Main Street shops before they close. The door to Papa's Pizza stays open with a steady stream of customers going in and out, and I sit in my SUV thinking about what Carmen said and knowing my answer was right.

I am doing what I please, and Bellegrave is where I want to do it.

Fifteen minutes later, I'm not surprised when I hear barking as soon as I open the door of my SUV in our driveway. Great-Aunt Marge's cottage, which we inherited right after we were married from Logan's great-aunt, sits back from the access road along the east end of the lake, and a curved concrete driveway bends up to meet it. Tamaracks and elms and some oaks tower around it. Sometimes the old trees look like a gathering of wizened souls. Other times, like now in the falling light, they look like sentinels guarding something precious.

I don't bother going into the house through the door off the garage but circle around to what would be the backyard, the stretch of green lawn between the house and the lake. I find my dad where I expect him. He's thrown the winter cover off part of the patio furniture and stretched out on a chaise, last year's dead leaves still curled beneath it. He's propped both hands behind his head, and his eyes are closed behind his tortoiseshell-rimmed glasses.

The barking is from Henry, the chocolate lab I rescued three years ago. I never thought I was a dog person until Carmen told me a colleague at the station was being forced to rehome her puppy. She was apparently allergic and didn't know it, and she hated the thought of having to give him to a shelter. Carmen brought him to me, and I fell in love for the second time in my life.

The honeymoon phase is short with a puppy, and I have an ugly scar on my shin to prove it, the remnants of one of many middle of the night trips out to the yard in the ongoing battle to potty train a fifteen-week-old puppy. I might see ghosts, but apparently I can't see coffee tables in the dark.

Now Henry coils, bowing before the automatic ball thrower my dad got him for Christmas two years ago. I frown even as I see it's made a reappearance, and I wonder how on earth my dad found its hiding spot. The machine ticks down as the mechanism inside winds up to shoot the ball. But when the bright yellow fuzz of tennis ball shrieks through the sky, Henry does not go after it.

Henry likes the machine more than the balls it throws.

He whirls around, yapping ferociously at the air, before coiling once more in a bow, ready for it to do it again.

"Henry."

He immediately breaks posture, his head coming up, eyes

locking on mine, and just like that I fall in love again. He barrels toward me, tongue and tail flopping in unadulterated joy, but before he gets to me he hits the brakes, careening to a sit that's ruined by his excited shaking. I offer him my hand, and he gives me his paw.

"How was your day, Professor Jones?"

Henry barks.

Only then do I kneel down and wrap my arms around him. He licks my face enough that I'll have to find a paper towel from the kitchen, but I don't care. Once he's covered me, the bags from Matt's Meats, and my backpack in fur and drool, he lets me stand up as he returns to the ball-throwing machine.

My dad's eyes are open when I turn to the patio door he's left open behind him.

"Your mom says you might want company for dinner." He grins unapologetically.

"So you called Matt to get what you wanted for dinner?"

He shrugs. "Seemed like a good idea."

Henry barks behind me, and I hear the rustle of grass as he spins. "And the ball thrower? We talked about this."

Dad shrugs again. "He likes it."

"It's a menace to world peace."

"So is your mother, and we've kept her for forty-three years."

"Where is dear mother tonight?"

"Glass painting," he says, swinging his legs over the edge of the chaise to stand.

"I thought she already did glass painting."

He takes the bags from me, including my backpack. "That was ceramics. This is painting on glass."

I shake my head. "How many more days until retirement?"

"Ninety-eight."

"And then what are you going to do?"

"Try not to lose my mind." My dad raises his eyebrows above the rim of his glasses.

"You've managed to keep it this long. I bet you'll do fine."

Dad grimaces. "I've never been subjected to the full force of Maxine Hopewell. She started working at the practice right after she pushed out Ryan."

Ryan is my younger brother. My mother wouldn't allow my father to name him Orion, and Ryan was the compromise. Yet my mother did allow my father to name me Delia, an epithet of Artemis, goddess of the moon, so I'm not sure how that checks out. I'm just grateful Della was an acceptable nickname given to me by Great-Grandmother Theresa.

I follow my dad through the open patio door into the kitchen where he sets the food bags on the island and my bag on a chair at the table pushed into the eating alcove.

He turns to me, the grimace still on his face. "I thought I would have more time than this. I've only gotten two years to enjoy my own retirement." He shakes his head. "The house is going to be filled with the remnants of whatever hobby she picks up next."

I go to the fridge for a couple of beers and hand them to my dad who opens them on the edge of the counter like I've seen him do since I was a kid.

"Maybe you two could find a hobby you enjoy together."

Dad takes a swig of his beer instead of answering me, and I hide my smile behind my own beer bottle. There's a clamor at the still open door, and Henry sails in, scooting right past me to sit at my dad's feet. He looks up adoringly.

Dad sets his beer on the island, his face serious as he looks from Henry to me. "I'm going to tell you something right now that you can never tell anybody else. Especially Ryan if he ever marries and procreates." Ryan is the golden child of the family. Not just by my parents' standards but mine too. Ryan is just the best and always has been. Dad's expression turns even graver. "Henry is my favorite grandchild, and there will never be one better than him."

Henry tilts his head when he hears his name and glances in my direction.

"You told me not to get him."

"I never said that." Dad is quick to defend himself.

"You said dogs were expensive and messy."

"I would never."

I look at Henry. "He said those very words, Professor. Don't let him lie to you." I set my beer down. "Want some steak?"

Dad and Henry both grin.

I fire up the grill and take out the steaks Matt had wrapped for me, fine cuts of sirloin with just the right marbling. I'm not sure how Matt does it in such a small town, but he consistently sources the best quality meats, which only enables my preference for grilling instead of preparing real meals.

While the grill is warming, I prep the steaks and find the makings of a salad in the fridge. I suddenly can't remember the last time I've done the shopping and sniff tentatively at a bottle of dressing. It isn't growing mold, so that's good enough for me.

When I step back outside, Dad has resumed his spot on the lounger, Henry collapsed on the ground after his bout with the ball-throwing machine. I put the steaks on the grill along with some peppers I found lingering in the fridge before I tug some more of the cover off the patio furniture and unearth a chair from the small table set that is somewhere under there. I brush off some spiderwebs, checking diligently for any lurkers, and sit. Dad is silent for a few seconds, but I know Mom wouldn't have sent him over here without instructions on topics to cover.

"So Logan's in Albany again, huh?"

"Launching right into it?" I ask before taking a sip of my beer.

"Your mother's going to ask," he replies.

"I know."

We're both silent as a motorboat crosses the lake in front of us. It's a fourteen-foot aluminum fishing boat much like my own, and I recognize Lester Kohl at the helm. Their cottage is down the access road from our own. He and his wife are retired teachers from Utica. They spend their winters in Boca Raton, and I'm surprised to see him back at the lake so early. I raise a hand, and he lifts his in return.

The light is fading quickly now, and we'll need to eat inside in order to see our food, but I enjoy the last of the early spring sun before it disappears completely behind the hills to the west. I glance in that direction, remembering Lisa Reynolds's room and the staleness that draped the house.

"Dad, do you remember when Lisa Reynolds went missing?"

Dad had been scratching absently at Henry's ears, but he looks up at this.

"Lisa Reynolds? That's a name I haven't heard in a long time. What brings this up?"

I can feel him studying the side of my face, but I keep my gaze on the lake as I say, "Carmen came to see me today."

My dad sits up, swinging his legs to the side of the chaise to put his feet on the patio pavers. He leans forward, elbows to knees, and finally, I meet his gaze.

"Marty asked Carmen if I would try to contact Lisa. Because of what's going on with Bob."

"And?" My dad has never been one to dawdle in emotion. It's probably why he was such a respected and successful lawyer.

I shake my head. "I went to their house today up on the

peninsula. There was nothing there." I pause before speaking my next words. "I don't think Lisa is dead."

My dad presses his hands together and apart between his knees. "What makes you think that?"

"For one, Lisa wasn't there. But more importantly, I didn't feel her energy on any of her things."

Dad's face doesn't change when he asks, "Is that that echo thing you're talking about?"

I had once tried to explain to my parents what I feel when I touch the possessions of people who have passed, and the best way I could describe it at the time was as an echo. I was nine. My vocabulary was limited.

"Yeah, that's it." I stand and check the steaks, turning them over to grill the other side. I spend too much time fiddling with the peppers, but Dad doesn't press me. I don't speak again until I sit back down. "There's something off about that house, Dad. Almost likes it's waiting for something. You know Marty Pruitt, right?" I gesture with one hand. "I mean, you know of her, right?"

Dad nods and presses the palms of his hands to his knees. "The Reynoldses have always been good about keeping up appearances. It helps if there are no cracks in the facade."

I nod. "That's the thing. The house was kept up and all, but there were parts of it that were just kind of frozen. It didn't seem right."

"Do you think it was something to do with Bob?"

I shrug. "I only remember Mr. Reynolds as being the quiet, handshaking type. He never really made waves when he was superintendent, and I get the sense Marty wears the pants in that marriage."

Dad lifts one shoulder. "It makes sense. Marty's always had a lot of pressure on her to keep face. The Pruitt name carries a lot of weight in this town."

"What was it like? When Lisa disappeared? I can only

remember how the kids at school talked about it, and the gossip of teenagers isn't exactly a reliable historical source."

Dad's grin is swift before his face settles back into its usual lines. "I don't recall much. Mostly just the shock of it so soon after that terrible accident with that teacher. You remember that, don't you? What was her name?"

It takes me a few seconds to figure out what he's talking about, but when I do, my stomach clenches. "Miss Gustafson." It's like that first moment of waking up when I can't remember the terrible thing that happened the day before, but it suddenly comes back to me, and my insides seize. "I had completely forgotten about that."

I picture her without trying, Miss Gustafson. She was tall and slender with long dark hair that had a natural wave to it, so it fell around her shoulders in a shimmer and made her look like a fairytale princess. She wore glasses that were too small for her face, but it didn't matter. Her smile made up for any flaws she might have had. When Miss Gustafson smiled at you, you felt like you were someone.

"What was her first name?" I ask suddenly.

She was a middle school teacher, and I had existed in that strange place as a student where teachers can't possibly have first names, and they definitely did not exist outside of school, and if you saw them outside of school, you had to run away. It was the law.

"Victoria," Dad says. "Her family moved here when Victoria and her brother were in elementary and middle school. I know because her brother, Kevin, was in my class, and back then, they always made a spectacle of it. Making the poor new kid stand up in front of everyone and talk about himself." Dad shakes his head. "No wonder we're a generation of people who can't name a feeling. We had to block them all out to survive."

"I didn't make that connection. That Miss Gustafson's accident was so close to Lisa disappearing."

Dad nods. "It was a tough time for the town. Remember your mother that summer? Wouldn't let you and Ryan out of sight. Thought something terrible would happen to you both."

"She wouldn't let me do the summer reading program that year at the library because Ryan was at camp, and she didn't want me to ride my bike into the village alone."

Dad nods again. "I don't know what she was worried about. You were always the one protecting Ryan. Not the other way around."

I smile at this memory. "Is her family still in town?"

"Kevin left for the city after graduation. I never saw him again, but I think her mom is still here. She was the postmistress, remember?"

I do and nod. I rise and take the steaks and peppers off the grill. Henry leads the charge back into the house and takes his spot under the table in the alcove.

The small cottage has no formal dining room, and the old oak table I rescued from an estate sale is where we take our meals. The chairs around it are mismatched and in various states of refinishing, a project I indulge in now and then when the time allows, but chairs are tough, and I tend to gravitate toward easier projects first.

I set the peppers and steak on the table and retrieve the salad. I get myself a glass of water and milk for my dad.

We're several bites in before I ask, "Did they ever figure out why Miss Gustafson crashed?"

Miss Gustafson had driven her car off the Bellegrave River bridge just outside of the village. She had been in the submerged car for some time before they found her, but that's all I can remember. Something as terrifying as that happening when you're a kid tends to leave holes in your memory.

Dad punctures some lettuce leaves. "Tom always figured she must have fallen asleep on her way to school. He was only an officer back then, but he was first on the scene. You know how early teachers need to get to school. At that time, the bridge had those old-style guardrails where the ends are buried in the earth. Tom figured she fell asleep, drifted, and her car went right up that guardrail like a ramp. Shot her right into the river." He stops, his fork going silent in the salad. "She might have lived, did you know that? She only had one nasty bump on her head from the impact, but the way the car fell, she was submerged." He stabs more lettuce again. "They changed out that guardrail that summer. Now it's that sturdy iron and concrete barrier."

"I remember when they put that in. It cut off the path down to the river. The high schoolers were so mad about it. They couldn't sneak off to smoke down there anymore."

Dad's fork stills. "You never did that though."

I blink, the bite I had been about to take paused on its way to my mouth, even though it wasn't really a question. "Dad, I got heart palpitations when I was late returning a library book."

He frowns. "Maybe you've always been a little too good."

Carmen's words come back to me, and I set my fork down, the steak uneaten on it.

"Logan's working on that new real estate development client he just took on. That's why he's in Albany again."

Dad only lifts his eyes from his plate before saying, "Are they the ones who are looking to take over the old hotel?"

He's referring to Bellegrave Manor, Peter Bellegrave's pride and joy, which sits empty at the top of the western hill that cocoons Bellegrave. It's a four-story structure with a red mansard roof adorning its top. It's all white except for the roof, and sometimes in the fall when the trees have emptied their leaves you can just make it out at the top of the hill like a specter in the trees. It's been empty as long as I can remember, and it would be hard to imagine someone taking it over now.

"No. It's some parcel out along the county highway. Do you think it would be profitable to take on a project like the manor? You know how long that outfit from Plattsburgh has been trying to get those rustic retreats built on the old girls' camp island."

Dad gestures with his fork. "That's not the same thing. They can't get those retreats built because the island is haunted." Now he points at me with his fork. "You think no one notices, but I've noticed since you were a kid you avoid that part of the lake."

I wrinkle my nose. "I don't know what you're talking about."

The conversation changes yet again, and we discuss Mom's current fascination with painting things, which follows her stint in macramé and basket weaving. While I scrounge up some ice cream for dessert, Dad fills me in on Ryan's latest gigs in New York.

When we were young, Ryan wanted to take piano lessons, and Mom thought it was only fair that I take them as well. Ryan swiftly grew bored with it, and it was soon discovered I was mostly good at it. Ryan got to quit, and I was forced to keep playing. My brother picked up the guitar to impress girls in high school, but it turned out that was what he was meant to play. He's now a popular and successful studio musician who splits his time between New York and Nashville.

I lick the last of the vanilla ice cream from my spoon as Dad asks, "Are you keeping up on your swimming?"

This is Dad's polite way of asking how much pain I'm in without actually asking.

"Of course. Three days a week at the aquatic center just like always."

"What does Doc Randy say about it?"

"He says one day my leg is just going to walk off on its own." I smile to let him know this is a joke, but he doesn't smile back.

I know the accident was difficult for everyone, something that changes so much so quickly always is, but if I don't make jokes about it, I won't be able to go on living with it.

By then it's time I walk my dad down to his boat tied up at our dock. He keeps a slip at the marina in the village, and from there, he can walk home. The sun has set now, and it's that half-light right before night falls so unexpectedly it never fails to take me by surprise even though I know it's coming.

Dad's aluminum fishing boat bobs in the water, knocking gently against the dock.

"I can come over this weekend and help you get your boat in if you want," he says, hopping down into the fishing craft.

"Thanks, Dad, but Logan should be home to help me."

Dad lifts his eyes, and even in the half-light, I can see he's questioning whether or not that's true. He doesn't say anything though and pulls the rope on the outboard to start it. The lights at the bow and stern come to life as the engine roars.

"Tell Mom I've been eaten by Sasquatches," I call over the din of the engine.

Dad looks up at me, real earnestness in the lines of his face. "Are you sure you're okay here alone?"

"I can literally see what goes bump in the night, Dad. Henry and I will be fine," I say. What I don't say is that when Logan started making these regular trips to Albany, I moved the safe for my Beretta M9 from the bedroom closet to mount it to the wall behind the bed's headboard where it will be in easy reach in the middle of the night.

Dad lifts a hand, and I catch the flash of his smile as he motors away. I stand there on the dock long after he's disappeared around the curve of the bay, Henry whining softly at my feet. I lean down and scratch his ears.

"Soon, boy," I say. "Soon the water will be warm enough for us to swim."

I had told my dad the truth earlier. I do keep up on the swimming my orthopedic surgeon prescribed for me when I was cleared for exercise after the accident, but I much prefer doing it in the lake. There's something about chlorine that never quite leaves the body, and I think at this point it might be burned into my nostrils. Henry prefers lake swimming too because I let him join me most mornings. He gives up after a couple of laps, but he loyally cheers me on from the dock.

I pat his head one more time and turn toward the house, but a noise on the wind catches me, and I turn back to the lake. My gaze travels unerringly across the water to the place where the old girls' camp sits on an island running west to east, vacant now, its cabins and facilities sitting, waiting, breathing.

The trickle of laughter comes again on the wind, and I turn away, holding on to Henry's collar as we walk swiftly toward the glowing lights of the house.

FOUR

I get to my office the next morning before the library opens for the day and let myself in through the employee entrance in the rear off the parking lot that runs behind the buildings on Main Street.

The library is still cool and dim in that early morning quiet before the day begins, and I stop a moment near the front desk to enjoy it—the smell of the books, the feel of the old industrial carpet spongy beneath my feet, and the quiet whir of the computers across the hall. There's something about that soft whirring that triggers a note in my brain, but I can't piece it together. I let it go and head up to my office.

I've gotten through my email when Frances shows up. I hear her greeting at the checkout desk and Miles Parker's reply. Miles is the only person who comes close to having worked in this building as long as Frances, and I enjoy their back and forth the few times their shifts line up.

Frances appears seconds later in my office, a small parcel wrapped in wax paper in one hand.

"Good morning, Della," she says and sets the parcel directly between my arms where they lie on my desk, stretched out to my laptop, and sails out of the room before I can utter a reply.

I know without having to open it that it's an egg and gouda sandwich on a fresh ciabatta roll from Shelly's Diner.

"I ate," I call down the hall.

"Trail mix in the car on the way here doesn't count," Frances calls back.

I eat the sandwich with my second cup of coffee that day.

By the time Allie arrives at nine, I've been on the phone with the vendor for the party favor bags for twenty-seven minutes and signal for her take over so I can inspect the boxes being delivered with the programs for the gala. She scoots into my seat, taking the phone from me as I swap places with her and meet the delivery person from the printers.

Before I can get back to my office, I'm waylaid by Diana Milton, our development director, who throws her hands in the air in a call of triumph. She's a small woman of barely five feet, and she's not entirely unlike a garden gnome come to life.

"I've gotten Prescott Motors to sponsor Wi-Fi in the conference rooms at the lodge!" she cries.

"Yes!" I fist bump her in solidarity. "How about a donor to replace the plumbing in the bathrooms?"

It's like I've taken away her balloon. She deflates, mutters to herself, and disappears into her own office.

From there it's the usual whirlwind of costume fittings as volunteers show up when they can throughout their workday, checking deliveries, tracking packages that say they're in Illinois when they've only shipped from Buffalo, and fielding questions of dire consequence from Frances. Like the caterer threatening to cancel because one of our volunteers said her watercress was wilted. Or Steve letting us know termites have been found once again in the milk house, and the only day the exterminator has open to fumigate is two days before Founder's Day.

It's in those sneaky doldrums of early afternoon when most of the staff has gone to find lunch, and Frances is out taking her usual afternoon stroll about the block, that the quiet starts to invade my mind.

I think about the conversation with Dad the previous night about Lisa's disappearance and how frightened the town was, already unsettled by Miss Gustafson's fatal accident.

Before I make a real decision about it, I minimize the donor database I'd been working in and open the digital archive program for the *Bellegrave Bulletin*. I search Lisa Reynolds's name, and stories appear that one would expect. The front-page headline declaring her missing, foul play suspected. There's a picture of Tom Reznick looking younger than I've ever remembered him looking on the front page, standing behind Marty Pruitt and Bob Reynolds. I study the picture for a moment, noting how Marty and Bob are not touching and try to remember if they ever did, at least in public. I remember what Dad said about there always being a lot of pressure on Marty, and a wash of sadness overcomes me. What had it been like to be unable to publicly mourn your missing daughter because you were required to keep your chin up?

I click through to where the story is continued on page A4. There's a picture of Lisa there. She's looking over her shoulder as though someone has caught her from behind, and her eyes are lit with surprise and the kind of joy you only find in young people. She has a denim backpack over one shoulder, and her hair is a messy braid down her back.

I click on the next result. The search for Lisa Reynolds continues. The police are asking for the public's help and lists a phone number to call if anyone saw or heard anything. The next result is nearly two weeks later and is more of a human-interest piece about Lisa, her life, and her impact on the community of Bellegrave at such a young age. I wonder if

Marty pushed for this when the search ran cold, hoping the newspaper story would bolster community interest and keep the case going forward.

There's a different picture included this time. Lisa is standing in the middle of a group of friends. I recognize a couple of faces of people who still live in Bellegrave, but the others are fading memories.

I'm about to click away when something in the photo catches my eye. Like at the Reynolds house, I'm not sure what it is right away, so I let my gaze linger over Lisa and see it. The strap of her denim backpack on one shoulder.

I text Carmen before I can talk myself out of it, asking her if any of Lisa's possessions were found in her car when police recovered it.

I'm about to click out of the digital archive when another headline at the bottom of the page catches my eye. It's an announcement of a village-wide memorial to be held in the town square for Miss Gustafson. It's brief and to the point, listing the time and date of the memorial service. A photo of Miss Gustafson is included, and I recognize the middle school cafeteria in the background.

I clear the search box and enter Victoria Gustafson's name.

The first return is the one I expect, the article detailing her accident. I scan it quickly, but nothing jumps out at me. I catch myself and wonder why I should be looking for anything at all. I glance at the included photo of first responder vehicles at the bridge just outside the village. There isn't much to see in the photo except the volunteer ambulance and the fire truck, a few people but their backs are all to the camera. I don't see Tom in this photo or any police response, but that's likely because they're just not in the frame. The photographer took a close shot of the bridge itself, and my eyes settle on the guardrail just as my father's words come back to me.

Tom thought she fell asleep, drifted, and drove up the guardrail. I enlarge the digital photo, and although the quality is grainy, I can clearly see the guardrail.

There isn't a single dent in it.

I lean back, my eyes glued to the photo.

Wouldn't the guardrail show some sign of damage if a car had driven up it?

I let my hands fall away from the laptop as I study the picture of the unblemished guardrail. It could mean nothing. Maybe she never hit the guardrail and simply drove off the road and down into the river.

I check the date of the story. April 2.

The spring melt would have been at its peak then. I could check the weather forecast, see if it had snowed recently and then melted. The river could have been high. She wouldn't need to have driven her car up the guardrail to go into the river the way she did.

I look at the date of the story again. The river now wouldn't be too far off from what it had been that day if the weather had been similar.

I'm startled from my thoughts by my phone buzzing. Carmen's reply is short. Nothing in the car except an old Belle-grave High School Softball Team sweatshirt. Why?

I click out of the newspaper archive and close my laptop lid. Frances is passing by my office door, the sneakers she wears for her afternoon stroll still on her feet.

"Frances, I'm stepping out for a minute. Call me if something comes up. I should be right back."

I don't give Frances time to say anything as I grab my bag and phone and escape through the back employee entrance. I dodge Allie as she's coming back in, juggling a salad container and an iced tea, phone wedged between shoulder and ear. I wave and say I'll be right back and hop into my SUV.

Main Street runs through the village west to east before it

joins Route 3 and heads north to Saranac. But if you go west, it leads out of the village onto the county highway. I follow it, keeping the image of the photo from the newspaper in my mind, trying to orient myself.

The bridge over the Bellegrave River is about a mile past the end of the lake. The county highway runs along the southern hill that brackets the lake until it drops down to cross the river before it heads south to Tupper Lake. Miss Gustafson was traveling east into the village where the middle school is when she drifted off the road.

I park on this side of the bridge though, grateful for the ground clearance of the SUV as I steer well off the road to avoid any accidental collision with traffic. I walk slowly up to the bridge, letting my senses open.

The light is not good, clouds hanging low and heavy in the sky, and I feel the zing of electricity of a coming storm along my bare arms. I hadn't thought to grab a sweater, lulled into a false spring by the morning's gentle weather, but the afternoon is pressing in, humidity rising, and I know it's not the temperature that has chilled me.

The county highway is a two-lane road, and the bridge is substantial to handle the kind of traffic moving through this part of the Adirondacks. The hill that cocoons Bellegrave rises up to my left, and the river rushes below to my right, already high from the spring melt and the amount of rain we'd gotten that spring.

I'm not sure how long I stand beside the road, staring down at the bridge, before I decide to move closer. I watch for traffic from both directions before crossing to the other side. I walk up the embankment and try to position myself where the newspaper photographer must have been that day.

My dad is right. The single corrugated metal guardrail has been replaced with a steel or iron and concrete structure that borders the bridge on both sides. Stone crunches under my feet as I walk closer, the sound of the river rushing up to engulf me until the chatter of birdsong is drowned out.

That's why I don't hear the car as it approaches from behind me, and although I'm safely off the road, it startles me, sending me up the embankment in a panicked scramble, my mind inexplicably snapping back to another time.

The rain on the windshield, my wipers unable to clear it even though I have them turned all the way up. Easing into the intersection. Hoping any incoming traffic can see the red light for their direction. The flash of movement to my left. The headlights, the car. The woman behind the wheel. The phone in her hand. The moment my eyes found hers in the dimness, the realization she was not paying attention the second before the impossible explosion of pain through my body, and the final thought before everything went black.

My baby.

I come up through my memories like a drowning person bursting through the surface of water, lungs starved for air, releasing a ragged cry as oxygen floods my bloodstream. The memory didn't last very long. They don't anymore, and I'm grateful for that.

I look around to see what has startled me though I already know it was a blast of cold air. My conscious mind just hasn't acknowledged it yet.

The clouds have darkened, and I know I can't linger, crouched like that in the tall grass of the embankment. A storm is coming, and I can't be caught here. I push to my feet, circle back to find the road again, and make my way to my SUV when I see her.

She's standing between me and my SUV on the other side of the bridge. Standing in the very spot where her car supposedly drifted from the road and launched into the river.

Victoria Gustafson.

She looks exactly like how I remember her, too small

glasses, long, wavy hair like a princess. She's wearing one of those gauzy dresses I remember, one of my favorites of hers with daisies embroidered at the bodice and beads hang in layered strands around her neck. She's just the same.

Except the back of her head is smashed in, a dark wetness glimmering in the flat light of the oncoming storm. My dad had said it was a small bump, but this is no small bump. The back of her head is caved in, and I know that was what killed her.

There's a second where relief floods me, knowing she didn't lie submerged in water, drowning, her life taken from her by the terrible happenstance of her car falling a certain way.

I'm too busy studying her to realize she's gesturing to me, her face imploring. She cups her hands and places them against her heart, presses her palms flat there, and then releases them, her arms extending outward at the elbow.

In my head, I hear her voice.

My heart. My heart.

It's clearly her head wound that has killed her, but she continues to press her hands to her heart and extend them, the same words playing over and over again in my head.

My heart. My heart.

Thunder sends my own heart racing, my already alert senses brittle with strain.

A look of despair enters Miss Gustafson's face, and I reach forward.

"I'll figure it out," I say out loud. I know ghosts only have so much energy to deliver their messages, and she's been standing there for so long. Too long. "I promise." Her head tilts as if questioning my resolve, and I say it again, the need to reassure her swamping everything else. "I promise."

She's already fading before the last word leaves my lips, and then she's gone before the next crack of thunder.

I tug the door of my SUV shut just as rain strikes the windshield, but I don't start the car, turn on the defroster, run the windshield wipers.

I sit there, my thoughts uncomfortable. I picture Miss Gustafson, standing there, the storm gathering around her, her hands against her chest where her heart would be.

I pull my seatbelt around me and start the SUV, the tires spitting gravel as I pull back out onto the road.

FIVE

Carmen struggles to hold her denim jacket over her head as she emerges from the stairwell that leads down to the Bellegrave Police Department, which is housed in the basement of the Opera House.

The police department was first installed in the old stables behind the village Main Street buildings that once offered visitors in town a place to keep their horses. There were eight sworn officials then, but the police force soon outgrew the converted stables as the village expanded to nearly seven thousand in population. In the late 1980s, the town held a fundraiser to restore the opera house, and it was determined the basement would be dedicated to the expanded police force. There it remains to this day with a total of eighteen full-time officials and six part-time ones.

Papa's Pizza sits at the rear of the building on Church Street, and the police department and its inhabitants always smell faintly of yeast as Carmen does now when she launches herself into the passenger seat of my SUV, shaking the denim jacket out at her feet.

"This had better be good," she says. "I don't know why you won't go in there."

I glance at the opera house. I found a spot in the angled parking along Church Street, and the view out of the windshield is of the side of the building that abuts Church Street. It consists mostly of the sign above the stairwell, which indicates the entrance to the police department and a row of windows at the back of the building where the dressing rooms used to be in the opera house. There's a movement of dark shadow at one of the windows, and I look back at Carmen.

"Do you want me to tell you why I don't go in there?"

Carmen shifts her gaze to where I had been looking and shudders. "Better not." She lifts her chin. "Get on with it."

"Remember Miss Gustafson? The teacher who died in that car accident right before Lisa disappeared?"

Carmen blinks and flicks away a drop of rain running down her forehead. "Victoria Gustafson? Her mom was the postmistress."

I nod. "That's her."

Carmen's hand stills where she's fixing the damage her denim jacket did to her black curls, and her gaze falls on me, the lines around her mouth firming.

"No," she nearly whispers.

"Murdered."

Carmen drops her jacket on her legs. "Woman, you are killing me lately." Her eyes lock on mine. "Lisa Reynolds is alive, and Victoria Gustafson was murdered. This is what you have to say to me? I thought we were friends." She throws out a hand toward the police department. "What am I supposed to say to Tom? Sorry, dude, my friend's been talking to the dead and now we got to undo some things we thought were old news."

I shrug. "You don't have to do anything. I just thought you'd like to know."

Her gaze narrows. "You're telling me this to absolve yourself of guilt when you start poking your nose in where it shouldn't be."

I look away without answer.

"Are you forgetting what happened with the Michaelson case? Do I need to remind you?" She goes on anyway.

I turn swiftly back to her, jostling my hair clip against the headrest of the seat, hard plastic digging into the back of my head. "That wasn't my fault. I didn't know that was an active investigation."

"I asked you to help with Lisa Reynolds. Not start digging up dead bodies."

"I can't help with Lisa Reynolds. She's alive. I only deal with the dead."

Carmen waves a hand. "Then what was that about her backpack?"

"I searched Lisa's name in the *Bellegrave Bulletin* archive. There are two photos showing her with a denim backpack. You said she stayed after school on the day she disappeared and then drove herself home. Wouldn't her denim backpack still be in the car when the police recovered it?"

Carmen's frown is fierce. "Weren't you the one who just said to me that finding blood in the trunk of a car doesn't equate to a murder having occurred?"

I lean against the console between us. "Lisa Reynolds was a senior in high school. The two photos of her in the *Bellegrave Bulletin* show her carrying that backpack. It wasn't found in her car."

Carmen only blinks.

"Come on. You can make this leap. You were a teenager once. What's a backpack to a teenager?"

"A place to hide the lunch you didn't eat until your mother and Jesus can smell it."

I frown now and wait. It isn't long before Carmen's face opens with understanding.

"She took it with her," she nearly whispers.

"She took it with her when she abandoned her car," I elaborate.

"That's speculation."

"That's a question that needs to be asked." I jam a finger into the console. "One that should have been asked twenty-seven years ago. A backpack to a kid that age contains their whole life. So where is it?"

Carmen presses a flat hand against her forehead and up into her curls. "It *should* have been asked." Her voice is flat, wandering, as if she's back there, but instead of being a kid in middle school, she's at the scene as the smart, experienced detective she is. She comes back to me in a minute. "What's this got to do with Miss Gustafson?"

I shake my head. "Nothing. My dad came over for dinner last night—remind me to thank you for that later—"

Her smile is swift and annoying.

"He mentioned how shook up the village already was when Lisa went missing. An announcement for a memorial for Miss Gustafson was in the paper next to a human-interest piece about Lisa." I shrug. "I went down to the bridge where she supposedly drove her car into the river, and she was there."

"Victoria was there?" Carmen's lips don't come back together after asking the question.

"She tried to tell me something."

"What did she tell you?" Carmen's asks as her breath hitches.

"She kept pressing her hands to her chest and saying *my heart*."

Carmen lifts one side of her mouth in confusion. "My heart? What does that mean?"

"I don't know, but I'm going to find out."

Carmen's finger appears quickly in my face. "You will be doing nothing, Dr. James. Victoria Gustafson fell asleep and drove her car into that river, and that's it. Don't go poking around where you shouldn't."

"The guardrail wasn't damaged."

Carmen's finger drops. "What?"

"The story in the paper about the accident included a photo at the scene. The guardrail wasn't damaged. My dad said the ongoing theory back then was that she went up that guardrail like a ramp and launched the car into the river, right?"

"That's why they replaced that guardrail." Carmen's eyes have narrowed, and I know if she doesn't believe me yet, she's at least curious.

"In the photo, it's undamaged. How would a car weighing at least a couple of tons drive up that guardrail and not cause even the tiniest mark on it?"

Carmen shakes her head. "Then she must have been coming the other way. Maybe you got it wrong."

"She was driving away from school? At six in the morning?"

"Maybe she forgot her coffee at home." Carmen's voice is pitched just innocently enough to let me know she's trying to throw me off the scent.

"Was an autopsy ever conducted?"

"Della, please. Victoria died in a car accident. Her cause of death was obvious."

"Was an autopsy ever conducted?"

I see the resignation play across her face. "No, there wasn't an autopsy. I believe her mom didn't want to put the family through that." She narrows her eyes as if thinking. "If I remember, my mom at the time kept saying Kevin was too upset about the whole thing. Kept blaming someone. Said he drove her to it."

"Someone?" I lean against the console. "Was this someone ever investigated? Was Kevin questioned? What was he talking about?"

"Della, do you hear yourself? Victoria died in a car accident. I know you want someone to blame. It's always easier when there *is* someone to blame. But she just died in a terrible, horrible accident, and there's nothing we can do about it."

There's a heavy moment of silence between us, but I'm tired of these silent gaps littering my life, so I ignore it.

"Why was Kevin in Bellegrave? I thought he left after graduating."

Carmen shakes her head and looks out the windshield. "I don't know. You would have to ask my mom." She turns back. "Better yet ask Victoria's mom. I bet she could tell you."

"Are you giving me your blessing?"

Her expression is tired. "I know you won't give up until you talk to someone, and it matters very little what I say." She reaches for the door handle and stops. "But what am I supposed to do about Lisa Reynolds?"

I shrug. "Find the backpack. Wherever the backpack is, Lisa is."

"Do you want a position in the department? I can talk to Tom."

"No, thanks," I say and start the SUV. "I always preferred history to criminal justice."

Carmen shakes her head and goes for the door handle only to stop again. "Should I know what's inside that building?" She pauses, licks her lips. "I mean for my own protection."

"Your gun isn't going to save you from what's in there," I say, lifting my chin toward the opera house.

"I don't know why I ever sat next to you at lunch that day. I've regretted it for thirty-two years," she grumbles as she jumps out of the SUV and back into the rain.

It's still raining when I slip back through the employee entrance at the library and up the back stairs.

"I was about to send a search party."

I'm so tense from the events of the afternoon I jump when Frances's pragmatic voice comes from behind me.

I turn to find her standing in the doorway to the break room, a cup of tea steaming between her two hands. Her head is tilted, her glasses at such an angle that it allows her to peer over them directly at me, and it's worse than any look my mother has ever given me.

"One thing led to another," I say. "You know how that goes."

"I don't." The two words are crisp and short, and I know she's trying to test me with unnerving silence, but Allie appears then, her arms filled with binders.

"I can't find the scripts for the children's choir," she says, her words distorted as she holds the stack of binders with her chin. "They didn't get put away with the fall pageant stuff, did they?"

I move to take some of Allie's burden, but I don't miss Frances's pointed look as she turns away back toward her office.

"Let's look in the basement," I say. "It's probably behind the stuffed replica of Roosevelt's dog."

Allie whines but not with heart. "You know I don't like the basement."

"And I keep telling you there's nothing down there. It's perfectly safe."

That's not entirely the truth. There's an Algonquin hunting party in the basement, but it's better that Allie not know that. They're harmless anyway. It's only a residual haunt, again sort of like an echo. They only repeat the same motions over and over and have never once in all the years I've worked there interacted with me.

I jump again when my phone dings.

"You okay?" Allie asks.

"Long day," I evade and fish my phone from my pocket.

It's a text from my dad, a picture of Henry in his anti-anxiety shirt, curled up on a sofa with a distinct mauve lily pattern. The very fabric my mother had to have when she declared Ryan and I grown-ups and finally bought a new couch that she no longer feared two children would destroy.

Ryan had immediately dumped an entire bottle of fruit punch on it.

I knew storms were predicted that afternoon and had left the downstairs bathroom door open for Henry. He liked to curl up between the wall and the toilet when the sky booms came, but it appeared my dad had rescued him and brought him back to the Hopewell house.

I text back a quick thank you and a heart emoji and put my phone back in my pocket.

"To the basement," I say to Allie who whines in response.

At five, the Friends of Lady Josephine Lodge start filtering into the second floor meeting room, chatting and catching up like they haven't just seen each other at work, school, or around the village. David is wearing a green button-down today with otters across it as he chats with Steve, and Dottie Uttin is trying to convince Sally Marsden, the owner of A Cut Above on Main Street, that all the volunteers of the reenactment should forgo underwear. They are followed by Matt Townsend from Matt's Meats, Pastor Jon Harding from the Methodist church, Reverend Earl Roderick from the Baptist church, and Lorna Hiddles from Bellegrave's Gardening Society. Frances brings up the rear, notepad and pen in one hand, and shuts the door to the meeting room behind her.

The Bellegrave Historical Society accepted the care and

responsibility of Lady Josephine Lodge after the Fairchild family who had owned it for over a hundred years went completely bankrupt and could no longer preserve it. Luckily, Lady Josephine Lodge had been recognized in the push in the 1980s to save the Adirondack great camps, and the Fairchilds received help in keeping it from falling to the ground. It was named to the National Register of Historic Places in 1994, but even that could not keep it alive. The Bellegrave Historical Society happily took on the care and keeping of the camp in 1998 and have been stewards of its history ever since.

That means I spend a lot of time cajoling historical society volunteers into helping me sweep the cobwebs from the corners and air out the musty smell in the spring when we open it for tours and events in the summer and operate a living history outdoor museum on its grounds.

Which is why we're here now.

Dottie gives up convincing Sally of anything, and I can finally bring the meeting to order. We go through the spring-cleaning checklist, and as this group of volunteers has been doing it for so long, they may know the procedure better than I do.

Dottie will secure the cleaning product donations and round up the usual suspects to do the dusting and sweeping. Steve has already reviewed the list of small maintenance projects that must be completed before the first event in the main house—a wedding the first weekend of June—and presents me with a budget for the repairs. It's a small number thankfully, and I can approve it without board consent. This means the repairs will be done more quickly, and the wedding will not be impacted, saving the much-needed rental fee the event will bring in. Lorna reviews the previous year's planting needs and confirms it for this year as well.

Once we've picked a day for opening the camp that works with both the reenactment rehearsal schedule and the gala preparation volunteer hours, we adjourn shortly before six. I gather my things quickly, hoping to escape another discussion about underwear with Dottie, but Sally touches my elbow.

"You know, Del, my offer still stands to do your hair." She leans against the table, bringing one finger to tap against her chin. She's tall and willowy with riotous curls that fall to her shoulders in big coils. Her features are both big and pointed and defined, and it gives her an air of authority.

I touch the clip at the back of my head unconsciously. My hair has never conformed to a style, being somewhere between wavy and curly but mostly just frizzy, and I've always worn it long and unstyled like Julia Ormond in *First Knight*. On Julia, it looks beautiful. On me, it just looks like I've let myself go.

It's practical though for me and makes it easy to get my swim cap on for mornings at the pool, so I've never taken Sally up on her offer to do something with it. She eyes me now though like Henry eyes his food dish.

I smile and shake my head. "I'm afraid I still can't accept that offer, Sally. I just can't be bothered with it."

She makes a sound of disappointment and straightens from the table. "Such a pity. You've got such good cheek-bones. It's a waste to wear your hair that long."

I touch it again, considering her words. "You would cut it?"

"Absolutely," Sally says, her lips not quite closing over her prominent upper teeth. "It would make you look ten years younger."

My only response is to touch the clip again, and then Dottie is there asking about the rehearsal for that Friday.

I make it out of my office just as the Wednesday night book club members are starting to filter in. I field a few questions about the reenactment, promising it will be exactly the same as last year—a promise I can keep after Allie and I finally located the scripts for the children's choir in a basket of old wigs—and one suggestion—that I turn the whole thing into a rap like that guy on Broadway did—I ignore.

I keep the cringe this idea invokes from my face, assure them I'll think about it, and escape through the front door, which is closest.

I'm nearly out of the village when I remember there's no food at home, and Logan is in Albany.

The rain that had let up around four is back and worse now, beating relentlessly against my windshield. Part of me just wants to go home, curl up on the couch with Henry, and put an Audrey Hepburn movie on. Maybe he'll share his dog kibble with me. But at this thought, my stomach lets out a disturbing growl, and I turn onto Water Street, which will bring me back around to Church Street and Papa's Pizza.

Twenty minutes later, a large meat lovers pizza is on the seat next to me, and I'm once more headed out of town to the east end of the lake.

A headache has nestled itself behind my eyes, and I try to remember the last time I drank anything, let alone water. I press my fingers to the bridge of my nose. All I need is a good night's sleep, and tomorrow I'll figure out what to do about Miss Gustafson.

The first thing that tells me something is wrong when I get home is the lack of barking. The second is the fact that the house is completely dark. I installed automatic lights in all the rooms in the house years ago, and they're timed to go on an hour before I usually get home. Not a single window is lit in the whole house.

It's not quite seven yet, but with the storm clouds blanketing the sky, it might as well be the middle of the night. I sit in my car for a solid thirty seconds, wishing my gun was in my purse and not in its safe in the house. I have a permit to carry, but the problem with carrying a gun is, you're tempted to use it.

My heart rate picks up, and I will myself to calm. Maybe the power is out. The power was still on at Papa's, but that doesn't mean a tree couldn't have come down somewhere along the access road and taken out one of the transformers. Maybe in my rush to get to the house I missed it. There is a lot on my mind after all.

I get out of the car, tossing my bag over my shoulder and grabbing the pizza. It's still hot to the touch, and right now it's the only weapon I have. Burning cheese is better than nothing.

I skip the garage and go right for the side door that goes into the mudroom at the back of the house. The headlamp I use when I take Henry out for his last pee hangs on a hook by the door there, and it will save me from walking into total darkness.

I press the key into the lock, turn the knob carefully, and let the door drift open.

Silence.

I open my senses, take in what's waiting on the other side.

All I can smell is garlic, and all I can feel is the hot box in my hands.

I step inside. The headlamp is where I left it, and slowly I reach up and take it from its hook. I don't shut the door. It's better to keep my escape route open and clear. Clutching the headlamp against the pizza box, I move toward the kitchen.

There's no hum of the fridge. No tick of a radiator. The house is entirely silent, confirming my suspicion that the power is out. Much as it had earlier in the day, that strange feeling of missing something washes over me, but the immediate threat in front of me keeps the thought from settling in.

I stand in the mudroom, clutching the pizza and now the headlamp, willing myself to think rationally. There is no reason to be afraid. The storms that afternoon were the unpredictable kind that spring often brings, and something might have happened. I'm just shaken up because of Miss Gustafson. That's all.

I take a step into the house, freeze on the threshold of the kitchen. Everything is exactly as I left it. Coffee carafe draining in the dish rack by the sink. This morning's paper on the island. The drapes closed over the doors to the patio.

My lungs collapse as I release the breath I'd been holding, and I take another step into the kitchen when I see it.

The half bath is just to my right, and its door is shut tight. I had left it open for Henry.

Henry.

Where—

The creak of a floorboard behind me has me spinning before the sound can connect with a sane thought. I lift the pizza, swinging it. Cardboard connects with the head of the intruder sneaking up behind me. I think I scream, but there are so many things happening at once I can't be sure.

The door to the basement is on the other side of the fridge, and I see now it's open. He was lying in wait for me. Ready to pounce the moment I stepped into the kitchen. I go to swing again, the primal need for survival inside of me controlling my movements.

The intruder grabs me, crushing the pizza between us as he holds on to my shoulders.

"Della, it's me."

I know that voice, and instantly my body calms, the flash of fight draining out of me. Of course, I know that voice. It was the first voice I heard when I woke up after the accident, the one that spoke the words that still haunt my dreams.

Our baby is gone.

"Logan?" There's only the light by the open mudroom door to see him by, but I don't need it. I know his face. The square jaw and forehead, the black slashes of eyebrow over blue, blue eyes, the smattering of faded freckles at one corner of his forehead that come out with his summer tan, the black hair now touched by gray in spots. "You're in Albany."

His face had been frozen in concern, but at this, it breaks into a knowing smile. "I *was* in Albany," he says. "But it was a false alarm. I got everything sorted this morning and drove back this afternoon."

"Where's your car?" The question comes out like the accusation it is. I need some sort of rational explanation in a day that has seriously gone off the rails.

"In the garage. Where it always is." He studies my face. "Are you okay?"

"I'm fine," I say, ignoring his concern. "What were you doing in the basement?"

His eyes travel over my head to the kitchen behind me, and his expression grows sheepish. "I wanted to surprise you. I was trying to find something to make for dinner."

He doesn't say anything more, and he doesn't need to. The relief that rushes through me is so complete I laugh.

"You turned on the teakettle and the air fryer at the same time again, didn't you?"

"I did," he confirms with a guilty smile.

"And when you tried to reset the circuit, you flicked the interlock for the generator."

He looks over my head again. "I must have."

I shake my head. "We've been through this. The one at the top is not a circuit."

"It's the only one that looks different than the rest. That's how I know which circuit I've popped."

"You didn't take a flashlight with you."

He won't meet my gaze now. "I thought I could just feel my way through it."

"You're going to get yourself electrocuted."

Now he does look at me. "I didn't get electrocuted. I got

assaulted with—" He looks between us where the pizza is wedged, hot and greasy against our chests. "Is this pizza?"

"Meat lovers," I say. "Want some?"

Even in the dim light, I see his eyes change. "Something happened today." His hands move, the gentlest of strokes up and down my arms. "What was it?"

"Where's Henry?" I ask, avoiding the question.

"I assume he's with your dad."

I close my eyes, let out a breath. I'd completely forgotten he was with my dad. Logan pulls the ruined pizza from between us, tossing it on the island behind me. He gathers me into his arms now, and the grease from the pizza box is sticky between us.

"Hey," he says. "Tell me what's happened."

I shake my head where it's buried against his shoulder. "It's complicated."

"Complicated can be interesting," he says.

"You just say that because you're my husband and you have to."

I can feel his grin against my temple where he presses a kiss. I erupt in a full body ache of longing. For this. The ease of it. So elusive in the past thirteen years of our marriage that it takes assault with a deadly pizza to allow it to come up between us.

"I say that because it's true." His hands wander over my back, tracing curves and valleys. "Tell me who you saw."

I lean back, my gaze finding his. "How do you know I saw someone?"

"Because the living never confound you this much."

I drop my head back against his shoulder. "Miss Gustafson," I murmur against him after a while.

"Why is that name familiar?"

I lean back again. "She was the middle school special education teacher. Remember?"

His eyes widen. "The one who died in that horrible crash?"

I nod. "Except I think she was trying to tell me she was murdered."

I've said enough wild things to my husband that his face doesn't change with this statement.

Instead, he squeezes my shoulders and sets me away from him.

"If you get the lights back on, I'll see if I can save the pizza. Then you can tell me everything."

SIX

While I go down to the basement with my headlamp in place so I don't make the same mistake as Logan while trying to fix the circuit breakers, he attempts to salvage the pizza. By the time I return to the kitchen, he has pried most of the pizza from the lid of the box, and while it doesn't look pretty, it's most certainly edible.

The fridge is once more humming, and the under-cabinet lighting is on, lifting the gloom from the small space. I check the mudroom door to make sure it's closed and locked and return the headlamp to its peg by the door.

Logan has placed two beers on the table in the dining alcove along with the pizza. We take our usual spots and eat straight from the box with the aid of a roll of paper towels while I explain about Victoria Gustafson.

When I've finished, Logan asks, "What does this have to do with Lisa Reynolds's disappearance?"

I pop a piece of pepperoni into my mouth and shake my head. "Nothing. It's just what started me looking into the newspaper archive when I found the photo of the accident scene."

Logan leans back, hooking one arm over the back of his chair, twiddling a paper towel between his fingers. "So no one's actually asked you to look into Miss Gustafson's death?"

I shift, recalling my conversation with Carmen earlier that afternoon. "Not really."

A smile lifts half his mouth, but I can tell he wishes he weren't smiling. "Delia James, most people don't go out searching for ghosts. You know that, right?"

I study him under the glow of the shaded light that hangs above the table. I try to pick out the pieces of the boy I fell in love with in high school that are hiding in his face or the man I married fifteen years ago, but so much has changed, so much is different between us that sometimes I struggle to find the people we used to be.

He's taken off his dress shirt after I ruined it with pizza grease, and he sits in only his black undershirt. His arms are well defined and already starting their summer tan, and it's hard to believe either of us has reached forty. I thought there would be so much more time.

"I think they find me," I finally say, taking a sip of beer.

We've been sitting there so long it's gone flat and warm, but I drink it anyway, washing down the last thirteen years since the accident that have suddenly clogged my throat.

He drops his arm and leans his elbows on the table. "What do you need from me?"

The yellow light hits his eyes in just a way, and suddenly they're bluer than they've ever been.

I set down the crust of pizza I've been nibbling and wipe my hands on a paper towel. "Do you remember anything about Miss Gustafson? I know it's weird because she was a teacher and all, but do you recall her ever dating? Coming to school events with a boyfriend?"

Both of his dark eyebrows lift. "I was a middle school boy. I wasn't even aware of you yet, let alone anyone else's love life."

Something warm and once familiar spreads through me, and now I'm smiling. I wipe my hands, although I've just done that, but at least it's something to do to distract me.

When I look up again, his eyes have changed, and for a second, I wonder if I'm wrong about Albany.

Suddenly I remember what he'd said when I hit him with the pizza box. "Why *are* you here?" I ask. "You said you'd be in Albany until Friday."

I regret the words almost at once because his face changes, and the stale separateness that has marked our marriage since the accident returns, disrupting the small quiet moment we'd been having.

He stands and takes his bottle to the sink to rinse before dropping it into the recycling bin by the fridge.

"Eh, it was a false alarm," he says, his voice deceptively casual. "Something came up with a vendor contract, and the DEC was disputing some conditions, but it turns out the wrong contract went to the wrong vendor." He grabs another beer from the fridge and turns around with a shrug and an expression on his face I've never seen. He's guarded, and something inside my chest flinches. "Just a mix-up. I didn't even need to be there." He gestures with the bottle. "Why are you wondering about Miss Gustafson's love life?"

It's a second before I can pull my thoughts together to answer. "Carmen said something about Miss Gustafson's mom being upset at the time. Apparently Miss Gustafson's brother was accusing someone of driving her to it. I thought it might be a boyfriend."

"Why a boyfriend?"

"Only love can drive someone to do something so extreme." My words are careless, and now a heavy silence hangs between us. I collect my soiled paper towels and take them to the trash under the sink. "I suppose I should speak to Miss Gustafson's mom. Does she still live out on the county highway?"

Logan opens his beer on the edge of the counter like my dad taught him, and the gesture stops me for a second.

"I think so. It's been a while since she retired, but with a federal pension, I bet she's doing okay in the house by herself. How old do you think she is?"

I pick up his dress shirt from where he's discarded it on the island and absently take it over to the sink to apply dish soap to the grease stains. "Well Kevin is my dad's age. Victoria was younger though. Maybe by about ten years? That should put Mrs. Gustafson in her mid-eighties at least."

"She always gave out lollipops, remember that?" Logan returns to his seat at the table and leans back again in his chair, one arm looped over the back. "She would save the orange ones for me."

"Remember her dog?" I say, the memory coming back to me out of nowhere like memories often do. "It would sit on the counter when she was in the back sorting mail and bark when someone came in. What kind of dog do you think that was?"

"Some kind of terrier," Logan says. "His name was Walter, and his wire hair made him look like he had a mustache." He bends one finger over his upper lip, wagging the end of it and twitching his nose in an imitation of Mrs. Gustafson's terrier.

I laugh until apprehension grips my throat. I stall in my attempt to get the grease stains from Logan's shirt, my hands settling on the edge of the sink.

"What do I say to her?" I ask, my eyes lingering on the empty sink. "The last time I attempted to intervene with a ghost it didn't go so well."

I hear him get up, but I can't move my eyes from the sink. I'm not startled when he takes my shoulders and turns me toward him. Logan has always been demonstrative. That's never changed. I look up at him as he holds my shoulders steady.

"You did what you could in the situation, and Becky Brewer is alive and without third degree burns because of you." He pauses, but I know he's not done. "You always know what to say, Del," he says. He shakes his head slowly as if in disbelief. "I don't know how. But you do."

Even though he's trying to reassure me, it's hard to accept his words. "I always feel like I'm fumbling about, trying to figure things out as they come to me."

I try to pull away, finish washing the shirt, but he holds me steady.

"The point is you *do* try to figure it out." He shrugs. "Most people don't even try."

Suddenly I don't think we're talking about Miss Gustafson anymore. His eyes watch me carefully, and I get the sense he wants me to say something. But that's not how our marriage works. Since the accident, I don't say anything, and he pretends everything is okay. That's how we've gotten this far. But right then, standing there in the kitchen, my hands soapy and him in his undershirt, I want to ask him about Albany.

The quiet is shattered by the sound of the mudroom screen door screeching open, the scrape of a key in the door, the stampede of paws across the wooden floor, and my dad's call of hello.

"In here," I call back automatically, but Henry has already found us.

Or rather he has found Logan, and he launches himself into the air. Logan catches him against his chest, burying his face into the neck of the squirming dog.

"Hey, buddy, I'm home," he says with a laugh as the weight of Henry pushes him back against the counter.

I watch the two of them, and the warmth that fills me is what keeps me where I am.

"Hey," Dad says, and I turn to see him standing hesitantly by the fridge.

"Logan's home," I say, waving a hand that sends soap bubbles fluttering through the air. "Albany didn't need him." I gesture to the half-eaten pizza on the table. "Want some meat lovers? It's a little smushed, but it's edible."

Dad's eyes haven't moved from Logan through my whole rambling speech, and tension creeps up my neck.

"How about a beer?" I say, going for the fridge, hoping to diffuse whatever is happening here.

Logan has put Henry back on all fours and is retrieving the dog's food dish when he says, "Hey, Greg. Thanks for taking care of the little man during the sky booms."

Dad nods. "How was Albany?"

I stare into the side of my dad's head, willing him to play nice.

"False alarm," Logan says, scooping kibble into Henry's dish. Henry makes the whistling whining noise he makes when he knows food is coming. "Contract mix-up. You know how it goes."

Logan is not only a lawyer, but he went to the same law school as my father, and the two often talk in code I can never understand. But not tonight. Tonight the messages they are sending back and forth are very clear. Henry has even probably figured it out. My dad is a grizzly bear up on his hind legs ready to defend, and Logan is shaking a measly can of bear spray at him.

I step between them. "Thanks for bringing Henry back. Are you sure you don't want a beer?"

I have never voiced my concerns about Logan going to Albany. If your husband goes to another city often enough, with enough regularity, other people start to notice. And when you've been through what Logan and I have been through, their first thoughts are not good ones.

My presence in his sightline seems to knock my father from the death stare he's directed at my husband, and his eyes focus on me.

He throws a thumb over his shoulder at the door behind him. "Your mother is waiting for me. She wants to try the square dancing class at the Gale Center tonight."

I cringe. "Square dancing? Does she not remember the salsa camp?"

"She still swears she thought it was a cooking class on making salsa. Not the dancing kind of salsa." My father shakes his head as his lips go flat. "Might as well get this over with."

By then Henry has finished his dinner and trotted over to the patio doors, giving them a light tap with one paw to be let out. Logan follows him and opens the door. He slips through only for Logan to call out, "Don't chase the—" But the last of his sentence disappears as he runs out the door after the dog.

I turn back to my dad to find him watching me cautiously, his tortoiseshell glasses pushed high on his nose.

"You okay, little girl?"

"Still fine," I say, the same thing I've said every time someone asks the question since my accident.

My father as usual doesn't seem to believe me, and his lips stay stubbornly flat.

I touch his arm. "I'm really fine. You know that. When it's not fine, I do something about it, so don't give me that pitying look. I'm not on my way to a square dance class."

My dad's grimace goes nuclear as he turns for the door. "If you don't hear from me in an hour, send help."

"What kind of help?" I ask as he pushes open the back screen door.

"The kind that comes in a bottle," he calls as he lifts his

hand in farewell, the screen door banging shut behind him as he heads for his car in the driveway.

———

My alarm goes off too early the next morning.

I haul myself from bed, careful not to disturb Henry, who will only die of sadness when I tell him it's not quite warm enough to swim in the lake. He's curled against Logan on the other side of the bed while Logan appears to cling to his pillow for dear life or risk getting pushed entirely off the bed by the Labrador retriever.

My bathing suit hangs on the back of the attached bathroom door, so I make little noise getting ready. I grab my swim bag from the bench in the mudroom and slip out the back, careful not to let the screen door slam.

The town aquatic center was built after vigorous fundraising back in 2009 when it was determined the area high schools could no longer afford to support the care and maintenance of individual pools, and the pool in the basement of the Gale Center was deemed run-down and inadequate. The Bellegrave Aquatic Center now hosts three area high school swim teams and a senior aqua aerobics program with enough vitality to solve world hunger.

It takes about ten minutes for me to drive there, and although the pool is clean and the center quiet at this hour, I long for the warm summer mornings when I can just drop into the lake outside my door.

I am not an athlete. I carry an extra twenty pounds on my five-foot-five frame because the healthiest relationship in my life is with cookies. I swim lazy breaststroke style for about forty-five minutes three times a week. The swimming is to keep up my mobility after breaking the femur in my left leg in the accident. So far it's working, and the dire predictions of my orthopedic surgeon, Dr. Swanson, called Doc Randy affectionally by my father, have not come true, and the leg continues to give me very little trouble. I also take the occasional yoga class with Carmen, which I think helps, especially the hot yoga, which turns all my muscles to liquid wax.

I wave to Bethany Marks, the center's director, who is manning the front desk at this hour as I walk through the sliding glass front doors.

The pool is kept at a steady eighty-two degrees, and I slip into the water with ease, my muscles finding the rhythm automatically. Forty-five minutes pass quickly, and soon I'm showering off and putting my sweats back on. I'll take a proper shower at home, but I like to get the chlorine off as soon as possible.

When I return home, Logan is in the kitchen, his hair still damp from his shower. He's pouring coffee into his to-go tumbler as Henry trots up to greet me.

"He's already had breakfast, so don't listen to his cries of woe," Logan says as he comes around the island, coffee in one hand, his leather satchel already thrown over his shoulder. "I'm headed in early. Trying to catch up on what I missed after being in the car for two days."

I turn my head to offer my cheek for his perfunctory goodbye kiss, but instead, he takes my shoulders in his hands, the coffee tumbler warm against my arm.

"No summoning bad ghosts today, okay? Only talk to the nice ones, got it?"

I nod, trying to keep my expression serious. "I will do my best."

Instead of the peck on the cheek I'm expecting, he kisses me. Soundly. On the lips. I'm so surprised I almost forget to return his call of goodbye as he goes out the door that connects the kitchen to the garage.

Henry and I exchange a look of befuddlement before he

follows me up the stairs to shower. I glance at the closed door opposite our bedroom door on the landing, but I don't linger there anymore. I head straight into the master bedroom, Henry on my heels.

He likes to lounge on the bed and make me feel as guilty as possible while I get ready for work. His eyes drill into me with their disappointment that I should even contemplate leaving him for an entire day.

His dog walker, Jenna, will be by around noon to feed him and take him on an adventure hike, but he will still act as though I buy the discount kibble and make him sleep on the floor.

The library is already open by the time I get there, and I go through the front doors. I like the feeling of walking into the library as though I'm a patron, and I never miss the chance to marvel at the front foyer. Things were done differently back in 1883 when the library was built. They took their time and paid attention to details, and it shows in the careful wooden craftsmanship and carved marble of the library foyer.

Sarah is back at the front desk, and I wave in greeting before Frances pounces on me before I've even set a single foot on the stairs.

"A pipe burst at the lodge," she says without preamble. "Gail Saunders was rowing by this morning and saw the water coming out of the wall where that back bathroom is. She called Steve. He's there now with Kenny," she explains, referring to the town's only plumber, Kenny Wallencratz. She dangles a robust key chain in front of me. "Thought you might want to head over now."

And so my day truly begins.

I make my way to the camp on the west end of the lake. It brings me by the access road that leads up to the Reynolds's camp, and I briefly think of Lisa and wonder if Carmen has followed up on my suggestion about the backpack.

The stench of a stale winter slumber greets me as I open the front door of the camp, and I recoil, pressing a hand to my stomach. The cleaning volunteers can't get here soon enough. I glance around as I make my way to the back bathroom and am pleased to see the winter wasn't too hard on the place. There are a few cobwebs in corners, a healthy layer of dust, and the tang of eau de mothball, but it's truly not terrible.

I discover Steve and Kenny with their heads both literally in the wall behind the pedestal sink in the bathroom.

"Hi," I say, interrupting their back and forth in the dank cavity of the wall.

Steve extracts his head first. "We've got a real problem here, Dr. James."

I wince. Steve only calls me Dr. James when it's expensive.

"Don't know how long the pipe's been leaking, but it's rotted the wall." He shimmies out from under the sink as Kenny finally pulls his head out.

"Hey, Della," he says with a grin, revealing the gap in his front teeth.

"Hey, Kenny," I reply before going back to Steve who has now managed to stand and wipe dust from his canvas coat.

"I've got to meet the exterminator this morning to go over the plan for the milk house, but when I'm done, I'll call some contractors for quotes. We're going to need to fix that wall, and with the wedding first weekend of June, you'd best hope for a miracle."

"Thank you for not sugarcoating it, Steve," I mumble.

One side of his mouth lifts in a smirk. "I know how you prefer to receive bad news, Dr. James." He turns back to Kenny who is still in the wall. "Later, Kenny," he says as he scoots out the door.

Kenny's reply is muffled inside the wall.

I check the rest of the lodge while Kenny finishes the

repair in the back bathroom. Luckily it's in the smaller bathroom that's typically only used by the staff.

The floor plan of Lady Josephine Lodge is helpfully split exactly in two, which made converting it to a living history center with conference space rather easy. From the main entrance, the original bedrooms are to the right down a long corridor. These rooms now serve as historical society offices during the season. To the left of the entrance are the public rooms, including a great room, dining room, library, and kitchen. The great room has been converted to conference space, but the rest has been largely restored to its original state.

Many of the outbuildings on the property have been restored as well, and it's in those buildings that Allie runs the living history portion of Lady Josephine Lodge.

When I step into the great room, I'm pleased to see the warm glow of natural wood and the cozy feel of the twig and branch decor. I find a cracked pane of glass in one of the diamond-pane windows in the library, but the rest of the lodge is in order. I pull out my phone and send a quick email to Steve to add the cracked pane of glass to his maintenance list before heading back to the main entrance.

Kenny is loading his tools into his van. "I'll email you the invoice," he shouts from the drive.

I raise a hand to acknowledge I've heard him and lock the front door behind me. My dreams of having a quiet hour at my desk to catch up on emails is dashed when I climb the stairs to the second floor of the library to find Allie has strewn a path of papers through the nonfiction stacks. She looks up from where she's perched under the table of new nonfiction releases by the stairs.

"The scripts for the townspeople have been entirely mixed together." She holds up a piece of paper. "Peter Bellegrave's speech was in with the blacksmith's explanation of the anvil. I have no idea what happened."

I toss my things into my office before joining her on the floor, glad it's a Thursday morning and the library is quiet enough for us to commandeer this part of the second floor.

It's noon before I have a chance to think of Mrs. Gustafson and what I might say to her. The problem with all of this is I was a kid when it happened. The human brain tends to fill in the blanks of our memories with events we think are plausible, considering the facts we actually remember, and on top of that, I could only remember those events from the perspective of the child I was at the time.

Deciding it's better to get my facts straight before I show up on Mrs. Gustafson's door to tell her I saw her dead daughter, I decide to call my mom.

I am finally in my office, and I have about ten minutes of peace and quiet before Allie comes back with iced coffees and sandwiches from the diner to continue our semi-successful attempt to get the script mess straightened out. So I find my phone in the piles of paperwork on my desk and hit the contact for my mom's office as her employer has a strict no cell phone policy.

"The office of Doctors Kirkland and Martinelli. This is Melanie. How may I help you?"

"Hey Mel, it's me. Is Mom available?"

"Oh, sugar, I thought that was your number. Is the rehearsal still on for tomorrow evening? They're calling for thundershowers, so I wanted to double-check."

I had been about to open my laptop to take notes on what my mom had to say and at this I freeze. "Thundershowers?"

"Mmhmm, sugar. Big ones apparently. I know we usually do rehearsals on the grounds at the lodge, but I don't know if you want to make a backup plan or something. It's looking to be a complete washout."

I lean forward and let my forehead strike the side of the

table. "Thanks for letting me know, Mel. I'll put something together."

Reenactment weekend and the gala are six weeks away, and the universe is determined to make everything go wrong between now and then.

"You got it, sugar. Let me get your ma."

There is a tone as if I was put on hold, and I let my forehead rest against the table a little longer, enjoying the darkness as this position shuts out everything else in the space.

"Delia Ann? Is that you?"

I sit up. "Hey, Mom, you got a second?"

"Is this about Logan?" There's a hushed tone to the way she says this, and I wonder if she's cupped her hand around the mouthpiece of the phone to keep Mel from overhearing her.

My mother has worked at the medical offices of Doctors Kirkland and Martinelli for nearly thirty-five years. As soon as Ryan was old enough to be shipped off to pre-K, she was out the door and back to her career in the medical coding field. Melanie Short, the transplant from Georgia who runs the front desk, has been my mother's cohort in hobby-acquiring crime for thirty of those almost thirty-five years. My mother's attempt at trying to keep our conversation private is just for show. She will tell Mel everything we say as soon as we hang up.

"No, Logan's fine," I say, brushing past the topic. "I wanted to talk to you about something else."

"Oh." Mom's voice is suddenly bright and clear. "I don't know anything about Lisa Reynolds, honey. You know I was just so scared that summer. I went to work and straight home. We didn't even go to Old Home Days that year, and they postponed the reenactment until July. That's how you know it was serious."

Maxine Hopewell is good at two things: collecting hobbies

and talking. If you don't stop her rush of words, you'll never get a word in edgewise.

"Mom," I say deliberately, and her words finally cease. "I'm not calling about Lisa Reynolds."

There's an intake of breath, and I wait. "I thought your dad said Carmen asked you to look into that."

"I think that was supposed to remain private."

Mom snorts. "In a town like Bellegrave? Shortcake, everyone knows about it."

I frown, wondering if it's gotten back to Bob Reynolds and hoping not for Marty's sake.

"Well, even if that's true, I'm not calling about her. I wanted to see what you remember about the accident that spring when Miss Gustafson was killed."

Another intake of breath but this one with a whistle of despair. "Oh, poor Vicky. What a tragedy." I hear a noise as if she's shaking her head against the phone. "She was such a nice girl too. Shouldn't have happened. They just work those poor teachers to death."

"What do you mean?" I say.

"Well, everyone knows she fell asleep on her way to school. Woman was overworked, that's what I say."

I play with a pen I find on the table in front of me, concentrating on twirling it between my fingers as I try to assemble my thoughts. "So you think she just fell asleep? That it was an accident?"

"Well, that's what everyone said at the time. There was no other explanation for it."

I tap the pen against the table now. "You didn't hear any rumors about a relationship Miss Gustafson might have been in that had gone sour?"

"Mmm, I never heard anything like that. I don't even remember Vicky dating to be honest. She was always working so much."

I lick my lips and say what I need to say. "So you don't think anyone wanted her dead, do you?"

There's a beat of silence then, which in a conversation with Maxine Hopewell, any moment of silence is a cause for concern.

"Want her dead?" Another beat, and I can hear what's coming next before she says it. "Delia Ann, you'd better tell me what's going on. You saw her ghost, didn't you?"

"Yes," I say.

"Gee—" I don't hear the rest of the words because my mother drops the phone. At least, I think she does because I hear a clatter and a thud as though the receiver has fallen all the way to the carpeted floor in her office. She's back in a second. "You saw Vicky?" she hisses, and I know she's trying to keep our conversation private because she's still scarred from that time Mrs. Nickelson suggested I be institutionalized.

"I did. I don't think her death was an accident."

"Oh, shortcake, this is like that whole thing with the Brewer wedding dress again." Her voice has gone shrill with concern.

I look at my phone as if I can't believe she just said that, but really, it's a fair statement. As I'd told Logan the previous night, the Brewer wedding dress was not one of my finer moments.

I put the phone back to my ear. "It's not like the Brewer wedding dress again. I have no intentions of turning a hose on a bride because the vintage gown she's wearing belongs to a dead woman who is really upset with the alterations her great-niece made to it and is threatening to set it on fire with the bride in it. I was saving that woman's life."

"Ghosts have some real strange hang-ups about things," my mother mutters.

"So do the living," I reply. "So do you think there was anyone who would want to harm Miss Gustafson?"

Mom lets out a sigh as if she's given up. "It wasn't possible to hate Vicky. Not enough to want to kill her. She was just a good person. If she got the wrong change at the Super Duper, she'd give the extra back. Heck, she'd even go back to the store if she noticed the error when she got home. She always helped Mrs. Delanzo cross the street for church, and she was always at the town square early on Old Home Days. She bought ice cream cones for kids and tied their shoes when she saw their laces were loose. She was just...nice."

"So no one had it in for her?"

There's a noise like my mom shrugging. "I don't know. There was that dustup at the school board meeting that one time. But everyone was heated that night."

"What night?"

Mom lets out a breath that sounds like a cloud of static traveling down the line. "Oh, you know. It was the board meeting that determined the budget for the next year, and everyone was there with their opinions, and it was hot. I mean temperature wise. We were going through some unbearable heat wave. So unusual for May, and there's no air conditioning in those schools, you know, so people were irritable. I remember your father calling Jerome Van Allen a luddite that night. That's how you know it was bad. Your father apologized immediately, of course. He felt bad that whole summer. Bought Jerome a new tackle box."

"Why was everyone so mad?"

"Eh, Superintendent Reynolds had announced a shortfall in the budget, and some programs were going to be cut. That was the year you decided you wanted to play basketball, but they were going to cut the girls' team for lack of interest and wanting to save money. That's why your dad and I were there."

"I never wanted to play basketball."

"Yes, you did. It was right after your M.C. Hammer phase."

The M.C. Hammer phase was very real, and something I didn't like to talk about (my grandma made me custom parachute pants), so I just assumed my mother was right, and at some point, I wanted to play basketball.

"So there wasn't money in the budget?"

"Mmm, no," Mom goes on, her voice distant as if she's filtering through her memories. "And I remember Miss Gustafson getting into it with the middle school science teacher. What was her name? Torres, Tara, Terrance. Something with a T. She wanted to start an after-school geology program, and Miss Gustafson wanted more special education programming of some kind. Bob said there wasn't funds for either, and the whole thing blew over. But I'd never seen Vicky get angry like she did that night. She really cared about her students."

I could never picture Victoria Gustafson getting angry about anything, but hearing about this confrontation shifted my perspective.

"Thanks, Mom," I say.

"You're welcome, shortcake, although I'm not sure I was much help. You going to go talk to Gretchen?"

"I plan to stop by her house before I head home tonight."

There's a pause on the other end of the line before my mother says, "Just be careful, Delia Ann. I know you say the dead can't hurt us, but the living still can."

SEVEN

Mrs. Gustafson—Gretchen—lives in an old federal-style farmhouse out on the county highway west of Bellegrave. The faded red brick of the farmhouse is still intact, but the old post and beam barn caved in long ago, the depression of the roof now covered in a blanket of moss with several saplings springing from its center.

I pull into the driveway and park behind a small old SUV with fading paint. I hadn't called ahead. I find when it comes to letting people know their dead loved ones have contacted me it's better to rip it off like a Band-Aid.

The lawn appears to have been raked already, evidence of winter's wrath already swept away, and the planters on the front concrete steps are stripped of last season's annuals. The trees that dot the front lawn are mature and just beginning to bud. I can picture them full in the summer, their heavy branches cloaking the house in shadows, which probably keeps it cool. Somewhere in the distance I hear a dog bark as I get out of my car.

I make my way straight to the front door before I can lose

my nerve and press the button for the bell. It's crusted over in rust, so I give the front door a good knock just in case.

I step back as far as the front stoop will let me, and I let my gaze drop to the planters at my feet. They're a cerulean blue pottery, and I bet they're beautiful in the summer.

The door is yanked open so quickly I nearly topple off the stoop. In the vacuum created by the door opening the outer screen bangs slightly against the frame, and I'm distracted enough to not notice Mrs. Gustafson right away, but when I do, guilt floods me.

She's holding her right hand up at her side, and it's caked in flour. There's even some smeared across her brow and in her gray hair, which hangs in braids along her shoulders. I had forgotten the intense green of her eyes, and I'm pleased to see they haven't faded as they stare at me, the corners as tight as her pinched mouth. I've clearly interrupted her in the middle of something.

"What—" She stops, arrested, those green eyes riveted to my face. "Oh." This word is said with a gentility I had never heard from the postmistress who was renowned for running a tight ship at the post office. Her right hand fades to her side. "I've been waiting for you. Took you long enough." She gestures at the screen door. "Come in, come in. I got dough on the board, and I don't want it deflating."

She hustles away down what I see to be a long hallway, and she's nearly disappeared before I can engage my muscles to wrench the door open. I step inside, and a coolness drapes over me. I look around quickly, but Victoria isn't there. I hadn't been expecting Victoria's ghost to show up here, not when it takes so much for them to materialize, but one never knows when dealing with ghosts.

The federal-style farmhouse is set up shotgun style, and I can see the back door straight ahead of me down the long corridor. I follow the sounds of dough being kneaded down the hallway, not surprised Mrs. Gustafson has already vanished from my sightline. The woman might be in her eighties, but she clearly hasn't slowed down.

I step out of the hallway into a light-filled room that expands through the back of the entire house. On one side is a large, scarred wooden table surrounded by tall wooden chairs with an ornate swirling design carved into their backs. Opposite this table is the kitchen, which appears to be original with wooden cabinets painted a forest green that stretch all the way to the ceiling. Brass fasteners run along the bottoms instead of knobs and under a single window at the back is a generous porcelain sink with built-in drainboard.

Mrs. Gustafson stands in the middle of the room at an island, its butcher block top covered in flour and bowls of varying sizes and contents. She's wearing an apron I can see now over a flannel she's pushed to her elbows. She's bent over the dough so far I can see a thinning spot in her hair at the very top of her head.

"You were expecting me?" I ask.

Mrs. Gustafson doesn't look up from her dough. "Of course, I was. I'm sure you didn't know my Vicky well—you were too young—but I know she wouldn't have gone down without a fight." She blows out a breath of air and wipes the side of her face with the inside of her arm. "Fell asleep at the wheel. Ha! I don't think so. Not my Vicky!" She looks up so suddenly I nearly take a step back, those green eyes piercing straight through me. "My Vicky did not fall asleep. That I can assure you. Someone killed her."

That's rather a surprise.

"You think someone killed her?" I attempt to clarify.

Again she looks up from the dough. "I know someone did. Tommy can keep saying otherwise, but I know the truth. Sit," she adds, pointing to the table, and I take a seat automatically.

"You mean Chief Tom?"

"He wasn't chief then. Just a deputy wet behind the ears and still hanging on to his mama's apron strings." She shakes her head. "Taking everyone else's word that Vicky must have fallen asleep instead of properly investigating."

"Can you tell me what happened?"

Her eyes flash to me. "Didn't Vicky tell you?"

I shake my head. "It doesn't really work like that. I think it takes a lot of energy for them to materialize for me, and then they don't have enough left over for actual speech."

Mrs. Gustafson's hands float down to the island, her fingers nestling into the flour there, and she looks odd, so still like that. "So you really do see the dead. I always thought that was a small-town rumor. You know how it is." She waves a hand, and flour floats into the air, catching in the last of the sun coming through the window. "Not much going on in small towns so people need to make stuff up to keep it interesting." She gestures to me now. "So what did Vicky say?"

"Well, it's not so much what she said but rather what I found." I lick my lips, suddenly feeling nervous, and I remember Logan's hands on my shoulders, encouraging and reassuring, and my heartbeat slows. "I was doing research in the newspaper archives, and I saw the photo of the accident scene. I know the assumption was she fell asleep and drove off the road, traveling up the guardrail so her car launched into the river. But the guardrail at the bridge wasn't damaged. You can see it clearly in the photograph."

Mrs. Gustafson's hands are quiet again. "Can I get you a drink? Iced tea?" I'm about to say no, I'm fine when she turns toward the sink, flicking on the faucet. "I always knew there was more to Vicky's death than what Tommy said." She shakes her head, her gaze lingering somewhere out the window, but I think really she's reviewing her memories. She turns the water off, wipes her hands on her apron, and walks to the fridge.

She fetches two glasses from one of the cabinets, and with the pitcher of iced tea she took from the fridge, makes her way over to me. She pulls out a chair and sits down without pouring the tea. She looks straight at me.

"I should have demanded an autopsy. It's my one regret in this life." She holds up a single finger, bent with age and likely arthritis. She shakes her head again, her hand falling to her knee. "I should have done more for my Vicky, but I was trying too hard to protect Kevin." Her gaze drops for a second as if in guilt or despair before it snaps back up to me. "It's tough being a mother. Especially when you're forced to choose between your children."

Something cramps in my stomach, but it hurts less than it used to. "What do you mean you were trying to protect Kevin?"

Mrs. Gustafson lets out a noise that hovers somewhere between frustration and annoyance. "After that dustup Kevin had with Daryl and then Vicky's accident. I didn't want anyone coming around here asking about my boy. He had nothing to do with this. He was just watching out for his little sister."

"Daryl?" I prompt.

"Daryl Walden. You know he and Vicky were seeing each other back then."

I sit back in my chair, this news rippling through me like a runaway train. "Daryl Walden? The custodian at the Gale Center?"

For the first time since I started this odd interview, Mrs. Gustafson won't meet my gaze. "He wasn't always like he is now. Back then he at least tried to help himself."

Daryl Walden is an alcoholic and generally known as a troublemaker about town, harassing innocent people out on a nice night in the village or cussing out people if they step on the lawn at the Gale Center. Nothing ever really bad, just...

disturbing. It was said he only held down the job at the Gale Center because his brother-in-law owned the building.

"He and Miss Gustafson were seeing one another?" So there *had* been a man. One with a troubling past and even more troubling behavior.

Mrs. Gustafson shakes her head. "Poor Vicky. She always gravitated toward those who needed the most help and look where it got her." She purses her lips, her eyes flicking to my face, and I wonder if she's trying to decide how much to tell me. She makes a fuss of her hands on the table and rearranges the empty glasses before saying, "Ah hell, Vicky probably told you anyway. Daryl could sometimes get a little pushy with her, and one time Kevin witnessed it. It was outside of Farley's. Kevin was home from the city visiting friends, and he was at the bar just having a drink when Vicky and Daryl came in. Vicky wanted to go talk to some of her friends, but Daryl never liked her giving attention to someone who wasn't him." She gives a shrug then as if domestic abuse is easily excused. "So he grabbed her. Wasn't really anything, and all Kevin did was make him stop. But Tommy was there and saw it, and as an officer of the law"—here she exaggerates her tone in mockery—"he was required to arrest Kevin for battery." She shakes her head and picks up the iced tea pitcher only to set it back down. "You know I changed Tommy's diapers when his mama would leave him with me when she went over to Saranac to the health clinic for her other boy. He had no right arresting Kevin. Thinks he's the All Mighty because someone gave him a badge."

"What happened then?" I ask, trying to keep her on track.

"Oh, the charges were dropped. Daryl knew he'd had too much to drink that night, and they made up, but Tommy never got over it. Said he was keeping his eye on Kevin. I told Kevin to get back to the city, and that's where he was when the accident happened."

It was odd the way she said that last bit, almost like an afterthought, and I wondered if she were hiding something.

"Did Vicky's behavior change in the days leading up to her accident?" I ask, remembering what Carmen had asked Marty Pruitt about Lisa's disappearance.

Mrs. Gustafson shakes her head quickly. "Oh no, Vicky was a creature of habit. There was nothing in her life except her students, and that was where her focus always was." Her expression turns vacant as though she's thinking harder. "She could have done so much good. That's the worst of it, you know." Her eyes meet mine again, that flash of piercing green. "I know I lost my daughter, but the world lost a force for good. That's the real tragedy here."

Vicky's voice comes back to me, and I hear it as though she's standing in front of me.

My heart. My heart.

"Mrs. Gustafson, was there anything Vicky truly loved? Something particularly special to her?"

She waves a hand. "Oh, call me Gretchen. Mrs. Gustafson is my dead and gone mother-in-law. And Vicky didn't have time to love anything. She was always busy up at the school." She taps a finger on the edge of the table. "Teaching is hard enough, but Vicky dedicated her life to her students. She stayed after, worked longer than her contract hours, was always spending her weekends at conferences or seminars learning new ways to help her kids." Her eyes are crinkled in grief. "Vicky would spend her own salary on things for her classroom if she knew it could help them. It's a thankless job, teaching is."

"There must have been something she was passionate about outside of work. We all need outlets."

Her eyebrows go up. "An outlet?" she says as if I've just asked her if she believes in aliens. She shakes her head again. "No, Vicky only had school and Daryl, I guess." Her eyes go vacant again, but I don't press her, hoping something will rise unbidden from her memories. "Although I'm not sure how much she loved Daryl in the end."

"Why is that?"

A line has appeared between her eyebrows as she looks at me again. "You asked if Vicky's behavior changed right before her accident. Well, I guess it wasn't her behavior as such, but rather her mood. She got awful quiet, and I sensed something had happened between her and Daryl." She shrugs. "She never talked about it though, and I never pressed. It was her business, and she didn't need her mother poking around in it. She had enough on her plate, what with the budget cuts and everything."

"My mom mentioned the school budget was particularly bad that year."

Gretchen makes a harrumph sound. "Worst ever. There was apparently some kind of unexpected shortfall. Some expense that came in far above budget." She held up her hands. "Nothing Bob could have done about it, but it's still frustrating. I know it was maddening to Vicky," she says.

"I understand Vicky got into a confrontation with one of the middle school science teachers over the budget."

She blinks, and I can almost see her thoughts arranging themselves. "Oh that was a year before the accident. I don't think that has anything to do with it. Do you?"

"Do you remember the teacher's name?"

"Of course. Gabriella Torres." She hooks a thumb over her shoulder. "She lives over in those new condos now. Got herself a new place and one of those fancy new cars where you just wave your foot under it and the back hatch opens up." She gives a sharp laugh and shakes her head. "All these problems in the world, and that's the one the smart people think to solve first." She leans forward and drops her voice. "Heard she made out good in her divorce." She taps the table again. "Good for her. She deserves something nice. Worked at that middle school for thirty years and put up with Marc's bullshit for twenty. The woman deserves a goddamn medal."

I make a note to speak with Gabriella Torres and stand. "Thank you for speaking with me, Gretchen. I hope you don't mind if I come back if I have more questions."

She stands with a slap of a hand to the table. "I knew sooner or later there would be justice for Vicky. I just had to have patience. There's a time for everything." She walks me to the door, but before she opens it, she looks up, her eyes dark. "You find out what happened to my Vicky."

It's not a question, but I answer anyway. "I will."

———

"Daryl Walden?" Carmen nearly shouts, and I blame myself for not breaking the news with greater warning.

"Shh," I whisper, my eyes scanning the other attendees of Mrs. Laura's House of Gymnastics' spring exhibition, but no one is paying attention. There are the usual over-bright smiles of moms catching up, dads swapping stories about lawn maintenance, and aunts overloaded with treats for the children they have the privilege of returning to their parents after indulging them on sugar. No one is listening to us.

"I know it's a bit of a surprise," I say.

"Surprise?" Carmen hisses, crossing one leg over the other, her magenta sandals flashing in the harsh overhead light. As soon as the snow melts, Carmen has her sandals out, and I'm not surprised she's sporting them so early in April. "How about a shock. Girl, you need to warn me."

"About what?" Raymond, Carmen's husband, leans forward on the other side of Carmen so I can see him. I always thought Raymond would look more at home on the starting line of an NFL team, which only makes Carmen look daintier than she already is. He wears his brown hair cut short on the sides, spiked on top, and somehow makes the whole thing blend with a beard that rivals Santa's.

"It's nothing," Carmen says, patting him gently on the thigh, which makes me worry for the folding plastic chair Raymond perches on.

He is six foot four, two hundred something pounds, and that plastic chair is saying the Rosary for the first time in its existence.

"It's something." He gestures toward me with his chin. "Who did you see now?"

Carmen squeezes her husband's knee. "Victoria Gustafson," she says, voice low.

He sucks air between his teeth, making a small whistling noise as his eyes go wide. "Oh dang. How about that?" He shakes his head, emitting a soft noise of sympathy. "Tragedy right there." Again he moves his chin toward me. "What'd she want?"

I look around to make sure no one is listening, and then lean over Carmen to keep my voice down. "I don't think her death was an accident."

His lips part, but sound doesn't emerge. Then he holds up one hand. "Nope, I'm out." He points a beefy finger at me. "I got a black eye trying to keep John Brewer from whoopin' you when you hosed his daughter at her wedding. I'm not doing this." He settles back into his chair, the plastic contraption squeaking ominously, and pulls out his phone.

Carmen can't quite keep the smile from her face as her husband slouches in his chair, his attention fully on the screen as he scrolls. "So you going to tell me about Daryl or leave me guessing?" she says.

I shrug. "There isn't much to tell. Mrs. Gustafson—Gretchen—just said they were dating when Vicky died."

"Daryl Walden has a criminal record," Carmen presses.

"Heck, I've picked him up more than once for criminal threatening. He's got everything from trespassing to DWI to assault on his record."

"But not murder," I point out.

"That we know of," Carmen is quick to correct. She sits up, dropping her foot to the floor again. "What if he went too far just one time? You know Daryl. He blows a lot of hot steam. There's nothing behind it but a sad man whose life didn't turn out the way he expected, but he has been known to be violent. Say he pushes around his girlfriend a little too much and accidentally kills her. He panics and gets rid of the body." She holds out both hands, palms up, as if she's cracked the case.

I shake my head. "It just doesn't feel right. Daryl's never truly harmed anyone. He's just more of an annoyance."

"Didn't you just say Kevin saw him get rough with his sister?"

I wrinkle my nose. "That whole thing seems weird, don't you think? Why would Gretchen be so worried about her son for a spat in a bar? He didn't even live here anymore."

Carmen blinks. "You're right. Want me to look into it?"

I glance at her. "I thought you said there weren't any resources for this investigation. Especially because it was a closed case."

She flutters her fingers. Today her nails are lime green, and I wonder when she's had the time to have them done. "That's an easy check. It would at least clear up one avenue of suspicion."

I lean back in my chair so I can see her better, the thing giving out not quite the ominous squeal as Raymond's but bad enough to have me getting my feet under me. "You think Kevin has a record?"

She shrugs. "Who knows. Kids in small towns do dumb stuff all the time when they get bored, waiting to take off for the big city. Maybe he's done something more than most, and that's why Mrs. Gustafson was worried about him drawing attention from the police."

"Do you think there might be something there?" I'm saying the same thing again, but there's a part of me that can't believe anything bad of Kevin Gustafson, a man who from what little I know ardently defended his sister.

"It's better to rule him out. Besides, I don't like this whole Daryl aspect. You going to go talk to him?"

"Of course," I say.

"Then I should probably come with you."

I frown. "I don't need you to babysit me."

"He could become belligerent if you corner him, Del. Remember he was in Kuwait. It did things to him."

"How do you know he was in Kuwait?"

"My mom told me. Remember back when we were kids and swim lessons were in that horrible little pool in the basement of the Gale Center? We didn't have that fancy aquatic center like the kids today. If you wanted to learn how to swim, you took lessons in the primordial swirl of the Gale Center basement."

"My dad taught me to swim in the lake," I say, which earns me a frown I'm sure Carmen learned from her mother.

"My mama is a city girl, born and raised. You know she's still afraid of water she can't see to the bottom of." She waves her hand again. "That's not the point. The point is when we'd take swim lessons we were all careful not to track water from the pool to the locker rooms because Mr. Walden would always get irate." She draws out the two syllables until it's almost a three-syllable word. "He had no problem cussing out little kids and everything. And that's when Mama told me he'd been in Kuwait. He came back scarred and hurt where we couldn't see because war is a terrible thing that does terrible things. That's what she said." She presses a lime green fingertip into her knee. "And my mama is never wrong. You know that."

Vanessa Wilder *is* never wrong. It's true. The woman has an intimidating ability to know people that I could never hope to match. Not even when it comes to knowing the dead.

"So you think the war left psychological scars that may have led him to hurt Vicky?"

She shrugs. "Maybe. You won't know until you talk to him."

I look away and back. "What if he can't remember? He's been an alcoholic for many years, and that takes a toll on the body and mind."

"You'll just have to cross that bridge when you come to it."

I don't get to tell her about Gabriella Torres because just then Mrs. Laura steps up in front of the plastic chairs that have been assembled at one end of the long, cavernous gym and claps her hands together three times in a prim, sharp fashion. I'm nearly startled completely out of my plastic seat when everyone around me claps back in the same manner.

"It's a gymnastics thing," Carmen mutters to me out of the side of her mouth, and then the students file out. I see Ella and Anna at the front of their classes, their hair carefully braided and coiled into a bun at the top of their heads, small flowers of blue, red, and white carefully tucked along the ridge.

I lean forward so Raymond can see me. "You're getting good at that," I whisper.

He presses a hand to his chest in mock embarrassment and flutters his eyelashes. "I've been watching some YouTube videos."

I give him a thumbs-up and lean back. Carmen has no patience for the kind of hair the girls want, so Raymond took it upon himself to learn how to style natural hair, especially because it's why the girls started this sport to begin with. Ella came home from second grade one day and declared gymnasts have the best hair, and she and Anna should immediately become world-class gymnasts. They've grown in their skills and abilities, and it shows in the more advanced stations they queue up to.

The gym is broken up into various tumbling skill sections such as the mat, the balance beam, and the uneven bars to name just a few. The girls are both lined up at two vaulting runs of differing ability. Last year they were just attempting to spring from that little board thing that sends my heart into overdrive and land on an airbag the size of Wisconsin. Now it looks like they're going to land on actual foam mats.

I turn to Carmen. "I don't know how much longer I can watch this."

She pats my bad leg. "Doc Randy will fix them up," she says.

"Dear Lord, help us," I say sincerely and turn back just as Ella springs into the air, the little board banging against itself at her feet, my heart thundering into shock. I keep my eyes closed more than open for the next hour.

EIGHT

My alarm goes off so early Monday morning it takes me several seconds to remember what day it is. The darkness has already lifted from the windows, and it suddenly occurs to me the days are getting longer. It's already the third week of April, and the gala is only five weeks away. It feels as though we've just closed up the camp for its winter slumber, and I wonder at the speed of time.

Henry is tangled in my legs, and it takes me more ninja skill than usual to slip from the bed. I gather my swim things, and in hushed, creeping tiptoes, make my way out to the car.

I go through my swim routine in a haze, my mind entirely on Daryl Walden. I plan to see him on my lunch break today, and the idea of facing the man has left me with only mild trepidation, which if I've learned anything about dealing with the dead, is not a good sign. It usually means I'm letting down my guard when I shouldn't be.

I spent Sunday opening the patio, hosing off the furniture, and helping Logan put my fourteen-foot aluminum fishing boat in the water. It's soothing to have the boat knocking against the dock again. There's something about menial chores that's good for clearing the fog from one's brain, and this morning I feel laser focused, although apprehensive.

I have never felt Daryl Walden is a threat. An annoyance most assuredly but not a threat. If anything, watching him sink deeper and deeper into alcoholism over the years has just been heartbreaking. I've been privy to some of his rows with tourists, but I unfortunately do not have the childhood connection Carmen has with him and so cannot feel that kind of instinctual guardedness I probably should feel around him. He is, after all, the prime suspect in Victoria Gustafson's murder after what Gretchen told me.

Which is why I decide to bring Henry with me.

Bringing my gun probably would be a better idea considering Henry once got himself locked in the bathroom, but deep down I know the seventy-pound lab will surely do his best to protect me if he thinks I'm being harmed. And as I've said before, carrying a gun means one is tempted to use it, and that's not something I want to risk. Not with someone like Daryl Walden who is misunderstood enough.

I bring Henry to work with me because it's easier than making the round trip back to the cottage.

The library is not exactly dog friendly, but it is Henry friendly. Sarah uses him during the morning story hour as kids are infatuated with a giant brown fluffy dog. Once Sally Marsden's toddler fell asleep on him, and poor Henry had never looked so scared in his life, as if he were afraid breathing would wake him up. Every once in a while Henry would turn his head and lick Brady's forehead to ensure the child was safe and sleeping. He lay like that for close to a half hour before Sally finally picked up her son, risking the grumpy tantrum that might have erupted if he'd woken.

Henry trots through the front doors of the library when we arrive, tail high, and heads right for where he will spend the entirety of his day despite the fact I allow him to sleep in the old recliner in my office that Logan and I hauled up there just for that purpose. He flies behind the circulation desk, and Sarah lets out a squeal of delight before she disappears, and I picture her on the floor giving Henry hugs and kisses.

I make my way over, balancing not only my stuff, but the bag of Henry's stuff I've brought with me. I reach over the circulation desk and plop it beside Sarah's keyboard. The metal water bottle inside clinks against the travel bowl, and the bag of treats rattles as I do so.

"Is this okay? I need him for something later," I say.

Sarah is sprawled on the floor, smack on her back, arms extended as Henry drapes his body over hers. She's incapable of responding as Henry is clearly trying to figure out the flavor of her lip balm, so instead, she gives two thumbs-up and a giggle.

I shake my head and retreat to my office just in time for Frances to appear.

"Arnold Fairchild requested a meeting," she says, her eyes pinning me over the rims of her glasses that are perched at a new impossible angle at the very tip of her nose.

Suddenly I want to sprawl on the floor like Sarah, but instead of giggling, I want to throw a temper tantrum. Arnold Fairchild is the last in the line of Fairchilds that built Lady Josephine Lodge, and while he has no legal ties to the camp because his father donated it to the historical society while Arnold was still in diapers, he feels the need to give his opinion on everything from building maintenance to our choice of toilet paper.

"Did he say why?"

"He wants to know where we are on installing the three-sixty cameras at the camp for conferences."

I drop my bag directly on the floor. "He knows we don't

have that in the budget. I keep telling him that. Unless he finds a sponsor to fund the project, it's not happening."

Frances shrugs. "Maybe he found a sponsor."

There's a muffled bark from downstairs, followed by the distinctive tinkle of dog tags.

Frances's eyebrows go up, and her face loses a degree of severity, an expression I know she only reserves for her grand-kids and Henry.

"Is that Henry?" She doesn't bother to wait for my reply and disappears down the corridor.

I haven't even gotten a cup of coffee before Allie appears. "I talked to Arnold Fairchild," she says without greeting. "He wants to know if you've installed those cameras he recom-mended at the camp." She tries to hide a smile behind her hand. "It sounded as though he thinks you're doing the instal-lation yourself."

I gesture toward her with an empty mug, but she shakes her head. I place the mug against my heart innocently. "And do you think me not capable of installing a network of confer-ence cameras in an Adirondack Great Camp from 1891?"

"Not if there are spiders."

I drop the mug to my side as the machine behind me hisses its final burst of steam. "You're right," I say. I take my coffee from under the espresso machine and head around the table to my dropped bag. "Let's go over the notes from Friday's rehearsal, and we'll take it from there. I really like what you did with Peter's entrance coming from the left and not the right. It flows much more easily."

Allie drops into the recliner reserved for Henry and draws up her legs crisscross applesauce style and balances her laptop on one knee and a binder with the script in it on the other.

"Thanks," she says with a smile before sobering. "All right, we should start with the Donaldson twins," she begins, and the next three hours are lost to me.

Steve stops by to let me know the repairs to both the plumbing and the structure are underway at the camp, and everything should be airtight by the end of the week. A local contractor offered to donate his time, so we're only footing the bill for materials. The correct bags for the party favors come in, and we decamp to the conference room along with Diana to stuff them. We finish up shortly before one, and everyone disperses in search of lunch.

I grab my bag and make my way downstairs to fetch Henry. I find him in the periodicals with the Historical Aviation Aficionados, a group that meets once a month to talk about old airplanes. They only let me have him after I promise to bring him back for their meeting next month.

Henry catapults himself into the back of my SUV like he always does before turning to me suspiciously.

"We're not going to the vet," I assure him.

His tail thumps once, but his eyes remain wary.

The Gale Center sits in the no man's land between the village and the new housing developments by the larger supermarket on the county highway. I remember when the community center seemed like it was on another planet it was so far out of town, but development has sprung up all along this section of the highway until it almost feels like the Gale Center is part of town now.

The center is mostly used for recreational sports, weddings, and fundraiser functions. Inside are two large spaces on the first floor for just about anything and the modular seating to go with it. The pool in the basement has been filled in, creating one large space that twice a month turns into a roller skating rink but usually serves as a place for groups to meet with a little more privacy than that provided by the other meeting spaces located directly in the tight-knit village.

The reception desk at the front is empty, but I turn right, heading for the stairs to the lower level. I've only been in the community center a handful of times over the years for various events, but everyone who has grown up in Bellegrave knows how to get to the lower level. The staircase is still composed of the original small square tile and marble treads with the brass railing bisecting the steps.

This is where every kid in Bellegrave goes to learn how to slide down a staircase railing. It's where I learned to do it with such dedication and determination I turned the seat of my black stirrup stretch pants red from the metal rubbing against my butt as I slid down again and again and again. My mother was furious until she decided to try to learn how to dye clothes and used my destroyed pants as a guinea pig for her experiment.

Henry wants to sail down the staircase, but I go a little more cautiously, holding him back on his leash, keeping my eyes open, but more importantly listening. The Gale Center is a cavernous space, and sound travels easily. I want to hear Daryl long before he hears me.

I also don't want to be surprised by a ghost.

A lot of people die in and around pools, and I don't want to be taken unawares. Especially if it's a kid. Children ghosts are the most heartbreaking, and I don't want to see one wearing a faded mermaid bathing suit and orange arm floaties.

Henry stays by my side when we reach the bottom, whining softly as if sensing my apprehension, and I wind his leash more tightly around my hand.

The staircase empties into the long corridor that runs parallel to where the pool used to be on the other side of a concrete brick wall to the right and what used to be the locker rooms on the left but are now just restrooms. I know there are some offices down here and think this is the best place to start my search for Daryl.

The place is neatly kept, the floor gleaming in the glare of the overhead lights, and a part of me is bolstered that Daryl might take pride in his work.

"Dogs aren't allowed in here!"

The shout is so loud, so close, and so unexpected I jump, tugging on Henry's leash, which only makes him whimper. I spin around toward the voice and find Daryl Walden behind me.

He's standing beside the staircase in front of an open door I realize must be his office.

He's not as tall as I remember, probably a couple of inches short of six feet. His hair is completely gray and outgrown its style. His chin is stubbled, as though he's shaved recently but not that day.

But what catches my eye most is his uniform. His gray button-down, short sleeve work shirt has been ironed. I can see the pleats in the sleeves. An embroidered name tag sits above the left breast pocket, *Daryl* spelled out in navy blue thread. His work pants are the same utilitarian gray and starched so much the knees almost don't bend as he takes a step toward me and stops.

It's a minute before I realize he's not coming any closer to me, and I look up to meet his eyes. I'm more startled than when he yelled because in his eyes I see fear.

"I don't want to talk to you," he says before I can speak. His voice is deep and ragged, from alcohol or from going unused is uncertain.

"Mr. Walden," I say, but he's already turned his back, walking away from me. I realize too late he's heading for the door that's tucked away under the stairs. "Mr. Walden, Vicky asked me to talk to you," I say to his retreating back because I can't think of anything else to say to keep him from locking himself in his office.

My words stop him, but he doesn't turn around. Henry

whimpers softly beside me and sits, nudging my leg with his nose in question.

"Vicky came to me. She wanted to tell me something. Something about her death." I think about the courtroom dramas I used to watch in college and try not to lead the witness. If Vicky's death wasn't an accident, I don't want to show my hand to the most likely suspect.

"I said I don't want to talk to you," he growls without turning around. "I don't believe in that nonsense. The dead are dead, and there's no way you can see them."

"I *can* see them," I say, a line I've used so futilely over the years when someone calls me a fraud. "I can see them and sometimes they're able to talk to me. Vicky said something to me, and I think she wanted me to learn more about her death."

He spins around so quickly any more words are caught in my throat. The fear in his eyes has burned away to something raw, almost like pain, and I wonder if suddenly this wasn't a good idea. Not only because Daryl is known to be violent but because what I'm saying is clearly upsetting him.

He was in a relationship with Vicky. That must have meant something. And as far as I can remember, he's never been with anyone since. Has he been grieving for Vicky this whole time? Or is it something worse than that? Something darker?

I brace myself, ready for him to come at me like I've seen him do with tourists who step out of the imaginary lines he's drawn, but he doesn't advance. He holds himself very still, three feet from his office door, his feet together on a single tile of industrial white vinyl flooring. But he doesn't move. He only watches me, that pain burning in his eyes.

"Something happened to Vicky, didn't it? Something you might be able to tell me about."

The corner of his mouth twitches, and I wonder if he's

trying to hold back his words, but his lips remain stubbornly fused shut. I press on.

"Vicky was a good person. She didn't deserve to die like that. Maybe you can—"

Now when he turns, his motions clipped and efficient, I'm not as startled. In two steps he's through his office door, turning back to me with those furious eyes.

"I don't care who you think you are or what you think you saw." His words fall out of his mouth with a healthy rain of spittle. "But I will tell you this. I don't regret doing it. I never have and never will." He clamps one shaking hand around the metal door, but before he can slam it in my face, the glare of the overhead light catches on the glass of a frame sitting on a battered metal desk just inside the door. Even from where I'm standing I can make out the picture inside of it. Probably because Miss Gustafson had looked just like that every day she'd come to school. Long wavy dark hair, too small glasses, and a flowing dress, her smile lighting the way before her.

The door slams with a hollow ring, metal against metal, and I'm left wondering why Daryl Walden has a picture of Vicky Gustafson on his desk almost thirty years after her death.

NINE

I don't remember climbing the stairs back to the main floor. I squint when I reach the outside, the sunshine suddenly brighter than I remember it. I hold up a hand to shield my eyes, and Henry tugs against the leash.

"Della? Are you all right?" I turn in the direction of the voice to find Lorna Hiddles standing beside me in her usual plaid button-down tucked neatly into ironed khakis, her wide-brimmed green hat covering her hairsprayed gray curls. She's out of context, and it takes me a moment to realize it's her. My hesitation must be alarming because she lays a hand on my arm, the other going to scratch Henry's head. "Della, it looks like you've seen a—" But she stops, color coming to her cheeks.

Like most people in Bellegrave, Lorna Hiddles is too sensible to believe in ghosts and doesn't quite know what to make of the rumors about me.

"Hi, Lorna." I find my voice. "I'm fine," I say with a smile that's only a little wobbly. "Just forgot to eat lunch. Think I'll swing by Shelly's on my way back to the office."

She nods, but her smile isn't quite sure as I wave goodbye

and load Henry into the SUV. As I start the car, I see Lorna unloading canvas totes from the back of her sedan as others pull into the parking lot of the Gale Center, and I recognize other members of the Bellegrave Gardening Society.

I don't stop at Shelly's. I'm too shaken by my encounter with Daryl to do anything but go straight back to my office where I tell Frances I need to get ahead on email and firmly shut my office door against the rest of the world. Henry whines to be let out to explore, but I coax him into his recliner with a treat and scratches and a promise to go for a walk when we get home.

I try to focus, but I can't, Daryl's words spinning through my mind like a sudoku puzzle that refuses to be solved.

What doesn't Daryl regret? Murdering Vicky? Was he admitting to his guilt? It couldn't possibly be that easy or that simple.

My heart. My heart.

Was Vicky referring to Daryl? The man she supposedly loved? Her sweetheart perhaps?

Or was Daryl confessing to something else entirely?

He has a history of violent episodes like Carmen had said. He could have been referring to any one of them. But why say such a thing after I told him I saw Vicky?

But that wasn't the most unsettling part of the entire encounter. It was the look in his eyes when I mentioned Vicky. The pain there was real and raw, and I knew I had done more than strike a nerve. I had ripped open a scar, one that ran deep, and what scared me most was how much I understood that kind of pain.

Instead of reading through the email from Diana on this month's gifts, I think of the picture on Daryl's desk. It was clearly a picture taken for the yearbook with the evenly blue background and studio lighting, and I imagined Vicky giving it to him so he would have a photo of her. It wasn't like today when you carried a million photos on your phone in your pocket. The photo on Daryl's desk had meant something. But why had he kept it all these years and why there, where he would see it every day? Was it a reminder of a love he had lost or of an evil thing he had done?

I wasn't getting anything done as my thoughts spun one over the other, and at five when Henry starts to whine for his dinner, I call it a day.

At home I give Henry his dinner, but I'm both too agitated and too stressed to feed myself. Logan usually stays later at the office on Mondays to catch up with whatever came in over the weekend. I decide manual labor is the only thing that will help me to settle, and once I set up the dreaded ball-throwing machine for Henry, I go in search of my workshop vacuum.

Allie's comment about spiders earlier in the day was both accurate and a reminder that I hadn't vacuumed out the shed the day before like I usually do in the spring. Spiders and I just don't get along. I daisy chain extension cords until I have enough to reach the small building at the back of the cottage, and I go to work. I will, of course, need to set this vacuum on fire when I'm done and get a new one, but that's the price I must pay for safety and peace.

I've nearly finished an entire wall when movement out of the corner of my eye has me swinging around, the wand of the vacuum raised like a sword. I nearly bean Carmen right in the head before I realize it's her. I give her an annoyed look before shutting off the vacuum and taking off my noise-canceling ear protection.

"Do not sneak up on a woman when she's killing spiders," I say.

There's a deep line between Carmen's brows as she stares at me. "What happened today? Are you okay?"

I frown. "Why do you think something happened?"

She spreads her hands wide as if it's obvious. "You're vacuuming the outside."

I put the wand away and step out of the shed so I can better see her. "As I said, I was killing spiders." I check to make sure Henry's still enthralled with the ball machine before turning back to Carmen. "Why are you here? Isn't it dance night?"

The girls recently decided to dabble in dance when Mrs. Laura offered a six-week introductory course, and Ella thought it might be an opportunity for more sequins.

"Something came up I've got to talk to you about, so Raymond took them." She points at the shed. "But I want to hear what this is about."

The infernal thwacking of the ball machine is setting my back teeth to grinding, so I nod toward the house.

"Come on," I say. "You'd better hear this."

I step inside the kitchen long enough to grab two waters from the fridge and an enrichment dog toy from the freezer I already packed with peanut butter now frozen solid. I distract Henry with the treat, and he abandons the throwing machine so I can finally turn the dang thing off.

I hand a bottle of water to Carmen who has pulled out a chair at the patio table.

"I saw Daryl Walden today," I start, taking a sip from my bottle. "Much like Gretchen, he didn't seem surprised to see me, but he definitely didn't want to talk to me."

"What did he say?" Carmen has both elbows on her bent knees, the water bottle swinging loosely in her fingers as she watches me.

"Not much," I say. "But right before he slammed his office door in my face, he said he doesn't regret what he did. He never has, and he never will."

I hear Daryl's voice in my head like an echo, and it's like

I'm back in the basement of the Gale Center with its fading scent of chlorine and too-bright lights.

"What did he do?" Carmen asks.

"He didn't say."

She shakes her head and straightens. "Then he could have been talking about anything."

I look at her. "I told him I saw Vicky."

Carmen deflates. "Oh." There's a long beat of silence as she thinks, and I study the lake, the water calm as the light fades along the western ridge of hills that cup the village of Bellegrave in a cocoon. "There's still the possibility he was talking about something else," Carmen says.

"He had a picture of Vicky on his desk," I say, still watching the lake.

I hear more than see Carmen slouch in her chair. "Well. That's rather suspicious then."

I move my gaze back to her face. "That's what I thought."

"Why would he still have a picture of Vicky on his desk? Did Gretchen give any indication of what kind of relationship the two of them had?"

I try to remember Gretchen's words when I saw her the previous week. "She said Vicky's mood changed right before her death, and she thought something happened between Vicky and Daryl."

Carmen sits up. "Did Gretchen say what it might have been?"

I shake my head. "No. Only that she wasn't so certain about their relationship anymore."

Carmen's eyes narrow. "I wish I could remember what Daryl was like back then. I only remember him being loud and demanding." She shakes her head now. "I can't imagine him dating someone like Miss Gustafson. I mean. What did she see in him?"

"How old were you when you took swim lessons at the

Gale Center?" I ask, trying to piece the parts of Daryl we know together to make a picture.

Carmen shrugs. "Ten or eleven. It was probably around ninety-two or ninety-three because it's when we got that caravan with the wood panel sides." She says this with raised eyebrows and a self-satisfied nod.

"You were the most popular family in town when you got that."

Carmen buffs her nails dramatically. "All the cool kids wanted a ride after school."

"You didn't even know who the cool kids were."

She drops her hand. "I didn't, but if I did, they would have asked for a ride." She sticks a finger toward me to emphasize her point.

"So you only knew Daryl after he came back from the Gulf War?"

She looks up as she thinks and lets her hand drop to the table. "I guess I did."

"I wonder what he was like before the war and when it was he met Vicky."

"Do you think Vicky stayed with him out of guilt?" Carmen asks.

I try to picture Miss Gustafson as I'd seen her in school. She was a middle school special education teacher when I was in seventh grade, so I saw her in the school halls a lot.

"I always thought she was so old," I say before meeting Carmen's gaze. "She was thirty-one, and I thought she was ancient. She wasn't married, had no kids, and I thought she was just the coolest. Living her life the way she wanted to even though I got the sense everyone else thought it was somehow weird she was still single." I shake my head. "My mom was always tired and cranky, and Miss Gustafson was always smiling. I could never understand how that was a bad thing."

Carmen's expression sours. "I swore I would never get

cross with my kids the way my mom did with us, and just this morning I yelled at Ella for opening the fridge wrong." She held up both hands, the water bottle swinging between two fingers. "The cats were antagonizing each other again, and Raymond had the TV on way too loud when he wasn't watching it, and Anna was telling me she no longer wants PB&J in her lunch when she's been having PB&J for eleven years. When Ella let the fridge door bounce against the counter, I lost my mind." She drags out the last words like an incantation, and I can't help but smile, picturing the domestic chaos. "Of course, everyone thought Miss Gustafson was weird. She probably got a full night's sleep every night."

"Do you think Daryl could have killed her? Is that what Vicky meant by *my heart*? She was talking about the man she supposedly loved?" I ask.

Carmen drops her arms. "I'm afraid it's not that simple."

My stomach clenches the way it does when I miss a step. "Why is that?"

"I looked into Kevin Gustafson's background," Carmen says. "He has a record."

"A record?"

She nods. "He was eighteen when the incident happened otherwise no one would be the wiser. But he was an adult so there it is." She taps the edge of the metal patio table with one finger. "He was charged with stalking, Del."

I sit up. "Stalking who?"

"A woman named Julia Hammond. Twenty-four-year-old white female employed as a teacher at the high school. Kevin was hot for teacher, it seems, and she was forced to call the police when he showed up at her house."

"Maybe he was looking for after-school help," I suggest, feeling the tension coiling along my shoulders.

"In the middle of the night," Carmen adds.

"Oh," I say, my stomach falling now. "What happened?"

"This Julia Hammond called the police when she woke up to the sound of a window breaking in her apartment. Her apartment was on the second floor, thank God, and Kevin couldn't get in. He claims he was only trying to wake her with the rocks he was throwing, and that it was a romantic gesture like Romeo to Juliet on the balcony. She dropped the charges once a restraining order was granted."

"Restraining order?" My throat is closing with each word as I try to picture this version of Kevin Gustafson.

"His midnight romantic gesture was apparently not the first incident. There had been several. He followed her out to her car after school and would wait by her apartment to follow her around the village when she would go out. She asked him to stop, but he didn't. There were no more reported incidents after the restraining order was granted."

"But does a history of stalking mean he killed his sister? What was his motive?"

Carmen shakes her head and stands. "I don't know," she says. "I've got to pick up dinner on my way home, but while you're trying to figure out what Daryl Walden doesn't regret, you might also want to find an alibi for Kevin Gustafson the day his sister was killed."

TEN

I'm meeting Diana and Allie at the lodge at ten the next morning to go over the improvement projects and additional living history programs we'd like to secure donors for this summer season, so I get some work done at the kitchen table before heading over to my parents' house on the way into town.

Carmen's visit the day before and her news about Kevin Gustafson's criminal past has thrown a curve into my investigation. It's not like Vicky told me the name of her killer. Maybe she was trying to tell me something else entirely with her message of *my heart*.

But if Kevin Gustafson is not in Bellegrave for me to question him, my parents are the next best thing. If anyone can give me more insight on who Julia Hammond was, it will be them.

I step into their kitchen just as my mom is packing up her lunch for work. Her lunch bag is a victim of her fabric-painting days, and it's covered in daisies she depicted with smiling faces that make them look more like insane clowns.

"Delia Ann," she says as I come through the kitchen door.

"We are seeing far too much of you lately. Shouldn't you be at work?"

My dad is at the kitchen island with the newspaper spread in front of him, a half-empty glass of orange juice at his elbow.

"Some parents don't see their grown kids at all," my dad chimes in without looking up from the paper.

My mom settles both of her hands on her lunch bag. "Well, what is it? What terrifying specter have you seen now?"

"Do you two know who Julia Hammond is?"

My dad looks up immediately at the same time my mother's mouth drops open.

"There's a name I haven't heard in forever," Mom says at the same time Dad intones, "Hot for teacher," invoking Carmen's words from the day before.

I frown. "She was really that stunning?"

Mom holds up a single finger. "I have a yearbook somewhere. Hang on." She disappears into her hobby addition as Dad sets down the paper.

"Julia Hammond taught twelfth-grade English, but she could have been a model. Never seen anyone like her in Belle-grave except for your mom."

Mom returns to the kitchen just as Dad says this and swats his arm playfully.

"Please, Greg. We all know Julia Hammond was a goddess." Mom sets a red leather yearbook on the kitchen island and starts flipping the pages. "If I were of a different sexual orientation, I would have salivated over Julia Hammond myself," she says, flipping to a page near the back where row after row of teacher headshots appear. "As it was, all the girls in my grade tried to emulate her."

Mom stops at a page of black-and-white photos and flips the book around so I can see it. She places a single finger on a photograph that I swear is a mistake. Somehow Farah Fawcett has ended up in my mother's senior yearbook.

"Whoa," I breathe because everyone is right.

Julia Hammond is a beauty. She has long hair that although I can't tell the color in the black-and-white photo I would assume is blonde from how light it appears. She wears it in flyaway layers that melt into spectacular curtain bangs. She has cheekbones that would cut glass and eyes sultrier than Sophia Loren's.

"What happened to her?"

"She got married," my mother says as if this were the worst fate that could happen to a woman.

"Married a doctor and moved to Utica," Dad elaborates.

Mom taps her finger on the yearbook page. "It was 1977. Women couldn't even have credit cards in most cases without their husband's permission. It was the best any of us could do, and she did it." She shakes her head. "Wonder what happened to her. She was always so nice and friendly with the students." She shrugs. "Probably because she wasn't much older than us, I guess." She looks at my dad. "Right, Greg? What do you think? She was just out of school when she came to Bellegrave, remember?" Now she looks at me. "I always thought her so wild and cool. I wanted to be just like her." She makes a tutting noise as if scolding herself.

Dad's expression sags, his lips pursed in annoyance. Mom notices and sets an apologetic hand on his arm.

"I'm very happy I married you, Greg. You know that." She glances at me, her brows knitted in concern. "You kids on the other hand." More tutting noises. "My insides were just never the same again." She holds out both hands. "To say nothing of our carpets."

"Why are you asking about Miss Hammond?" Dad says now, likely trying to steer my mother away from more exclamations of regret about her younger days.

"Apparently Julia Hammond had a restraining order against Kevin Gustafson," I say.

"Oh my," Mom says with an intake of breath.

"Restraining order? Against Kevin?" Dad asks.

I nod. "Apparently Kevin had been giving Julia Hammond unwanted attention, and she finally got a restraining order when he showed up at her apartment in the middle of the night."

"Kevin Gustafson?" my mother asks, her nose wrinkled in confusion. "But he was so quiet. Wasn't he quiet?" she asks this last part of my father.

"So quiet," Dad confirms. "Are you sure it was Kevin Gustafson?"

I nod. "Carmen pulled his record."

"Oh I don't like this, Delia," Mom whispers.

Dad taps the yearbook. "Where's Kevin's senior picture?"

Mom makes a soft noise and picks up the yearbook again, flipping pages to the middle. She holds it open for me, pointing out a nondescript male that looks like any other teenager from the seventies. Longish dark hair, clean face, bigger chin, but otherwise just a teenager. The quote under his name reads *the future looks bright from here*.

"You said Kevin went to the city after graduation. Do you know why? Was it college or a job?"

Dad shrugs. "No idea. He never really shared much, and we didn't think to ask. We were just kids, you know."

"I know he lives in the city now. Gretchen mentions it from time to time when I run into her at the Super Duper," Mom says, referring to the small grocery store and gas station located in the village. "But she's never really said anything else about him."

"She made it sound like Chief Tom was suspicious of Kevin when Vicky was killed. She said she didn't have an autopsy done because she didn't want any more attention on Kevin after the dustup between him and Daryl."

Mom's nose wrinkles again. "Dustup? You mean that little

spat they had at Farley's?" She snorts. "That was hardly a dustup. It was just two males marking territory. It's barely worth mentioning."

"You were there?" Farley's is the local bar, and while a perfectly respectable establishment, I find it hard picturing my mother there. She is most likely to frequent Wine and Dine, the wine bar on Water Street, after one of her hobby classes.

Mom shakes her head. "No, I just heard about it. Me and everyone else in town." She touches my dad's arm again. "Remember that?"

Dad nods. "It really wasn't anything. A small town just likes to have something to talk about."

That I can understand.

"Mind if I take this?" I ask, picking up the yearbook.

"Not at all, sweetie," Mom says, coming around the kitchen island to press a kiss to my cheek. "I need to get to work. Ninety-two more days until retirement!" she announces, kissing my dad on the cheek. "See you both at trivia night," she adds as she sails out the door.

I gather the yearbook, but my dad stops me with a hand on my arm. I meet his gaze as he asks, "Does Logan know you're looking into Vicky's death?"

I think about our one discussion about it when I attacked him with the pizza last week.

"Of course, he does," I say.

What I don't say is how Logan didn't get home until after eight the night before, and I'd resorted to a dinner of store-bought cupcakes and lemonade. What I don't say is how I'm worried the already separate lives my husband and I lead are getting further apart.

I move my arm, so I can squeeze my dad's hand. "It's fine," I say when my dad's expression turns ominous. "I know how to keep myself safe." I kiss his cheek like my mom did. "Don't forget trivia night," I call after him as I leave.

It isn't until I'm knee-deep in the conference linens at the lodge that I realize the phone in my pocket is not mine.

Allie and Diana are at one of the round tables that fill the conference space going through the list of programming needs for the season that Diana can use to appeal to major gift donors and our recurring donors. I've already gone through the list with Allie at her debrief last fall at the conclusion of the summer season, and my list of improvement projects that required donors with Diana, so I'm using this time to sort through the conference linens used for the tables and luncheons we offer to mark something off of my reopening list.

Allie's and Diana's voices are occasionally garbled by the construction sounds emitting from the bathroom where the contractor Steve found is fixing the damage from the burst pipe.

I count and recount the napkins, but I still come up five short, and I need to make a note to replace the ones that have somehow gone missing the previous conference season. I pull out my phone to do just that, but when the screen comes to life I see a picture of me on the dock in front of our cottage instead of Henry, upside down in his favorite napping position on the couch.

It's so startling I almost drop the phone. I realize not only that I have Logan's phone, but also that at some point he took this picture of me. The sun is setting to my left, and the profile shot means I'm lit up in oranges and gold. I look pretty and unguarded, and I wonder when he took it.

Before I can stuff the phone back into my pocket, a terrible urge passes over me to unlock his phone and go through it.

I've never once pried into my husband's business. I've never had reason to. Not until Albany.

I hold the phone carefully in one hand, wondering. What would I find in there? Would there be answers to this undulating feeling of mistrust that keeps slipping just out of my grasp? Would there be an explanation for the pitying looks I get from my mom and dad and Carmen?

I stuff the phone in my pocket before I can think about it anymore. There's a line I won't cross when I haven't done all I can in a healthy and respectful way for the relationship between me and my husband.

I push to my feet, my legs wobbling slightly as I've been perched in the cupboards of the sideboards for the better part of an hour now, counting. I grab the back of a chair before turning to Allie and Diana.

"Have the two of you got this?" I ask when there's a break in their conversation. I pull out Logan's phone and hold it up. "I switched phones with Logan again. I'm going to swing by his office and get mine, and then I need to update the inventory on these linens. Looks like we're missing some napkins again."

Diana purses her lips. "I don't know how we always lose napkins. Are people throwing them away? Who is throwing away cloth napkins?"

"They probably just get swept up when the servers are clearing the tables. You know what a mess it can be," Allie says.

Diana's pursed lips turn into a frown. "Heathens. Why does everyone turn into a heathen when they aren't required to do the washing up?"

"I blame social media," Allie says, which is her answer to everything.

I steal a scrap of paper from the stuff spread out on the table between Allie and Diana to make a note of the linen count and stuff it in my pocket.

"I'll see you both back at the office later. I need to approve the mockups for the table stands at the print shop, and it's easier if I just go into the shop instead of emailing back and forth."

Diana holds up a finger. "Make sure they spell Bellegrave correctly this time."

I flinch. Last year's table tents proclaimed it the *Bellgrade Founder's Day*.

"Noted," I say. I grab my bag and head for the car.

It's one of those flat spring days when the sky can't seem to decide if it should rain or not, and after all the pounding from inside the camp, the sudden silence makes my ears ring, and a headache begins to brew behind my eyes.

I roll down the windows, hoping the fresh air will set me to rights as I head into the village.

Logan's office is in the Russell Building, which sits just off the town square. It's one of the original office buildings along Main Street, the first floor consisting of retail shops, a cafe, and an art gallery, and the second floor housing professional offices ranging from a dental practice and podiatrist's office on one end to legal services and pet psychology on the other.

I find street parking along the square and take the central wrought iron staircase up to the second floor. The thing that always amuses me about the Russell Building is the fact that it was renovated sometime in the eighties, and the public hallways all consist of bright orange industrial linoleum, orange tiled walls, and peach ceilings. The linoleum still looks brand new, and I often picture it being the only thing remaining after the zombie apocalypse.

Bridget looks up from her desk when I slip through the door of the offices of James and Bartlett. Logan had worked for a couple of different firms straight out of law school before settling into real estate law. Navigating the tricky waters of the Adirondacks with the stipulation of "Forever Wild" embedded in the New York State Constitution appealed to him, and he soon found his niche helping developers bring jobs to the region while also preserving the landscape and reducing environmental impact.

"If it isn't the missus," Bridget says. Bridget is a small but stout woman on the other side of fifty with bottle red hair that goes a little brassy before her next hair appointment and green eyes the color of the hills in her home country of Ireland. "I don't see that feisty young fella with you," she says, referring to Henry.

"He took another day off. I can't get him to hold down a job."

Bridget laughs a full-bodied guffaw just as the phone on her desk starts to ring and the door to the right of her opens. Philip Bartlett, Logan's partner in the firm, steps out into the reception area with who I can only assume is a client.

"We'll have that squared away by the end of the week," Philip is saying. "Bridget, can you—"

He's cut off when Bridget holds up a finger, her ear still pressed to the phone. The door behind me opens, and two women come in, both speaking rapidly, clearly in a conversation they started somewhere down the hall.

I smile at Philip and point to Logan's office door before slipping out of the chaos.

It's too late when I hear Bridget call after me, "Oh, honey, you can't go in there. He's in a—"

The last word is probably *meeting*, but by then I've already opened the door, and the pounding of my heart stops me from hearing anything else.

Logan is bent over his desk, studying what appears to be a survey, and standing next to him is a woman I've never seen before. A woman who has her hand on my husband's shoulder in an inappropriately familiar way.

"Logan," I say because they clearly haven't heard me come in.

Is that surprise I see in my husband's eyes? Does he step away from the woman too quickly?

"Della, what are you doing here?"

For a second, I forget why I'm there, but the sudden, unfamiliar rage inside of me takes over before rational thought can return.

I step forward and extend my hand to the strange woman. "I'm Logan's wife. We haven't met."

The woman straightens, and I see she's tall, probably five nine or five ten, giving her an elegance I'll never have at five five. She sweeps her long, straight blonde hair over one shoulder as she reaches her other hand out to me. When she smiles, I see veneers that match the tips of her French manicure.

"Oh, Della, what a pleasure to finally meet you. I'm Heather Russo from the Rivendale Associates in Albany."

Albany.

Finally.

She takes a form. Instead of notes of suspicion, she's a woman now made of flesh and blood. Instead of worry about the late nights, the phone calls taken in another room, and the frequent trips to Albany, she has a name, and her name is Heather Russo.

I let go of her hand before she's ready, and her hand lingers awkwardly between us.

"It's Dr. James, actually," I say, and the light in her blue eyes dim, the corners narrowing. "Logan has been forced to go to Albany a lot lately," I add.

Her lips part on an aborted reply as her eyes skate over to Logan as if for help.

Logan laughs uncomfortably. "That's a little dramatic, Del." His eyes nervously meet Heather's. "It isn't torture, I promise." He laughs again in a way I've never heard him laugh before. He almost sounds nervous, uncertain.

My stomach turns over, and I'm suddenly sick of being there. I reach into my pocket and pull out my phone.

"We switched phones again," I say, placing his on the desk, my finger brushing the surface, so it lights up, the picture of me on full display between them. "You probably didn't notice because you've been in—" I pause looking between both of them. "Meetings," I finish.

The regret that I didn't go through his phone stabs me in the stomach.

Logan makes another nervous noise and rubs the back of his neck with one hand. He's taken off his jacket and rolled up his shirt sleeves, exposing his forearms and the dusting of dark hair there. Am I relieved to see he's still wearing his wedding ring?

Heather laughs now too, the sound brittle and false. "I know I've been taking up a great deal of Logan's time, but we've almost reached the end of this deal. Just a little bit more to go, and we'll have it."

"I love that for you," I say, lifting the corners of my mouth. I extend a hand toward my husband. "May I have my phone please? I need to get back to work."

Logan hesitates, and I think he might ask something, but he doesn't. He reaches for his suit coat discarded on one of the chairs at the small table he usually uses for client meetings. He fishes out my phone, and when he hands it to me, I avoid touching his fingers.

"Thanks," I say. "Nice meeting you," I say to Heather before turning for the door.

Even when I reach the sidewalk outside and draw in a deep breath, my nostrils sting with the cloying, citrusy perfume of Heather Russo.

ELEVEN

I almost don't go to trivia night. I'm not sure I'll be able to control my face, and I don't want to answer any questions my mood might arouse. But if I don't go, there will certainly be questions, and those I'd rather not face either. So I go.

Trivia night is held every other Tuesday at Domingo's, the only Mexican restaurant in the village. Located on the lakeside of Water Street, its deck is a popular spot in the summer season. Terra cotta tiles adorn the floor while blue ceramic tiles spell out the names of Domingo's family members along the top of the walls around the entire circumference of the restaurant. Domingo, whose real name is Walter Ramirez, Domingo being a nickname he'd picked up in college, and father to our beloved Sarah Ramirez, can be found behind the bar every Tuesday night where he shouts out ridiculously incorrect answers to rile up the patrons, which results in uproarious laughter. I'm looking forward to both that and the margaritas tonight.

Not having been able to focus at work, I left early to take Henry for a long walk and feed him dinner before heading back into the village. I arrive at the restaurant before anyone else I'm expecting, and I snag a high top in the bar area. I mindlessly munch tortilla chips with salsa until Carmen appears, somehow looking more frazzled than I feel.

She shucks her giant baby blue leather bag on a stool and signals to a server for a margarita before hauling herself onto the stool beside me.

"Delia Ann, you have gone and walloped a hornet's nest that has landed directly in my lap." She thrusts a salsa-covered chip directly into her mouth without elaborating.

I break apart a tortilla chip between my fingers and let the crumbs fall to my napkin. "How's that?"

"Chief Tom heard I've been poking around in the Lisa Reynolds case."

I point with a broken chip. "That is a hornet's nest you poked yourself. Don't bring me into this."

Carmen smiles at the server when he sets down her margarita, but as soon as he leaves, she turns on me. "I wouldn't have kept poking if you hadn't been all like Lisa is alive." Her voice drips with mockery.

"I sound just like that," I say, playfully sticking out my tongue at her. "Did you find the backpack?"

Carmen's eyes were closed in what can only be called bliss at her first sip of margarita, but at my words, her eyes fly open, and she sputters in her drink. "That's what I was trying to find out," she says, wiping her mouth. She looks around us surreptitiously before leaning in. "There was no backpack recovered in the vehicle. I double and triple confirmed with the guys who found the vehicle that night and with the evidence log."

"I thought we already knew this," I say, confused.

Carmen rolls her eyes. "We did, but after what you said about the backpack, I had to double check because—" She stops, and I see the war waging in her head that she doesn't want waged.

"Because Lisa took it with her when she fled," I finish for her.

Carmen's stare turns to annihilation.

"Lisa took what?"

Raymond pulls out the stool next to his wife and gives her a flamboyant smooch on the cheek before sitting.

I can't stop the image of Heather Russo's hand on my husband's shoulder from entering my mind, and I take an overlarge scoop of salsa and shove it in my mouth, making my eyes water.

"Della thinks Lisa Reynolds is still alive, and that she fled the scene of her abduction with her denim backpack."

"I'm not sure she was abducted," I say, and Carmen's expression turns icy. I shrug. "I'm just not."

"If she wasn't abducted, then what?" Raymond asks, both hands in the basket of chips on the table.

"She ran," I say.

"That doesn't make sense," Carmen retorts. "Lisa had everything, and she was about to embark on an amazing future."

"That's what we know of it, yes. But we can't possibly know Lisa's inner life. You said so yourself. We can't say what demons she had to run from."

Raymond appears puzzled. "You think Lisa Reynolds was struggling with some inner demons that made her run away?"

"Aren't we all struggling with some kind of demon?" I say and try not to think again about Heather Russo's hand on my husband's shoulder.

"Usually only until about June fifteenth or so," he says with a sarcastic chuckle.

"Surely Chief Tom isn't angry with you for digging into a cold case, is he?"

Carmen takes another sip of her margarita. "It's not the cold case part. Apparently—" Again she looks around to see if anyone is listening. The bar has filled up since I arrived, but the tables immediately next to us are empty. I check my watch. Ten minutes to trivia time. "Apparently Marty Pruitt asked for the investigation to stop."

"She what?"

"Are you serious?" Raymond says. A beer has appeared in front of him, and he holds it halfway between the table and his mouth.

Carmen takes a long sip of her margarita before replying. "Tom said after two years of investigation, after countless interviews, and false hope, Marty came to the police station and told Barry—you remember Barry Wise, the chief before Tom?" She goes on after we both nod. "She told Barry she and Bob couldn't take it anymore. They couldn't take having their hopes exploited like that. She and Bob had put Lisa to rest, and they wanted to move on with their lives."

"Then why ask me to try to contact her dead daughter's spirit all these years later?"

"That's different," Raymond says.

"How so?" Carmen asks.

"Della can provide comfort. Not hope."

"Should I be offended by that?"

"Nah," he says, popping a chip in his mouth. "Comfort's a beautiful thing, and not everyone can offer it." He shrugs. "I bet Marty just wanted Bob to have some comfort. You know, before he dies."

Carmen lays a hand on her husband's arm. "You are a wise and benevolent soul."

He gyrates his eyebrows at her as he shoves two chips into his mouth.

"But what does this mean? For the investigation?" I ask.

Carmen shakes her head. "Tom told me to leave it, but when I told him about the backpack, he admitted to being curious."

"Did you tell him I was involved?"

"For God's sake, of course not." She splays an innocent hand against her chest. "Do you think I'm stupid?"

She looks and sounds so much like her mother just then I can't help but smile.

"So what are you going to do?" Raymond asks.

"I told Tom about the photos and the denim backpack and asked him if such a bag was recovered from the car. As I said, it wasn't logged into evidence, but he suggested I reach out to old Chief Wise to see if he can remember any other details. You know how things go with a small-town police force and a big investigation like Lisa's disappearance."

"Didn't the state troopers get involved?" I ask.

Carmen nods. "Yeah, and the Bellegrave boys then never did appreciate their interference. But, with a possible homicide, the Bellegrave police back in the nineties didn't have the resources it does now. They couldn't handle a suspected homicide investigation then."

"So are you going to find Chief Barry? He retired almost twenty years ago. Where is he now?"

"I heard he has a place on Key West," Raymond says. "Met some woman in Fort Meyers after he snow birded there one winter, and she asked him to marry her in like a year. Turns out she's some kind of millionaire. Doesn't leave Key West now unless he has to."

Carmen eyes her husband. "How do you know this?"

"It's every man's dream, baby," Raymond says around a mouthful of chips, eyes incredulous. He swallows when Carmen's expression darkens. "I mean, except mine, of course."

"Of course," Carmen repeats.

Raymond is saved by the arrival of my parents who greet Raymond and Carmen with hugs and catching up. By the time my mom finally settles from cooing over Carmen's pictures of the girls at their gymnastics recital, the emcee has made his first announcement that trivia will be starting soon. A plate of nachos and a pitcher of beer appears on the table, and I assume my mom ordered them as she came through the door.

She takes the stools beside me as she asks, "Where's Logan?"

I'm about to say he's working when Logan himself answers.

"Late as usual," he says, appearing from the crowd like a ghost.

I start at the sight of him, crumpling the tortilla chip still in my hand. I don't miss Carmen's quizzical look in my direction, but I'm too focused on my husband to acknowledge it.

He's much the same as I saw him earlier that day in his office, shirt sleeves rolled to the elbow, but now he's discarded his tie and undone the topmost button of his shirt.

He looks so much like my husband it hurts.

"Hi," he says, pressing a kiss to my cheek like I didn't catch him with Albany in his office that very same day.

I'm stiff under his kiss, but it's more from shock than anything else.

He pulls a stool over to our table, somehow finding room between me and my mother to sit, and when he does, he drapes an arm possessively around my shoulders, and it's like the episode earlier that day in his office never happened.

I'm once more at sea in the muddled waters of suspicion, and I hate how good it feels to have Logan's heat at my shoulder, his fingers playing with the lock of hair that has slipped from the clip at the back of my head.

"Where has he been?" Carmen whispers in my ear, but the emcee takes the mic again and asks everyone to silence their phones and drop them into the boxes on the table, and the only questions I answer that night are the trivia kind.

———

It's late by the time we get home, and instead of talking about what happened that day, I claim I'm tired and go straight to bed with Henry. I should sit up and talk to my husband, but I close my eyes instead, burying my face in my pillow. Because what people don't understand, when they ask me if my leg hurts, is that after the accident, the thing that hurts the most is talking.

So I don't do it.

I pretend I'm asleep when Logan finally comes to bed.

I eventually drift off, but it's a near sleepless night filled with disturbing dreams that jolt me awake. At five, I give up and sneak into the bathroom for my swim stuff.

I wave to Bethany as usual when I walk through the sliding front doors of the aquatic center ten minutes later. She looks up from the computer, her eyebrows going up.

"You're early this morning. You must be getting busy with Founder's Day stuff, I bet. Almost a month away, right?"

I smile. "Sure thing."

I take longer than usual to do my swim, my laps lazy and wandering. When I finish, I slip into the teaching pool, which is about ten degrees warmer and feels like a comforting bath instead of a swimming pool. The water hugs me, and I float aimlessly, letting the cradle of the water slow my heart and unwind my muscles. Since I turned forty, I don't have the luxury of indulging my emotions in a dozen black and white cookies from Cake & Cookie, and I try to tell myself swimming is pretty much the same thing. This works zero percent of the time.

By the time I make it home, Logan is in the kitchen making coffee.

"Good swim?" he says as soon as I step into the room from the mudroom.

I'm so jolted by his overly cheery tone that I nearly poke Henry in the eye when I go to pet him.

I look up to find Logan smiling at me so hard his teeth are showing. I hate this awkwardness between us more than the silence. It comes now and then, when we're aware of how fragile we are and are afraid our very words might shatter whatever is left between us.

"You've never asked me about my swim," I say, scratching Henry's ears until he moans in pleasure.

Logan shrugs, smile unwavering. "Better late than never. How's the sauna since they put the new one in?"

I straighten and watch my husband pack his bag where it sits on one of the stools at the island.

He glances up when I don't answer, so I say, "I stopped using the sauna when I saw Gladys Norwich go in there bare-foot. You know she has warts."

He cringes theatrically. "Oh, yeah, smart move."

"That's what you said when I told you that the first time."

He freezes, and his eyes meet mine. There's a beat of silence in which I think he might tell me what's going on between him and Heather Russo, but instead he just smiles and shakes his head, and the space between us grows.

I take Henry out so I don't have to kiss my husband good-bye. I tell him to have a good day over my shoulder as I go through the patio doors, and I stay outside with Henry until I can hear Logan's car in the driveway.

Maybe I'm being ridiculous. Maybe not. If I could talk to my husband, maybe then I'd know, but I can't.

I sit at the kitchen table until 8:01 before I call Frances. She picks up in half a ring.

"The moon has fallen from the sky," she says when she answers, and I can't help but smile.

"No, I'm afraid it's just that I'm behind and want to spend a day working from home to get caught up," I tell her. "Can you cover my calls? I still owe Diana some numbers, and I want to get everything ironed out before we start opening the lodge next week. I just want to clear the deck before we open another can of worms, you know?"

"I'm afraid I know all too well. I'll let everyone know you're working from home today. Are you available by cell?" I hesitate just long enough for Frances to say, "Or should I tell them only for emergencies?"

"That one," I say.

After I ring off, I take a long hot shower, put on my comfiest jeans and sweater before making an entire pot of coffee just for myself. I lose myself in donor spreadsheets, mailing campaigns, and fiscal projections for the next several hours. By noon, I'm feeling more human, and my mind, if not settled, is less squirrelly than it's been since my encounter with Heather Russo.

It's funny. This thing that has existed between me and my husband suddenly has a face when before it was only suspicion and instinct. Is it better now that I've seen her? That I can give my suspicions a name?

I take Henry out on my lunch break and throw several balls into the woods at the same time. If I throw one, he doesn't care about it, but if I throw several, he goes crazy trying to bring them all back to me. The dog thrives on chaos.

I spend the afternoon reviewing the summer season's marketing plan to ensure all campaigns are on target, and somehow during coffee breaks manage to load and run the dishwasher and wash, fold, and put away a load of towels. By four o'clock, I'm pretty sure I'm invincible and take Henry for a walk before dinner.

My mind must not be as settled as I thought because it starts to wander, going back and forth about whether or not I know anything at all. Logan's behavior the night before at trivia tells me there's nothing to suspect, but his manner this morning tells me there is. I realize we've been gone from the house for more than thirty minutes. I call Henry back to me and turn us in the direction of the cottage, staying focused this time so we get back before five.

I wrap up my work and unload the dishwasher before feeding Henry dinner. The evening looms in front of me, and I can't help but wonder when Logan will be home. I haven't heard from him all day, which isn't unusual when he's working on a deal, but I also wonder if Heather Russo is still in town.

Henry sits beside his now empty bowl, and his eyes seem to wander over me suspiciously.

"I know," I say as if he's asked the question. "I'm not going to do anything stupid."

So instead I do a quick search for Gabriella Torres. I find an address at the new condos on one of those people search sites and decide to try it. If Gabriella doesn't live there, I've simply made a mistake.

I tell Henry I'll be right back and head for my car. The new condos sit up in the hills along this side of the lake, so I arrive at the address I found online within fifteen minutes.

The condos are all cookie-cutter replicas of each other, garage on the bottom and three stories stretching up against the hill behind it. If they have yard space, I can't see it from the parking area in front. I pull into a visitor space close to number nineteen.

I walk directly to the unit as if I belong there, keeping my peripheral vision sharp, but nothing jumps out at me, real or supernatural.

I ring the bell at number nineteen and wait. A door opens on the other side of the complex, and a bent man in a golf polo walks out carrying a brown paper bag that is clearly bulging with whatever is in it. He walks to the middle of the parking lot where a small structure sits. There's a clatter as he lifts the paper bag into the small structure, and I realize this must be where the garbage goes.

The door to number nineteen opens unexpectedly, and the tendrils of hair that have escaped my clip drift along my cheeks. When I turn back to the door, there's a woman there whom I can only assume is Gabriella Torres. I say assume because if I didn't know how old this woman should be, I wouldn't have been able to tell.

The skin of her face is artificially plump but not overly so, her eyebrows unusually lifted, and the hair that's swept back into a complicated bun on the top of her head is a color not found in nature. Gabriella is wearing workout clothes, the expensive kind. I can tell because they look like butter melted down her incredibly toned body. She wears a bright green halter top that presents her full breasts to me in greeting.

"Oh," she says, her brown eyes intent on my face. Slowly she lifts the fingertips of one hand to her lips. She's wearing a thick rounded silver band on her pointer finger, and I notice her chin is smaller than it should be, her face narrowing at the bottom into what might be called a heart-shaped face.

"Hi," I say. "Are you Ms. Torres?"

"Who is it?" she says, dropping the hand.

"I'm Della James," I say, slightly confused. Her reaction would suggest she already knew who I was.

She shakes her head. "Not you. Who is it that came to you? It's probably someone I know—er, knew—if you're at my door."

"It is," I say. I gesture to the stairs behind her. "Do you mind if I come in?"

She presses that same hand to her generous breasts. "I'm so sorry. Where are my manners? Come in. Come in."

I'm disturbed by how rumors of my ability to see dead people get me into people's homes with such ease. I could be a serial killer for all they know.

The stairs lead up to the main floor of the condo. It's a middle unit, and there are no windows on either side but the generous windows at the front that look out over the parking lot are wide and cast light through to the kitchen, which has a slider at the rear of it. Through the slider I see the backyard space and almost understand why people live here. The condos back up to the hill, and it's nothing but trees and tranquility out the back door.

The interior is decorated mostly in shades of white, including a white couch and a shag white rug underneath it. Gabriella Torres obviously doesn't have a dog. There's a blue yoga mat rolled out in front of a large television, and beside the mat is a phone set up in a tripod with a ring light behind it. On the television screen is a frozen image of a woman in clothes similar to Gabriella's doing a pose that looks like it's meant to dislocate your spleen.

"Sorry about this," Gabriella says, moving to turn off the television and the light. "I was just doing some yoga." When she turns back to me, her face is unusually pinched as if being caught in such a state is unpleasant for her. She gestures to the table that sits between the couch and the kitchen that seems to be the dining area in the open space. "Please sit. I'll get us some cucumber water."

She sweeps into the kitchen and pulls a glass pitcher from the refrigerator with cucumbers floating in it, and I try to remember the last time I had a cucumber. I expect her to pour a couple of glasses of water, but instead she sets the pitcher on the counter before going to a door by the stairs. When she opens it, I see it's a pantry, and all its contents are divided into plastic containers with little handwritten labels on each of them. She pulls out a gold gilded tray and returns to the counter.

She takes out two glasses from a cupboard that have white roses hand painted on them, places them on the tray, and fills them with water. To this she adds a glass straw and a sprig of some green stuff from a pot on the windowsill above the kitchen sink.

Finally she comes to the table, sets the tray down in front of me, and takes a seat across from me. She sits with her back very straight, one leg crossed over the other, hands folded at her knee.

"So who is it?" she says, her eyes intense.

Everything about her is intense really. From her posture to her manners, to her gaze, Gabriella oozes confidence and almost a discomfort or fear of stepping out of place.

"Do you recall a teacher you used to work with named Victoria Gustafson?"

Again, she presses her fingers to her lips before saying, "Oh my word, Vicky." The hand again goes to her breast. "That is the most awful thing I have ever witnessed. What happened to her I mean. Just heartbreaking."

"Do you remember Vicky well?"

"Oh, of course, I do. We both taught middle school then." She moves her chin back and forth deliberately, and her lips thin. "Middle school. Awful place to be. Those poor kids going through so much change and being forced to interact with one another. The Lord knows I tried to make things better for them, but the way public education is treated in this country is appalling."

"Did you ever find your efforts to improve their education stymied by outside forces?"

Her expression flattens. "You mean the time Vicky and I had a cat fight at the board meeting?" She lays a hand on the table between us and leans forward. "Let me assure you. Both Vicky and I were mad as raccoons—" she draws out the word until its two long, distinct syllables—"that night but not at each other." The hand tents until a single finger to poke the tabletop. "It was the school board we were mad at. Wasn't a single financial mind in the whole bunch. Put us in a terrible position with their mismanagement."

"Did that make you angry?"

"Of course, it did." The hand goes back to her breast. "Their poor planning meant my students didn't get what they deserved. Vicky and I were fighting for the same thing that night, but I was too clouded with rage to see that." Gabriella Torres doesn't seem like a person familiar with rage. No one who takes the time to transfer cereal from a perfectly good box to a plastic container screams rage to me. "I realized the next morning what I'd done. I got some cinnamon rolls from Cake & Cookie and brought them to her classroom before home-room. After that, we promised to fight together to get our students what they needed."

"And did you?"

Gabriella frowns. "We tried to. I don't know what the board was thinking, but they were always allocating the budget to funds that were already maxed out. Said they were being cautious. Ha! They just didn't want those kids to have the education they needed." She shakes her head slowly this time. "And then she died." Her voice has gone hollow. "I can't believe she died." There's something about the way her gaze drops to the floor as if she's lost in her memories that strikes me as sincere.

The Gabriella I see before me is not one I would associate with the Miss Gustafson I knew. Where Miss Gustafson was soft and flowing, Gabriella is tethered and controlled, perhaps even controlling. But maybe Gabriella is telling the truth. They really had tried to fight for more funding for their kids, and some bond was struck there that even death and time couldn't sever.

Suddenly her eyes snap back to me. "You saw Vicky."

"I did." I don't see the point in keeping this from her.

The one item I had against her is too quickly explained

away, and I don't find it logical to keep her on my suspect list. Gabriella Torres simply doesn't have a motive for killing Vicky from what I can tell.

She leans forward, both hands spread wide on the table in front of her. "What did she say? Is she—" She may have been about to ask if Vicky was all right, but I see understanding dawn. "Oh my God. She's—I mean—" She waves both hands at herself as if overcome. "She hasn't passed on. She's trapped here. She's—" When her words spiral together and end in a wet, choked noise, I push the tray of waters toward her until she takes one.

She sips greedily as I explain how I saw Vicky that day at the bridge. I tell her everything except what Vicky's voice said to me in my head.

When I'm done she sets down the glass, nearly empty now, and her lips part without speaking. I take the other glass still on the tray because it would be rude if I didn't at least try it. It's surprisingly good, and I take a longer sip, enjoying the pleasure of the whole experience. I set the glass down and eye it, wondering if what my life has been missing this whole time are glass straws.

"Poor Vicky." Gabriella leans back, recrossing her legs and wrapping her hands around her knees. "You're trying to finish her business for her. The thing she's left undone. Did she tell you what it is?"

I explain how it doesn't work like that, and that I only get what the spirit has enough energy to get through to me.

"It's often a code or a hint of some kind because it's short enough for them to convey. Kind of like that game *Password*." I smile, but Gabriella's stricken expression doesn't change.

"You have to get it in one word? God." She waves a hand away. "The pressure. I couldn't do it."

"You get used to it." I take another sip of cucumber water because usually at this point people tend to start asking questions about the first time I saw a ghost and if I've seen any famous dead people.

Gabriella surprises me when she drops her foot to the floor, and I get the sense she's getting serious.

"This is about Kevin, isn't it?"

"Why would you say that?" The lovely cucumber water is suddenly overpowering, and I set my glass down.

"There was that thing he did with the English teacher. Miss Hamill. Hamilton. Something like that. I remember when we were in school Vicky got really upset about that."

"You were in school with Vicky?"

Gabriella shrugs and rolls her eyes. "Small town," she says. "If we weren't in school together, we were in Sunday school together, and that was even worse." Gabriella nods. "I bet Vicky knows something about what happened with Kevin. He was a lot older than us, you know? He was always the dangerous, moody teenager type to us. Are you supposed to tell me what Vicky knows? Is that it?"

I shrug with less sarcasm than she did. "I don't know. I'm still just trying to gather the facts."

"Well, if you ask me, Vicky knows something about Kevin, and she went to her grave with it."

"You're quick to point the finger at Kevin, but what about Vicky's boyfriend at the time? Daryl Walden?"

Gabriella gives a bark of laughter. "Daryl? The man wouldn't hurt a fly." Her expression sobers, and her gaze drifts far away again. "Kuwait really messed him up, you know? He had a good future ahead of him. He was learning welding over at the community college. I don't know what made him sign up for the Army. He had a good thing going for him." Her voice fades away again, and I picture two different Gabriellas.

The real one and the one she dons in front of the camera on her phone that sits in the tripod, light at the ready. It seems exhausting.

"Thank you for speaking with me today," I say and stand. I need some fresh air and time with Henry. "I'll let you know if I get anywhere with this."

Gabriella stands too, her lips parting until I see her very white teeth. "Oh sure. You let me know if I can help with anything else."

"I will," I say. "Thank you."

By the time I get to my SUV, I mentally check Gabriella off my suspect list, which leaves me with Daryl and Kevin. Instead of thinking more about it, I go home and split a jar of peanut butter with Henry.

TWELVE

The rest of my week is taken up by Founder's Day rehearsals and the official start of the move to the lodge for the summer. The lodge won't fully open to the public until Founder's Day, but that's only four short weeks away. Anyone who needs to be on site at the lodge starts moving as soon as the power is back on in the building and snow no longer makes a regular appearance in the weather forecast.

I'm grateful to have work as a distraction, but I know in the back of my mind at some point I'll need to talk to Logan. But even as I acknowledge the thought, I push it down like I've done for thirteen years.

Instead of unpacking any of the boxes I've moved into my office, using the dolly I stole from programming, I scroll on my phone, something I only do when truly resisting the thing I don't want to do. But periodically, I check in on the historical society's social media outlets, and I do so now.

"The boxes will not unpack themselves," Frances says as she sails by my office door.

I hunch my shoulders, but there's a crash at the other end

of the hall, and I picture the crew that's there to repair the broken windowpane in the library as Frances homes in on them.

"Gentlemen, please, the floors are original," I hear her say as her voice fades down the hall.

"Have you found a stapler yet?" Allie appears in the doorway, her long black hair escaping her Boston Red Sox baseball cap, a generous smudge of dust marring her nose.

I triumphantly pluck a stapler from the debris on the desk in front of me. I go back to scrolling, my arm still extended, holding out the stapler to Allie, when a photo in my feed makes me stop.

"Allie," I say when she's almost back to the door after retrieving the stapler. "Did you give this to Hannah to post?" I ask, referring to our social media coordinator, Hannah Nowak.

I show her my phone.

Allie peers at my phone and shakes her head. "Nope. Wasn't me." She looks up, a line between her brows. "But I wonder where she got it. Great photo. It would be nice to have that in the archives."

The photo shows Marty Pruitt with her daughter, Lisa, at Founder's Day. Marty looks as though she's been caught unawares, her smile is surprised, her eyes bright. Her face is so alive and happy, so unlike the Marty I saw only a few days ago, that I can't help but think I'm looking at a different person. Lisa stands just behind her mother as they are both half-turned toward the camera with the green of the lodge's park spread out behind them on what looks to be a beautiful spring day. Lisa has one arm bent, her hand wrapped around the strap of a denim backpack.

The caption reads, "Throwback to Founder's Day 1996. Marty Pruitt and her daughter, Lisa, on the way to the festivities. Who's ready? #countdowntofoundersday."

Hannah is only twenty-four and likely doesn't know about Lisa Reynolds. Allie who is a transplant from Massachusetts wouldn't know either. For a second, I wonder if Marty has seen this photo yet. I think of how carefully she held herself together when talking about Lisa, how she asked Chief Tom to stop the investigation, and my stomach churns.

I stand. "The girl in this photo went missing a year after this photo was taken. The police suspect she was murdered."

The hand holding the stapler goes slack. "She what?" Allie says. She holds the stapler against her head then, which I think is more of a reflex. "Oh my god, we need to take that down."

I'm out the door before she's finished her sentence and hope Hannah has already transitioned to her lodge office for the summer. I find her at her desk, turquoise headphones in place, knees drawn up in front of her as she stabs viciously at her keyboard.

"Hannah," I say and then wave my arms because I know she can't hear me over the sound in her headphones.

She straightens and blinks, her smile coming slowly as she holds up a single finger, indicating I should wait while she takes off the headphones.

"Hey, Del. What's up?" She turns to see Allie behind me. "Whoa, five alarm fire. What's going on?"

I show her my phone with the post of Marty and Lisa. "You need to take this down."

Hannah holds up both hands. "All right, all right. But can I ask why? Just so I don't do it again."

I point at Lisa. "This girl disappeared in April 1997. She was never found. The police suspect she was murdered. I don't want her mother to see this post."

I don't add that I'm positive Lisa is still alive somewhere nor that her mother asked me to try to contact her spirit.

Hannah's expression clouds. "Is that the girl's mother?" She points to Marty in the photo.

"Yes," I confirm.

Her expression grows murkier. "But that's the lady who sent me the photo to post. She said she saw my countdown to Founder's Day series on social and wanted to contribute."

I pull my phone back as if Hannah has just accused it of being ugly.

"She what?" Allie says beside me.

Hannah nods and leans back in her chair, crossing her arms behind her head and showing the small tattoos that run along the insides of her arms.

"Yeah, she emailed it to me last week. Thought I could use it. Do you still want me to take it down?"

I look at Allie as if she could make sense of this, but she's looking at Hannah as if the young woman has just reinvented the wheel but made it fly.

"You're sure Marty Pruitt sent this to you?" I try again.

Hannah straightens, dropping her arms to her desk. "Yeah. Marty's sometimes in the same yoga class with me. Nice lady. She's really helped me find balance in my tree pose. Want to see the email she sent me?" She takes hold of her mouse, but I hold up a hand to stop her.

"No, I believe you. I'm just..." But I don't know how to word it. Surprised? Shocked?

"Disturbed?" Allie says.

I glance at her with a frown. "I'm sure Marty is just trying to keep her daughter's spirit alive," I say, but when I look again at my phone, I'm once again positive there's no need for Marty to do so. Lisa is out there somewhere, and I wonder if Carmen has made any progress in finding her.

I thank Hannah for explaining the post to me and wander back to my office where my boxes remain unpacked. I put my phone in my back pocket and get to work, determined to keep Lisa and Vicky from my mind until the end of the workday.

Instead of going straight home after work though, I go to see Gretchen.

This time when she answers the door, she's not covered in flour.

"Did you talk to Vicky again?" she says in that forceful way she has of speaking, her eyebrows raised in hope.

"Not yet," I say. "I need you to tell me about what really happened with Kevin and Julia Hammond."

Her eyebrows drop. "Oh. You found out about that, huh?"

"I found out about that," I repeat flatly.

She lets go of the door and turns into the house. "Well, c'mon then. I might as well get through this."

I follow her back to the kitchen, and I see I've interrupted her at the crossword puzzle in the paper as the folded paper sits on the table next to a coffee mug.

I tap it as I sit down. "Five down is a doozy."

Gretchen returns from the fridge where she's retrieved the pitcher of iced tea I saw the last time I was here. The glasses she sets on the table do not match, and there are no glass straws. But this time, she does pour me a glass, which I accept.

"Kevin has never been very good with girls."

I nearly spit out the iced tea I've just taken a sip of. "Never been very good with girls? You mean even now? Isn't he sixty something?"

"He's sixty-six," Gretchen says. "Been single his whole life. I had him too young, I think. I was only a kid myself." She points toward the hall then. "That psycho doctor they had on that afternoon program once said it was probably something to do with how his daddy left when he was still a boy." Gretchen puts her hand down on the table and shakes her head. "I don't think that was it. I think it was just how he was made. To be alone, you know?"

I feel tears sting the back of my eyes unexpectedly, and I

take a sip of iced tea. Gretchen's words have probably caused a bigger reaction in me than they would normally if I hadn't so recently seen the likely cause of my husband's slow drift from our marriage.

"So you think Julia Hammond misunderstood Kevin's advances?"

"Oh no," Gretchen says with a quick shake of her head. "Kevin's an idiot. Went to her house in the middle of the night, for criminey's sake. He was just a dumb kid."

"So why didn't you tell me about it?"

Gretchen looks down at her hands on the wooden table. "Because Kevin was always different, and then when he got in trouble, it made him really different, and I didn't want anyone looking at him like that. Like he was some kind of sex-craved weirdo. Especially not after that spat he had with Daryl." Gretchen looks up and meets my gaze with a sudden intensity. "Do you know what it's like? Choosing one kid over the other? Kevin always needed me more than Vicky did, and I think in the end, I let Vicky down."

There's a force about Gretchen Gustafson that's unexplainable. It's like the power of her personality is so strong it precedes her by several feet, and you can feel her before you see her. But now that force is diminished, and I see real pain in her eyes.

"My husband and I weren't able to have children," I say because I don't know what else to say.

Her eyes clear, and her lips pinch. "Oh shoot, look what I did. I'm sorry, Della. I really am. I forgot for a minute where I was."

Just like Vicky's accident, mine is well known in Bellegrave.

Gretchen sets her hand on my arm. "Kevin didn't have anything to do with Vicky's death. I know it. It's just—" She cuts off abruptly, her teeth worrying her lower lip.

"What is it?" I get the sense there's something else happening here, something Gretchen has tried to keep secret all these years because she's afraid of the truth.

She sits back, dropping her hands to the table again. "That morning when I called to tell him Vicky had died, he wasn't home. I got his machine. I left a message, and he called me back almost right away and said he was on his way up here. Only..." Again her voice trails off, and I can see in her face she's making a decision, one she's made before, but the last time she chose Kevin over Vicky. She sits up, and I know she's made a different decision this time. "Kevin got here before noon that day. He wasn't in New York, Della. He couldn't have been." She thumps a palm against the table. "To this day, I've always wondered where he was because he wasn't in New York when his sister died. He was somewhere much closer to Bellegrave."

"Do you think Kevin killed Vicky?" I ask the question I know Gretchen doesn't want to answer.

Her eyes spark for a second, but the resistance to my question fades quickly. "I don't know." Her voice is the softest I've ever heard it. "I just don't know." She shuts her eyes then, and when she opens them, they're damp with unshed tears. "I should have demanded an autopsy. I should have asked more questions. Everyone told me it was an accident. That she fell asleep and lost control of the car. But I didn't believe that for a second. Vicky was always up early." Gretchen shakes both fists in the air as if she's shaking someone by the shoulders. "She was one of those annoyingly chipper people who wake up ready to embrace the day. She wouldn't have fallen asleep on the way to school. She just wouldn't have."

This time I lay my hand on her arm where it's come to rest on the table. "I know," I say. "And I'm going to find out what really happened. But from now on, you need to tell me the truth. Is there anything else I should know?"

Gretchen's shoulders slump, and I can't help but feel as though she's unloaded something heavy she's been carrying for almost thirty years.

"No," she says. She shakes her head again, but I get the sense she's shaking it at herself. "I know Vicky and Kevin were close. Kevin always told her things he wouldn't tell me." She looks at me, fear and self-recrimination in her gaze. "What if Kevin told Vicky something he regretted, and he killed her for it?"

This is a question I can't answer, and it's one I know cost Gretchen a great deal to ask.

"Do you know what happened to Julia Hammond?" I ask. The only thing I can do to help that torment in Gretchen's eyes is to move this investigation forward.

Gretchen perks up at this. "She married a doctor. Moved to Utica. Smart girl, if you ask me," she says, repeating the same story I heard from my parents.

"Now women just become doctors themselves," I can't help but say.

"Like you?" Gretchen replies, a smirk on her lips.

"Wrong kind of doctor unfortunately," I say. "But I did marry a lawyer."

"Smart girl," Gretchen says again.

If only she knew.

———

"So Kevin is your main suspect?"

"I don't have a main suspect," I say around a mouthful of Reuben at Shelly's the next day. "I have suspects."

"Kevin and Daryl?" Carmen pokes at her Caesar salad.

I think about my initial meeting with Daryl Walden, and his words run through me like a bad chill.

"Yeah," I confirm, setting down my sandwich. "I'm going

to have to talk to Daryl again. I just can't figure out how to make him more amenable to speaking with me."

"Maybe he's afraid of dogs," Carmen suggests.

I picture Henry as he was that day, cowering against my legs. "I'm not sure Henry was exactly a threat."

Carmen looks up, her fork paused in the pile of lettuce on her plate. "Did Daryl have a mop?" she says, her voice grave.

Henry has always had an unhealthy fear of mops. I shake my head. "Actually no. I think it was the space. It's cavernous and echoey down there."

Carmen grimaces. "Imagine having to take swim lessons there."

"No, thanks." I give a mock tremble in solidarity.

Shelly's Diner is busy as it usually is on a weekday lunch hour, and Carmen and I were lucky to snag the last two-top even if it's by the door, which bangs open periodically. Shelly's brings in all kinds from the suits at the booth in the corner to the DPW workers at the counter. The buzz of conversation and the clinking of silverware against dishes is comforting as I try to sort through my thoughts.

"I wonder if Daryl and I have a connection. Something I can use to make me relatable to him."

"I think the kind of ghosts Daryl sees are not the same ones you do."

I frown. "That's not helpful."

Carmen smiles her elementary-school-teacher smile, but I don't register it because just then the door behind her opens, and my husband steps in.

With Heather Russo.

He doesn't look around as he comes into the diner, his focus remaining on Heather as she glides in behind him. They go straight to the counter where one of the servers is holding out a brown paper bag that usually contains to-go orders. She hands the bag to Logan who moves to take out his wallet, but

Heather lays a hand on his arm, stopping him as she reaches for her purse.

"Hey, you okay?"

Carmen's voice breaks through the trance the sight of my husband has cast over me. It's not enough to move my gaze away from them, but I hear myself say, "It's Albany."

Carmen doesn't hesitate. She turns in her chair until she's following my gaze, and I know the moment she sees them because she lets out a sound I've only heard once before, and it's when we both failed our driving test the first time.

"Are you sure?" Her voice has gone soft and serious.

"Yeah," I say.

"Do you want me to arrest her?"

The server hands back Heather's credit card, and Heather puts it in her wallet, some expensive leather looking contraption she handles delicately with her long French-manicured fingers.

"For what?" I ask.

They turn to the door, and I know now they'll see us. But neither of them is looking at us. They're only looking at each other, their expressions intent as their lips move. They're too far away for me to hear what they're saying though.

One of the DPW workers stands unexpectedly, nearly knocking Heather over, and Logan reaches for her to steady her. But instead of a simple hand to her shoulder, he wraps an arm around her, pulling her against him as he moves her out of the way. I see apologies being made between the DPW worker and them, but I can't hear anything at all over the roaring in my ears.

"What am I saying," Carmen says then. "I have a gun. I'll just shoot her." Carmen makes to stand, but they turn back to us, and like me, Carmen freezes.

They walk to the door, and I think they'll just move through it and out of my sight, and my heart will start beating normally again. Except at the last possible moment, Logan shifts as he pulls open the door, and his left hand goes to the small of Heather's back as he guides her outside.

"Oh shit," Carmen breathes.

But I can't breathe. I can't do anything except play that small gesture over and over again in my head.

"That probably didn't mean anything." Carmen has turned back to the table now. She reaches across and places a hand on the arm I'd forgotten on the table. "It was probably an automatic gesture. Habit. He didn't mean—"

"He doesn't do that when I walk through a door." My tone is emotionless, and it's that that scares me the most, the absence of feeling, like all the feelings I've ever had were removed from me when they took my dead baby girl out of my body.

Carmen lets go of my arm and sits up, her hands useless in her lap. "Oh God, Del, I'm so sorry."

My eyes finally focus, and I see my best friend sitting across from me. I wish suddenly, fervently, that instead of our lunch between us it was a basket of curly fries and two milkshakes, vanilla for me, strawberry for her, and after this, we'd get on our bikes and go down to the creek to catch crayfish. But that's not who we are anymore. Now I'm a wife whose husband is cheating on her.

I don't have time to let this realization settle because at that moment a man appears beside our table. It's a moment before I can look up, and I'm startled by how close he is.

"You that psychic that's been questioning my ex-wife?"

The man is a stranger to me, but even I can figure this one out.

"I'm Della James," I say and gesture to Carmen. "That's Detective Carmen Neil. You are?" I ask just to confirm what I already suspect.

"Marc Dabrowski. I'm Gabriella's ex-husband." He shifts,

his hands going into the pockets of his creased chinos. He's wearing a worn brown leather bomber jacket that looks too hot for the crowded diner, but it's April in the Adirondacks where days start out in winter and end in summer. His nearly black hair is cut excessively short and bends to one side where a deep cowlick breaks up his hairline. "Look, I don't know what she said to you, but I'm here to tell you the truth."

"Oh God," Carmen mutters and leans back in her chair, arms crossed, lips pursed.

I can't imagine how many times she's heard a similar line.

Marc glances at her, his brow as creased as his chinos, but he turns back to me without comment.

"Listen, I didn't say anything before because Gabriella is a teacher. She's a public figure in a small town, and I'm just not that kind of guy to do something like that."

I'm tired of looking up and gesture to an empty chair at the next table. "Do you mind sitting?"

He glances toward the chair and shrugs before pulling it over. He turns it around and straddles the seat, leaning against the back of the chair with his crossed arms.

"Listen," he says again. "I don't know what Gabriella told you, but if you're looking into Vicky Gustafson's death, there's something you need to know."

I picture Gabriella Torres that day in her expensive workout clothes, her perfect hair, and teeth so white they matched her furnishings.

"And what is that?"

"Gabriella isn't who she seems. I let everyone think it was me that was no good, but Gabriella is a narcissist. She'll do anything she needs to, to get her own way."

"And what way did she want?"

"Back then they didn't have the things they do now. Then it was only television that could really give you a break, and as a science educator, Gabriella didn't have much going for her.

But she'd been approached by some local programming out of Albany about hosting a science show. You know, like one of those Bill Nye type things. You remember those?"

"Yeah, I remember. You're saying Gabriella was interested in becoming a TV personality?"

Marc shakes his head. "That was just the start. She was going to get a local show and then expand from there. The woman could cure cancer if she just focused her energy the right way."

I think about the yoga mat, the ring light, the glass straws and gilded tray and think Marc might be right.

"But that television show was going to be her launch pad. Only Vicky ruined it for her."

"How so?"

"The producer from Albany said Gabriella had to show her experience at presenting to a large group of kids beyond the classroom, so Gabriella was going to form some after-school program for all ages in the Bellegrave middle and high school. Only she couldn't get the funding. Vicky fought her, saying the limited budget was needed for in-class education."

"So Gabriella never got the show?"

Marc shakes his head. "The producer got tired of nothing happening and went somewhere else. I've never seen Gabriella so upset. She took it out on me, of course. That's the thing about narcissists. They make you think it's your fault. I didn't even realize what she was doing to me until we were married for like fourteen years. Gaslighting me. Getting defensive. Blaming me when things didn't work out for her. Telling me I shouldn't feel a certain way. My therapist helped me to understand that. If she treated me, her own husband, that way, imagine what she might have done to Vicky."

I shake my head. "That's a nice motive, but I don't think it makes Gabriella a killer."

Marc leans forward, the chair creaking ominously beneath

him as he slams a blunt finger into the table. "That's not all. The night before Vicky was found in the river, Gabriella didn't come home. I don't know where she was, and when she finally did come home, she wouldn't tell me."

Carmen sits up. "Your wife doesn't have an alibi for the time Vicky died?"

Marc looks at her, his eyebrows up as though he's surprised she's taken an interest. "So you *are* investigating Vicky's death as a murder."

"Answer the question," Carmen says, ignoring Marc's comment.

"Yeah, that's what I'm saying." He gestures with both hands. "Gabriella wasn't home the night before they found Vicky. I don't know where she was. And you can take it from me, Gabriella is a vindictive woman. One time she was doing her nails, and I bumped the coffee table, making her mess up. I apologized of course. I'm a good guy. That bitch took my steak out of the fridge long enough to let it go bad and put it back in the fridge so I wouldn't know. I had food poisoning for three days. Ended up in the hospital." He wraps both arms around the chair and shakes his head. "And you know what? I didn't even realize it was her. Just thought it was bad steak. It took me years to catch on she was always doing stuff like that. Little stuff to get back at me. Little things to remind me she was in control." He scoffs, and his expression turns dismal, but I recognize the feeling there. It's one of disappointment in one's self. "I just always thought I could try harder. Be better. Make it work. That it was my fault. Took me so long to see who she really was." He looks up again, his expression clearer. "My therapist says that's how narcissists work, and I shouldn't blame myself."

I don't know how to respond to this and look at Carmen for help. She touches Marc's elbow.

"That's really good that you're getting help. Thank you for letting us know about Ms. Torres."

"Yeah, sure." He unwinds himself from the chair and puts it back at the table where he took it from before turning back to me. "Did you really see Vicky?" he asks, shifting his weight from foot to foot.

"I did," I say.

"What did she say?" he asks, the question everyone asks.

"I'm afraid that's not how it works."

"Huh," Marc says. "Well, I hope what I said helps her. Vicky was a good person. She didn't deserve to die like that." He says goodbye and heads for the door before we can say anything else.

When Carmen meets my gaze, I say, "This is why I eat lunch at my desk."

THIRTEEN

When Gabriella Torres opens the door of number nineteen later that day, her expression immediately brightens upon seeing me until I say, "You lied to me about your relationship with Victoria Gustafson."

Her smile wavers until it turns into a grimace. "I didn't exactly lie. What I said happened did, but yeah, maybe I did harbor a little resentment toward Vicky." She doesn't invite me in, and as she speaks, she slowly closes the door against me with the hand she still has on the knob. "I guess Marc found you?" This is said with a distinct sneer.

"He did. He said Vicky stopped you from getting some television deal."

Gabriella rolls her eyes and flicks her hair, which is in a ponytail today, a gesture more suited to a recalcitrant fifteen-year-old than a fifty-something-year-old woman. I guess she's not putting on her usual show for me today, and I'm seeing the real Gabriella, the one Marc was married to all those years ago.

"She didn't stop me, okay? I could have gotten that deal another way. It was those morons on the school board that stopped me." I raise an eyebrow but don't comment, so she continues. "They wouldn't approve the expenditure for the after-school program I needed. I even offered to fundraise, but it was too late. The producer from Albany had moved on."

"And so you took your anger out on Vicky?"

She scoffs, the sound causing her upper lip to curl unpleasantly. "Hardly. Vicky wasn't worth it. I just looked for another way to get my break."

"And what was that?"

"Radio," she says without hesitation. "I took over Rick Harris's spot on Saturdays on Tupper Lake's public radio station. I did it for about twelve years. Established myself and grew my fan base so when I made the transition, I was met with success." She shrugs as if she did nothing more than take the trash out.

"I'm sorry," I say. "Transition?"

She points above her to what I assume is the main floor of her condo. "To social media influencer obviously. It's really the right fit and where I should've been all along. I'm an early adopter."

I realize she's pointing to where I'd seen the tripod and ring light set up.

"Social media influencer? I don't understand what that has to do with teaching."

She laughs, a terrible sound. "It has *nothing* to do with teaching. I got out with an early retirement offer and haven't looked back." Again she points to the ceiling. "I have over a hundred and fifty thousand followers, and Hydro-Plates alone pays me ten thousand dollars for every video I post for them. That producer from Albany doesn't know what she missed out on."

The idea of anyone being paid to make a video for a social media platform boggles my brain, let alone ten thousand dollars.

"So you didn't have a reason to kill Victoria Gustafson?"

She laughs again but this time with absurdity. "Oh God, of course not. What would have been the point?"

"Then where were you the morning she was killed? Marc says you weren't at home."

Her gaze goes instantly icy, and I no longer have any trouble picturing her harming another human being.

"Marc told you that, did he?" Her modulated tone is gone as well, replaced with a raspy quality suggesting a deep-seated hate. "Well, I'll tell you where I was. I was with Tony. All night long. Several. Times. All. Night. Long." The last few words are nearly spit, spaces between them large enough so I don't miss the emphasis.

I cringe at the picture her words make but ask, "Tony?"

She rolls her eyes again. I see her hesitate, and I know she's choosing her words for impact instead of accuracy. "My lover," she finally says.

"Can I have Tony's full name to verify your story?"

She lurches back in disgust. "You're not the police, and I'm done talking to you. I don't care if Vicky's ghost haunts me for the rest of my life. I don't owe her anything."

She slams the door in my face.

I go straight home from the condos, and Henry's excited wiggles lift the tumult of the day. I take him for a walk, which mostly involves a slow procession down the access road from the county highway to our cottage with regular sniffing sessions along the ditch. I don't mind though. The day is warm enough not to require a jacket, and the mosquitos haven't descended on Bear Lake yet. It's the exact right time of year to enjoy a Henry walk along the road while my thoughts play topsy turvy in my head.

He soon tires of the sniffing and races back to the cottage where he knows he'll get food and cuddles. After placing his dish on the floor, I fish through my bag for my phone. I nearly drop it when I see Logan's name on the screen. After lunch, I had set it on do not disturb, not wanting any human interaction without my intention for the remainder of the day, and after having a door slammed in my face, I'd nearly forgotten about the day's earlier upset. But seeing Logan's name on my phone screen has that episode at the diner earlier coming right to the front of my mind, my husband's hand on the small of Heather Russo's back.

I swipe open the phone and see three missed calls from Logan and a text that says he's working late.

"Working late, my ass," I mutter at the phone and glance at Henry to see if he heard me.

He's sitting by his empty dish now, head tilted in question.

"You didn't hear that, did you?"

He thumps his tail.

"C'mon," I say. "Let's call Grandma."

His tail thumps harder at one of his favorite words, and we head into the living room where he catapults onto the couch, anticipating the cuddle session that's about to happen. I flop down next to him, and he launches himself upside down onto my lap, melting across my legs as I press the speed dial for my mom.

"I swear to God, Delia Ann," she says in greeting. "What happened now? I just saw you."

"Hi, Mom. Love you too," I say. "Do you remember Gabriella Torres dating a guy named Tony?"

There's a brief pause in which my mother releases a heavy sigh. "Tony Wottesley. What a dreamboat."

I almost vomit in reflex. "*Mister* Wottesley?"

My mother scoffs. "He's let himself go since then, but back in the nineties, Anthony Wottesley was a dreamboat."

Anthony Wottesley was, and as far as I know, still is the tech teacher at the high school.

"Mr. Wottesley carries all of his weight in a beer gut that rivals a beach ball."

"I know," my mother says wearily, as if something precious has been lost. "You should have seen him when he first started at the school though. I think he worked out then. He would do the bass tournament every summer on the lake, and me and Mel always scoped out a spot on the docks first thing just to watch him take off his shirt before getting into his boat. It was like a ritual. He'd tear off his t-shirt for the spectators. Oh, those were the good old days."

Now I'm sure I'm going to vomit. "Mom, please stop talking about Mr. Wottesley without a shirt on."

"You should have been there, Della." She pauses. "Why are you asking about Mr. Wottesley? Is this to do with Miss Gustafson?"

"Do you know if Mr. Wottesley ever had an affair with Gabriella Torres?"

There's a sharp intake of breath through the line so loud even Henry picks up his head from its melted position against my thigh to look at me in concern.

"I knew it!" my mother practically hisses. "I can't wait to tell Vanessa," she says, referring to Carmen's mother. "I always knew something was going on, but Vanessa told me I was seeing rain where there were only clouds."

"So there was some gossip at the time about an affair?"

"Well." My mother always states the word *well* like a preface to an encyclopedia because what is about to come next borders too closely to gossiping than her morals will allow, but she is not one to omit facts when called upon. "There was some scuttlebutt at the time about the Torres-Dabrowski marriage. Everyone knew it was on the rocks. Marc worked too much. He took over his father's home design business at the time. You know the tile and fixture place out on Route 3? So he was working extra-long hours then, and—" She pauses, and I know she's placed her hand against her heart without having to see her. "This is just me surmising, you understand? Gabriella always seemed like someone who required a little extra work to love. Do you know what I mean? I don't think she liked Marc working all those hours." She snorts now. "Although it paid for all those fancy clothes she wears. Don't tell me she afforded those on a public school teacher's salary." She grumbles for several more minutes about this rumored affair between Gabriella and Mr. Wottesley before proclaiming the need to call Vanessa and hangs up on me immediately.

I set the phone on the arm of the couch. Henry has fallen asleep on my lap, and I let his steady breathing slow my own heart rate until I'm in danger of falling asleep too.

I still haven't figured out how to approach Daryl Walden again, and every day that passes feels like a waste of time. If anyone knew Vicky well enough to know who might have killed her, it would be Daryl. Even if he's not the murderer himself, I can't help but feel he knows something important, and every day I avoid approaching him again is time lost.

Then there's the problem of Kevin Gustafson. Where was he the morning of Vicky's death? Was he truly not in New York as Gretchen seems to think? And if so, then where was he? Was he in Bellegrave all along and waited a reasonable two hours before showing himself in order to throw off suspicion? But even if he had opportunity, what was his motive to kill his own sister?

On top of everything, I now must confirm Gabriella's alibi for the morning of Vicky's death. I make a mental note to stop by the school one day to see Mr. Wottesley. The very idea of having to approach one of my former teachers to ask him about an affair he had is unpleasant and one I will put off for as long as possible.

Henry slides from my lap, curling into the cushions beside me. He maintains contact with a single paw pressed against my leg, but it's easy enough to swap the pressure of my thigh with another throw pillow as I ease off the couch.

I retrieve my laptop from my bag and grab a water from the fridge before settling back down on the couch, putting my thigh back into place against Henry's paw. He doesn't stir.

It takes a little longer to find Julia Hammond than it did to find Gabriella Torres. But through a careful cross-referenced search between social media sites, I find her. She did, in fact, marry a doctor, and from her profile picture on one site, has had several children and then several grandchildren. Her profile says she's still in Utica.

I click the button to send her a message. The story I fabricate about interviewing her for the historical society comes easily. I press send before I can feel guilty about luring her into speaking with me. I'll feel guilty when I'm dead.

FOURTEEN

I could have spoken to Julia Hammond over the phone. It would have been easier. The drive to Utica can take more than two and a half hours. But I want to see Julia's face when she responds to the questions I have for her.

Saturday rehearsals for Founder's Day start the following Saturday, so if I want to speak to Julia Hammond in person, I must go straight away. I planned to bring this up to Logan the morning after Julia responded to my social media message, but when I found him in the kitchen after getting back from my swim, he was on the phone as he made coffee.

I tried not to eavesdrop, but our cottage is small, and unless I went outside and stood in the cold, dim morning, I couldn't avoid what he was saying. So I sat down on the floor of the kitchen, braced my back against the cupboards, and drew Henry between my legs until he fell against my chest. He purred as I rubbed his belly.

When Logan hung up, he turned to me, coffee tumbler in hand. "I need to go to Albany this weekend," he said. "The developers are flying in from California, so it's all hands on deck."

I could have told him about Julia Hammond, but I suddenly felt so tired I couldn't form any words at all. So I just nodded and wished him luck and told him I'd see him on Sunday night.

I made plans to leave Henry with my mom that Saturday, but Carmen offered to take him. The girls had been begging for a dog, and she wanted to borrow Henry for the day to show them what kind of work a dog was. I didn't think Henry was a good example as he is happy to sleep on the couch all day, eat scrapes from under the table, and drink water from the lake. But Saturday morning I drop Henry off with the Neils and head south.

Julia Hammond—now Trenholm—lives in a standard colonial painted none other than colonial blue in a suburb north of Utica. The colonial sits at the end of a cul de sac, and I'm disappointed it's not surrounded by a white picket fence. I park on the street out front, and my knock on the burgundy front door is answered quickly as though Julia has been waiting for me.

I keep my face neutral when the door opens, but I honestly have been waiting to see if she still looks like Farah Fawcett. I'm not disappointed.

She's a few years older than my parents, and the time shows in the lines that now bracket her mouth and eyes, but the woman who opens the door still radiates beauty the way she did in the yearbook photo my mom showed me. Her blonde hair is still worn in waves coaxed to frame her face with generous curtain bangs, but now the blonde is highlighted with streaks of silver. She wears simple black ankle pants and a red blouse made of a fabric that looks expensive.

"Mrs. Trenholm?" I say.

She holds the door with both hands as she smiles. "So you're the daughter of Maxine Barnes and Gregory

Hopewell." She says this as if it's an accomplishment of unheard of valor.

"That's me," I say awkwardly with an equally awkward shrug. I suddenly feel bad I lied to her to get here.

"Come in. Come in." She opens the door wider and gestures me inside. "Nick just left for the club. He has a standing eleven o'clock tee time every Saturday with our sons-in-law as soon as the snow melts," she explains as she leads me into the house, and I assume Nick is Dr. Trenholm.

We pass through a double-story foyer of cheerful yellow paint, a pristine floral carpet running down the wooden stairs, and a gallery above with polished warm wood spindles. The wall along the stairs is filled with photos, evidence of a rich and wide life. I pause for a moment to take them in. There are only two photos framed and hung on a wall in our cottage, and one of them is of Henry as a puppy. The other is our wedding photo.

I swallow and continue after Mrs. Trenholm.

The back of the house is split between an open-concept kitchen and a small family room, almost a nook to one side with French windows that open onto a brick patio. The cheerful yellow paint continues in here and is complemented by blue tones in the rugs and chair cushions. There's a small table in an eating nook in the kitchen already adorned with a tea set and a plate piled with scones.

She gestures for me to sit. "So we'll have plenty of time to catch up without the boys interfering."

The guilt threatens to clog my throat. I take the seat she indicates.

"Help yourself," she says as she sits, pulling a cloth napkin onto her lap.

"How lovely. You didn't need to go to all this trouble for me," I say, selecting one of the scones. I nearly drop it when I find it's still warm and realize Mrs. Trenholm must have baked it that morning.

"Oh, I love an excuse to bring out this set. It was my grandmother's. She gave it to me when Nick and I wed."

The guilt is too much, and I set down my scone on the blue China plate in front of me. "Mrs. Trenholm—"

"Julia, please," she interrupts with a smile.

"Julia, I'm afraid I lied to you to get you to talk to me."

Julia's face hardly changes. "I only taught in Bellegrave for one year before I married Nick. I didn't think your story about a project for the historical society was true." Her smile is knowing, and my estimation of her changes.

I remember what Gretchen said about Julia being smart to marry a doctor when the choices women had were limited. I ease back in my chair and set my bag at my feet.

"I'm here to ask you about Kevin Gustafson."

Her lips firm the slightest of degrees, and had I not been watching her so closely, I might not have noticed.

"I see," she says, placing her own scone delicately on her plate and wiping nonexistent crumbs from her hands on her cloth napkin. "What is it you wish to know?"

Against the wall behind Julia is a hoosier that appears to have been restored, the enamel of its counter unmarred, the wood polished like the rest of the house. Above it is a row of three pictures, which I identify as senior portraits. Each photograph shows a blonde teenage girl with the same smile as the woman seated in front of me.

I meet Julia's gaze. "I really am Maxine and Greg's daughter. That much is true. I'm also really the director of the Bellegrave Historical Society. The thing I didn't tell you is that I can see and sometimes communicate with the dead."

I have had years of practice at telling people about my ability, and I've found it's best to simply get it over with. I wait for Julia's response, but there is none.

Finally she says, "And?"

She seems entirely nonplussed by my revelation. I go on.

"I was contacted by the spirit of Victoria Gustafson. I'm not sure if you met her in your short time in Bellegrave, but she was Kevin Gustafson's sister. She died in a terrible accident when her car left the county highway and crashed into the Bellegrave River. She indicated to me her death was not the accident everyone assumes it to have been, and I'm now investigating on her behalf."

"Investigating?" Julia's mouth tenses with a mixture of concern and suspicion. "Are you also some kind of detective?"

"More like a concerned citizen."

Julia lifts both eyebrows and picks up the teapot. She fills my cup and hers with a dark, rich liquid that steams pleasantly through the sun filtering through the windows that surround the eating nook. The entire scene is terribly domestic for such a macabre topic of conversation.

"And you're here to ask me about Kevin Gustafson. Do you think he might have had something to do with it?"

"I honestly don't know yet."

Julia pauses in adding milk to her tea, and several emotions pass across her face before she says, "How sad. Such a tragedy for that family." She puts the milk down. "I'm afraid I haven't much to tell you, but what I do have to say might not help you at all if you're looking at Kevin's possible involvement in his sister's death."

"And why is that?"

"Because I blame myself for what happened with Kevin." She stirs her tea languidly.

"Why?" The word comes out bluntly.

Julia looks up from her tea. "It was my first and only year teaching," she explains. "I'm afraid I couldn't manage a professional degree with my students. I let them get too close. I made them think we were friends. I'm afraid I led

Kevin on, and I'm sorry what happened"—she shrugs—"happened."

"You obtained a restraining order against him."

Julia sets down her spoon, her expression disappointed, but I know it's a disappointment in herself. "I did." She shakes her head. "It was so foolish when I think about it now. I was just so frightened and unsure of what I was doing. I was hardly more than a kid myself, and I was so far away from Nick." She stops and meets my gaze. "I met Nick through a friend. He was doing his residency in Syracuse then, and we wanted to marry, but not until he was done with his residency and knew where he would end up, so we could start growing our family." She adjusts her napkin on her lap in measured, steady movements. "I suppose I just let Robbie get to me, and I shouldn't have let him spook me with his nonsense about stalking."

"Robbie?"

"My cousin," Julia explains. "I was living with him at the time. That's how I ended up in Bellegrave actually. My cousin, Robbie, was always going on about this little village he'd found up north. He found work up there with an architecture firm—he was a surveyor—and when I was looking for a teaching position, he invited me to come stay with him." Her fingers play with her napkin, methodically folding and unfolding the corner. "It was supposed to just be for fun. A year of teaching, a different and exciting place up in the mountains, and planning for my wedding." She brushes her hair over one shoulder. "I suppose I was already too tightly wound with everything going on with the wedding planning and waiting to hear where Nick would end up, and when Kevin showed up at our apartment that night, I let Robbie talk me into calling the police." She grips the napkin with both hands now as she looks directly at me. "Kevin Gustafson was just a child. He didn't know what he was doing, and I was just as guilty as he was for not knowing how to be an ally to my students while maintaining a professional relationship. I never should have called the police that night."

"Did Kevin ever threaten you?"

Her expression turns horrified. "Oh heavens, no. Kevin wasn't like that. He was...quiet." She settles on the word as though she's plucked it from a shelf. "He didn't seem to really have any friends, and he mostly kept to himself. But when he did act, it was out of kindness. I just wish—" She stops and shakes her head.

"What is it?"

She looks out the window briefly before answering. "I just wish I had asked him what he was doing there that night."

"The police report says he thought it was a romantic gesture."

"How do you know what the police report says?"

"It's public record," I say even though I'm not sure if that's true. I just don't want to bring Carmen into it.

"Oh," Julia says quietly, and a line appears between her brows.

For the first time, I realize what I've come to speak to her about might upset her, and I regret not telling her the truth from the outset.

I reach across the table and touch her arm. When she meets my gaze, her eyes are glassy with tears.

"It's not your fault," I say. "We're not responsible for the actions of others."

"You're right," she says, her voice slightly hoarse now. "But I could have done better that night."

"What's done is done, and we can only hope to do better next time." I gesture to the house around me that exudes love. "I think you did better."

She laughs reluctantly and dabs at her eyes with her napkin. "I suppose I did." She places the napkin back on her lap, and I feel the mood has lifted. She confirms this when she tilts her head and asks, "Have you ever seen the ghost of someone famous?"

"I saw the Bellegrave High School star quarterback from the class of 1958."

"Oh heavens," she says, picking up her teacup. "What was that like?"

"Awkward," I say. "I had to tell him they lost the championship that year without him. You know...because he was dead."

"How did he take it?"

"Not well." I pull apart my scone, and my tastebuds scream just at the sight of steam rising from the fluffy inside. "He crossed over instantly."

"Oh dear," Julia says. "Can you summon someone you want to talk to?"

We finish our tea and scones over a discussion about speaking with the dead, and I learn everything there is to know about Julia's three daughters, their husbands, the grandchildren, and Nick. It's afternoon by the time I step through the front door again, and Julia stops me with a hand on my arm.

"If there's anything else I can help with, please let me know." She shakes her head slightly. "I just can't imagine quiet Kevin Gustafson doing anything to harm someone."

"You said when he did act it was out of kindness. What did you mean by that exactly?"

She leans against the doorframe. "Oh, one day after school, my car wouldn't start. He helped me get it going again so I could take it down to the garage in town. Seemed to know his way around cars a great deal. Said it was the one thing his father taught him before he left."

We say our goodbyes, and on the drive home, I have plenty of time to think about whether or not Kevin Gustafson would know enough about cars to use one to cover up a murder.

FIFTEEN

I'm not sure when Logan gets home Sunday night. Henry and I fall asleep on the couch, watching *Charade*, waking up only when Audrey Hepburn proclaims she'll marry all of Cary Grant's identities. Henry is sound asleep beside me, and I contemplate letting him out for one last pee. I look to the glass patio doors and can almost hear the eerie laughter floating across the black water of the lake.

But if I don't let him out, I might have to face the same thing at three in the morning, and that's far worse. The witching hour as it's called. I don't go out in the night during the witching hour because that's the funny thing about superstitions. They're always couched in fact.

I coax Henry from his slumber and lure him to the back door where his leash hangs unused by the door. He looks at me, furry brow creased, as I put the leash on him.

"I know they're dead, and they can't hurt me, but they're still creepy. C'mon."

I open the back door and walk out just far enough to let him go wee. I try to remain as alert as I can, but my senses are foggy from the kind of groggy sleep only falling asleep on the couch can produce. No paranormal sound drifts from the direction of the lake, but as Henry examines the bushes by the back door for a possible spot to do his business, I can't help but feel I'm being watched.

I peer into the woods around us, and for the first time since living in Great-Aunt Marge's cottage, I feel how isolated we are. The forest is an impenetrable black surrounding us, as though a natural wall has sprung up between us and the rest of the world, keeping us tucked in, yes, but also keeping help out.

Henry finishes his business and heads for the door, more interested in a treat than in further exploration. I close the door swiftly behind us and lock it, taking an extra moment to peer through the glass as if someone followed us back to the house. There's nothing there but darkness, but still, I can't shake the feeling of being watched.

I know it's all in my head. After my discussion with Julia, I don't know what to think about Vicky's death, and I'm jumping at shadows.

I leave the under-cabinet lights on in the kitchen, grab a bottle of water from the fridge, and after accepting his reward for doing business, Henry follows me upstairs. I check to make sure my gun is in its place in the safe mounted to the wall behind the headboard of the bed before crawling beneath the covers. I turn the TV on to an old sitcom and fall asleep, exhausted from the strain of the investigation into Vicky's death and the unsettledness of my own life.

I wake with a start somewhere near morning to find Logan beside me in bed. He has an arm flung over his head against the pillow, and it's a minute before I remember he wasn't there when I went to bed. I wonder when he got back, but like all thoughts this close to waking, none of them make sense.

I slip out of bed and head to the bathroom, not sure what time it is, but knowing I won't be able to fall back asleep now.

Luckily I've slept late enough for the pool to open soon and gather my things before heading out.

The swim works, as it usually does, to clear my head, and I feel focused and recovered from my interview with Julia when I arrive at the lodge later that morning.

I'm surprised to see David at the door with Steve. The lodge's main entrance faces the water as at the time it was built, it would have been customary to arrive at the camp via boat. So the grand entrance was always built facing the water. At some point this rear entrance was added, along with a small porch built to shelter the door from the elements. It's not as detailed and ornate as the main entrance, but the small porch serves its purpose.

David and Steve stretch out a yard of fabric that appears to be bunting, but it's in far better shape than the bunting David was concerned about only weeks ago.

"What's that?" I say as I stop by the door, adjusting my bag on my shoulder.

David looks up from the porch railing where he's secured his end of the bunting.

"Sue Sews did it," he says, his smile triumphant, as he refers to Sue Fitzsimmons who owns Sue Sews in the village. "Isn't it great?"

I step back off the porch to look at the bunting they've hung so far. "It's gorgeous. All of this fabric must have cost a fortune. Plus her time." I meet David's gaze. "How did you get her to do it?"

"I didn't," he says. "Marty Pruitt talked her into it."

"Marty Pruitt?" An odd coldness settles over me as I remember what Carmen told me at trivia night, that Marty wanted to end the investigation into her own daughter's disappearance and possible murder, followed quickly by that social media post.

"Yeah, I ran into her at the Super Duper and told her

about the bunting. She said she'd take care of it." David stands and puts his fisted hands to his hips. "Never thought she'd manage this."

"Yeah, it's great," I say, but my voice has lost its enthusiasm. "Thanks, David."

I go inside to find the usual chaos a Monday brings but with the added bonus of Founder's Day stress. I tell Frances to put everything in order of priority on my desk and slip out the main entrance through the conference space.

Ice-out was officially declared at the end of the previous week even though the lake has been mostly ice free since the beginning of April, and I want to check the condition of the boathouse. I catch Allie coming in and wave her along with me. The boathouse sits down the embankment on the very edge of the water where there's a break in the trees allowing it to be admired by those passing by boat.

The boathouse is circular, and while the bottom has three bays to house boats, the upper floor is a ballroom. It's here that we hold the Founder's Day gala every year, and every year, I make this walk, with great trepidation, when ice-out is officially called to see how the ballroom made it through the winter.

The sun is warm on the side of my face as we make our descent, and Allie tells me about her weekend spent in Tupper Lake with her wife and her nieces.

"We couldn't get Mabel away from the otters," she says, referring to The Wild Center's otters. "We had to bribe her with ice cream. In April. We were all still in jackets."

"Did it have its little hands up like this?" I hold my hands in front of my chest and make a dopey face.

Allie frowns. "That's not helping."

I make kissy noises, and she dissolves into laughter as we reach the boathouse.

There's the usual debris strewn along the walkways, small

branches and piles of dead leaves where the wind has blown them. It's nothing the clean-up crews can't handle and shouldn't be a concern for Founder's Day.

I take my ring of keys out and try the boathouse door. There's a sickening crackle that can only be the splintering of wood, and Allie and I instinctually freeze. I stare down at where the door has moved an inch but can't see anything visibly wrong. I tentatively push a little more, and that's when the flap of paint separates from the door and drifts to the floor. Allie and I bend to inspect the damage, but it looks like the paint has just come loose in the winter, likely from the wood swelling and shrinking with the humidity and changing weather.

"We should have Steve come down here," I say as we try the lights next.

"He would probably appreciate a reprieve from the bunting. Although it does look really nice," Allie says.

"Marty Pruitt got Sue Sews to make them."

Allie steps inside the boathouse, her feet scuffing along the wooden floorboards. "That makes sense."

I turn to her, puzzled. "What do you mean?"

Allie shrugs as she moves toward the stairs that lead up to the ballroom above. "She's always doing for Bob. It makes sense that she could talk someone into sewing new bunting for the lodge."

The water laps at the three slips, empty of boats now, but I can still hear their ghostly echo.

Knock, knock, knock.

I feel the eyes on the back of my neck before the cold can hit me, but I don't turn around. I'm still amped up from letting Henry out the night before, and I don't have my senses under control the way I would wish.

"What do you mean she's always doing for Bob?" I say, ignoring the presence I feel building behind me.

The boathouse was a point of transition in life, and in death, it attracts wandering spirits. An encounter with a wayward ghost happens more often than not when I come in here, and I simply walk with Allie to the stairs to the upper level.

Allie opens the door to the stairwell, and besides some spider webs, it looks much as it did when we closed it up for the winter.

"Marty never comes out and says it, but I get the feeling he can be pretty demanding."

"How do you know Marty?"

We reach the top of the stairwell, and I need to blink a few times to allow my eyes to adjust to the sudden light. While the stairwell is enclosed, the ballroom is surrounded on all sides by windows, and the morning spring sun streams through as though we're standing at the very top of a lighthouse, windows circling us.

"She's on our bowling league." Allie makes her way to the opposite wall where a series of French windows lets out onto the porch that wraps around the entire ballroom level.

"Marty bowls?"

"Oh yeah," Allie says over her shoulder. "Has been for years." She tries the doors, and they squeal when opened but still work.

I start checking the windows for cracked panes of glass. "Why do you think Bob is demanding?"

I see Allie shrug again out of the corner of my eye. "Just little things she says. I didn't have him for a superintendent, so I can't speak to it really, but it sounds like she's been helping him win favor in this town for years. You know how approachable she is. I think Bob takes advantage of that."

I think about Bob Reynolds the superintendent who told me to join the Navy and can't picture him demanding anything of anyone. But then I recall that day at the Pruitt camp, how carefully Marty held herself, how she wanted Carmen and me to reassure her that Bob wouldn't find out about my being there.

Distracted, I touch one of the windowpanes, and I remember what Carmen said about the investigation. How Marty asked for it to end. Was that really Bob's doing? Did he make Marty ask the police to stop the investigation? And if so, why? Why would he not want to find his daughter?

Frost prickles against my fingers, and before I can pull my hand away, a spiderweb of ice forms over the windowpane. I jerk my hand away, but it's too late. The window has filled with a pattern of ice.

Allie comes to stand next to me, her eyes fixated on the glass.

"Maybe we should come back another time," she says, taking me by the shoulders. "Let's take the outside stairs."

"That's probably a good idea," I mumble, and I keep my eyes averted from the boathouse stairwell and the presence lurking there as we slip through the French windows and down the outside stairs.

I spend the rest of the day keeping myself firmly rooted in the present. I usually have better control of my senses, keeping the ghosts at bay, but I'm too rattled, my head a confusing mix of Vicky Gustafson and Marty Pruitt.

I told Carmen the truth about Lisa Reynolds. I couldn't feel her presence, and if she was alive, that was Carmen's concern, not mine. And yet Marty keeps intruding into my life in ways I hadn't noticed before.

But perhaps it was like buying a new car. You suddenly start seeing the same make and model everywhere on the road. They were probably there before, but you just didn't notice them.

It's after five before I make it out to my car, and the drive home is a blur. I roll the windows down, the warm evening air keeping me awake until I can get to Henry and a much-needed walk in the woods.

He's as excited to see me as I am to see him, and he flies out the door as soon as I can get it open. He turns back to check in, and I give him the signal to go. We're outside of the village, and he is free to roam off leash here. He never strays far from me though. Once at the vet's office, he slipped his collar in the parking lot. He immediately sat on my feet, his whole body shaking in fear, as if I intended to leave him there. He only settled when I got his collar back on.

The woods are damp and cold as we enter them, and I wish I had gotten a thicker jacket. It may be spring everywhere else, but in the woods, winter still has a firm grip.

Henry sniffs his favorite trees and one fallen log before making a wide circle back to the access road. Kay Hemlock, whose cottage is at the start of the road, has a small mutt she walks along the access road, and Henry enjoys the pee-mail that's left there. Zoomies overtake him when the driveway appears, and he knows his dinner awaits him.

I'm laughing so hard at him that it's too late before I see the man waiting for me at the back door. I'm dangerously close when I finally set eyes on him, and I jerk backward, my hand reaching for Henry to stop him from greeting this stranger.

The man is tall, menacingly so, and I have to arch back to see him clearly.

"What do you want?" I blurt.

I have nothing with me but a trembling Labrador retriever who only wants to lick this stranger into capitulation.

The man takes a step toward me, and a slice of fading sun cuts across his face. I don't recognize him, and my heart thuds in my chest. But then my mind flickers, and it's almost as if I do know him. Maybe. But not like this. It's as though I've seen another version of him.

"Della James?"

"Who wants to know?"

The man rubs his hands together. "You've been asking questions, and I can't have that." The man's voice is deep, terrifyingly so.

It's then that my mind finally morphs the image of the man before into the one I saw in a yearbook, and I suddenly have a name. A name I don't care for as I stand there all alone with help too far away to do any good.

"Kevin Gustafson," I say.

SIXTEEN

His head tilts, and his eyes narrow as if he doesn't understand.

"I've seen your yearbook photo. You were in school with my parents," I explain.

I don't have Henry's leash, and I only keep him at my side with a hand signal for sit. He's vibrating against my calf with excited energy, but the last thing I want him to do is get any closer to Kevin Gustafson.

His eyes narrow even more. "Who are your parents?"

"Greg and Maxine Hopewell," I say automatically and then correct. "You would have known her as Maxine Barnes."

His face changes then, his features lightening as the names seem to register. "Max and Greg got married," he says softly, a small laugh at the end of his words.

I've never in my life heard my mother referred to as Max, and I realize she was almost a different person in high school, changing to fit her life as her life changed around her. Just like we all do or at least sometimes do.

"Yeah, they did," I say.

Some of my initial apprehension has cooled, and I can take

in more of the man in front of me. He's wearing loafers that look expensive, a white button-down tucked into dark jeans, and a corduroy sport coat. His gray hair is short and styled with some kind of hair product that makes him look like a catalog model. There are deep lines around his mouth and eyes that I hadn't seen on Gretchen, and I wonder if he looks like his father.

"Well, look at that," Kevin says, and his voice has lost some of its confrontational tone. "When Ma said someone by the name of James was looking into Vick's death, I didn't know."

"My husband is Logan James," I say. "Mitch and Sarah's son."

"Mitchell James?" Kevin says, his voice lifting in question. "That's a name I haven't heard in a long time."

"Mr. Gustafson, I assume your mother told you why I'm looking into Vicky's death," I say now.

The sun is setting, and I don't want to be standing there in the dark with a stranger who may or may not have murdered his sister. There will be time for reminiscing later, if he turns out not to be the murderer, of course.

"She said you saw her ghost." He says this with the same disbelieving tone most people do when talking about my ability to speak to the dead.

"Yes, I did. She indicated to me that her death wasn't an accident."

He crosses his arms, rocking back on his heels to make himself taller, a move that's entirely unnecessary because at five foot five, everyone is already a good deal taller than me.

"How is that exactly? Did she move around the planchette on a Ouija board? Turn a flashlight on and off like on those ghost-hunting cable shows?"

"She stood in front of me and told me."

His mouth had been slightly open in mockery, and at this, his lips close into a firm line.

He shifts his weight from one foot to the other. "I think you're lying about that."

"She was wearing her blue dress the day she died. The one with the daisies embroidered down the bodice."

Something goes out of his eyes then, a heat I think has carried him all the way from New York.

"How do you know that?"

"Because I saw her." The answer is simple because it's the truth.

Kevin's face loses color, and he sways ever so slightly. "You saw her."

It isn't a question. It's more like he's reassuring himself of something he can't quite believe.

"I did," I say. "And if you're willing to answer some questions I have, I'd like to find out what really happened to your sister."

He looks away briefly, and when he looks back, his gaze has hardened. "Ma always thought something bad happened to Vick, but I told her to let it go. She was so..." His voice trails away, but his lips remain parted as if waiting for the right word to come to them. "Crushed," he finally says. He shakes his head. "I knew I should have done more. I knew I should have —" He runs an agitated hand through his hair and looks away.

"Death is upsetting in more ways than humans are equipped to handle. We can only do what we can in the moment it's happening. We can't blame ourselves later."

He looks at me, his eyes assessing. "I guess you would have a lot of experience with death."

"More than I'd like," I say. I gesture to the side of the house. "Why don't we sit, and you can tell me what you believe happened to your sister?"

He doesn't say anything, but he follows me around the house to the patio, and I gesture for him to sit in one of the chairs. I let Henry back into the house through the patio doors, and while he does go inside, he sits by the glass door, watching.

Kevin has taken a chair with his back to the house, his gaze lost on the lake below. I pull a chair a little farther away from the table, keeping much needed space between us. I don't offer him hospitality because he's shown up at my home unexpectedly, and well, he might be a murderer.

"I understand Vicky was dating Daryl Walden at the time of her death. I heard there was an altercation of some kind between Daryl and yourself shortly before Vicky's death. Do you want to tell me about that?"

Kevin's eyes take longer than I would expect them to, to come back from the lake. "Daryl asked Vicky to marry him, and she turned him down. That's why I think he killed her."

This doesn't answer my question in the slightest but rather opens an entirely new line of questioning none of my interviews have uncovered so far.

"Daryl asked Vicky to marry him?"

Kevin nods once. He has placed both arms on the armrests of the wrought iron chair he sits in, and now his fingers curl around them. "Daryl was a drunk even then, and Vicky didn't want to find herself married to such a degenerate."

His language is strong, and I wonder if he's chosen his words to upset me. They don't. After you've seen the thing that lives in the Bellegrave Opera House, words seem rather tame.

"You think Daryl is a degenerate?"

"Vicky did," Kevin says.

"That's speculation on your part."

"I'm telling you that's what Vicky thought."

I hold up both hands. "Vicky's not here for me to ask her, so I'm going to take that as your observation until I can clarify with her."

There's no guarantee I can ask Vicky her thoughts on this

marriage proposal or her relationship with Daryl, but Kevin doesn't know that. My revelation of what Vicky was wearing when she died clearly shook him, and that's an ace I'm going to hold on to.

The lines around Kevin's mouth grow more distinct. "I'm telling you she refused him, and he went crazy. Said if he couldn't have her no one else could." He makes a slashing motion with one hand. "That's why he killed her."

"Did you think this then? When the accident occurred?"

"Of course I did."

"Then why didn't you say anything to the police?"

He makes a scoffing noise. "Small-town police with small-town views. Wouldn't know a murder if it bit them in the ass."

"So you didn't press for an investigation? Your mother said she didn't ask for an autopsy."

He looks at me quickly. "What would that have done?" He leans forward. "Daryl made it look like an accident for a reason. An autopsy wouldn't have proven anything."

I remember that day on the side of the road, the way the back of Vicky's head was smashed in, matted with hair and blood. I simply can't believe the crash into the river was the cause of it, but I don't say as much to Kevin. I need to know his true feelings, and I can't muddy them with what I've seen.

"What happened that night at Farley's?" I say, trying to get him back to the original question.

He waves a hand now as if batting away a fly. "That was nothing. Daryl got handsy with Vicky, and I wouldn't let him get away with it. We pushed each other around, and Tom decided it was time for a pissing contest, and with a badge, he could piss farther than both of us."

It occurs to me only then that Tom Reznick is probably the same age, if a little younger, than Kevin and my parents. How much had it grated Kevin to get his hand slapped by an underclassman even so many years after graduation? High school, like taxes, never goes away.

Did Kevin blame Vicky for his public shaming?

"I understand the charges were dropped though."

Kevin makes that scoffing noise again. "Who cares. The damage was already done. And after—" He cuts off abruptly, but I can fill in the blank.

"After the incident with Julia Hammond you had quite a reputation," I finish for him.

He eyes me, and there's an edge to his gaze now as if he's trying to decide how much to say. I wait, letting the silence push his words from him.

He sits back and runs his hand through his hair again, messing up the carefully gelled style. "Listen, I don't know what you think you know—"

"I know Vicky was murdered. I know her relationship with Daryl changed immediately preceding her death, and I know you had an altercation with Daryl shortly before Vicky was killed. And I know you weren't in New York the night Vicky died."

The edge I'd glimpsed in his gaze sharpens, and surprisingly, I would say he flinches at my words.

"How do you know that?"

"Your mother told me."

Kevin pushes to his feet, and I can feel the tension coiling in him as he paces away from me. I regret not going in the house with Henry and calling Carmen. I shouldn't have let down my guard. There in the dusk I can see the lanky teenager with the too long hair has turned into an angry and maybe bitter man.

He turns on me at the edge of the patio. "I was in Plattsburgh that night. I can give you the name of a witness, and he can verify where I was, but that's it." He takes three steps toward me, his expensive loafers scuffing on the stubbled finish of the patio pavers. He points a threatening finger at me. "You don't get to ask these kinds of questions. I didn't kill my sister. I didn't—" Just as surprising as the flinch, his voice crumples, choked by emotion, and the tension that had been coiling inside of him evaporates in a cloud of despair.

I stand and go to him, laying a hand on the arm he seems to have forgotten is stretched in my direction. "Kevin, what aren't you saying? Is it about Julia?" His eyes were vacant with pain, but now they zero in on me. "One of Vicky's classmates said Vicky knew something about you and Julia."

He shrugs off my hand and returns to the chair he so recently vacated. He collapses into it, dropping his head into his hands, bent elbows on his knees.

He doesn't look up as he says, "I was in Plattsburgh that night with the man who is now my husband." He straightens, and his face is ashen in the waning light. "My mother doesn't know that I'm..." He can't bring himself to say the last word, but he doesn't need to. My heart clenches in understanding.

I find my chair again. "Your mother doesn't know you're gay," I say for him.

There are real tears in his eyes now, and he pinches the bridge of his nose, looking away.

I reach over and grab his arm, keeping him grounded.

He looks at me. "Vicky knew. She was the only one I could tell." His voice cracks now with tears, and I squeeze his arm.

"I'm sorry, Kevin," I say. "I really am."

The pain he is feeling envelopes me. It's impossible to keep it away. He's not only led a life of careful secrets, but the one person from his own family he had confided in was murdered.

"I understand why you haven't told your mother, and I promise I won't be the one to reveal your secret." His eyes dart to my face, and slowly I watch his apprehension fade away. "I know what it's like. Being different in a small town." I give a weak smile, and slowly it coaxes one to Kevin's lips.

"I suppose you do."

I let go of his arm. "But I can't imagine what it was like for you. Not back then." I shrug. "It was bad enough in the nineties when everyone compared me to Haley Joel Osment."

He barks a laugh that seems to surprise him. "Did they ask you if you see dead people?" he whispers dramatically.

"All the time." I enunciate each word for effect.

He laughs again, and the tears dry on his cheeks. He looks to the lake a moment as he gathers himself.

"Vicky did know. About me being gay. And she knew about...my husband." Even then he can't seem to bring himself to say the man's name, and I wonder if keeping the name to himself keeps his secret safer. The pain I feel for him blossoms anew. "She was going to help me tell Ma." He swallows, hard, and grips the armrest of the chair. "And then she was killed."

"Do you really think Daryl did it?"

This question seems to sober him, and he says simply, "Yes."

I nod. "Thank you for telling me. I hope you can find a path forward. One that's better than the one you're on now."

He laughs. "I think it's too late."

"It's never too late," I say, and then my mind flits to Albany, and I wonder if I really believe that.

Kevin studies me before saying, "You're really going to find out what happened to Vicky."

"I have to," I say.

It's only when we've walked back to the driveway, and I see Kevin's small sedan hidden between the forest on one side and my bulky SUV on the other that I think to ask, "I don't know if this is rude or not, but if you're gay, what was the thing with Julia Hammond about?"

Kevin's expression sours. "I wasn't stalking Julia. I had a crush on her cousin, and I was trying to find a way for him to notice me." He shakes his head. "I was a stupid kid, and I had no idea what I was doing. I was a gay teenage boy in a small town in the middle of nowhere in the seventies."

"We're all stupid sometimes," I say. "All we can hope is that we grow out of it."

He smiles as though my words have reassured him. We say our goodbyes, and he gets in his car and backs out of the driveway. I wait until his taillights have disappeared into the darkness along the access road before going into the house to do an Internet search for security cameras.

Seventeen

"What the fuuuuuudge," Carmen breathes as we paste cotton balls onto blue poster board the following evening in Carmen's dining room.

"Yeah," I say. "I already ordered one of those security camera systems. The kind you just stick to the wall with those hanging strips. Should have put them in years ago before a possible murderer randomly showed up at my house."

"I told you you needed more than a dog out there," Carmen says.

Carmen snatched up one of the new colonials in the development out by the supermarket when they were built in the early 2000s. She said she wanted square walls and wall-to-wall white carpet, which is not something you readily find in the old homes along the lake. She got everything she wanted plus a perfectly fenced yard, a two-car garage, and a first-floor laundry room.

The entire house is still painted builder white, and she has never replaced any of the builder-grade finishes. It feels like living in a rental condo to me, but it smells of the Bolognese Raymond made for dinner, and the occasional tinkle of girlish giggles floats down the stairs. Ella and Anna were supposed to be working on homework, but the distinct sounds of makeup tutorial videos accompanied the giggles, and Raymond went up to play referee a half hour ago. Carmen and I are taking bets on how quickly he fell asleep on their bottom bunk.

"Did you get a sense he was lying to you about Daryl and Vicky?"

I shake my head. "I don't see why he would have reason to lie about Daryl proposing marriage."

"Speaking of marriage, we still good for Friday?" Carmen interrupts.

I place a cotton ball with the precision of a plastic surgeon. "Yep. Henry's already packed his sleeping bag."

Carmen and Raymond are going to Syracuse for a family wedding on Friday. The invitation said no kids, so I'll be staying with the girls Friday night and then Carmen's mom will take over on Saturday. I always bring Henry for sleepovers with Ella and Anna. I think he enjoys it even more than I do.

"He's picked out a rom com for us to watch and everything," I add.

Carmen wrinkles her nose. "You should show them something like *The Exorcist*."

"No way. Ella still wets the bed when she has nightmares. I'm not dealing with that."

"Well, neither am I. That's why you should do it," Carmen returns.

I only glare at her.

She gives her second-grade-teacher smile. "So have you checked Kevin off your suspect list?"

"Kevin texted me today with the names and phone numbers of everyone he was with that night in Plattsburgh." I look up from selecting another cotton ball. "Everyone," I emphasize. "Apparently he went there with a bunch of grad school friends to see a production of Shakespeare's *Hamlet* one of their professors was producing in a stock theatre there. Some off off off Broadway thing." I don't mention Kevin's now husband. That's not my secret to tell. "I called a couple of the numbers, and I got the same story each time. They all rented a single hotel room because they were poor grad students, and at the time of Vicky's death, Kevin was asleep on the floor of that hotel room."

"So how did he get his mother's message?"

"Called his answering machine and played his messages back. Remember when that was a thing?"

"Stone Age," Carmen confirms. She shakes her head now. "Poor Kevin. I can't imagine what it's been like for them." Carmen pastes another cotton ball onto the poster board. "What did Logan say about Kevin showing up like that?"

I adjust the cotton ball along the box Ella has outlined on the poster board where the graphic she's supposed to be making upstairs about water condensing to form rain should go.

"I didn't get a chance to talk to him. He had a client dinner last night."

Carmen's fingers freeze on a cotton ball, her nails pastel blue now. "Client dinner?" Her words are heavy with innuendo.

Carmen sets down the cotton ball without putting paste on it. "Delia Ann," she says in a great imitation of Maxine Hopewell. "When are you going to confront that man?"

"There's nothing to confront him about. So he has a pretty client. Am I supposed to be jealous and suspicious with every pretty client he has?"

"Yes," Carmen nearly yells, and I almost drop my cotton ball in surprise. "Yes," she says again, grabbing my hand for emphasis. "Get jealous. Get suspicious. Keep that man in check."

"I don't like the idea of keeping tabs on my husband. I should trust him."

"*Should* trust him?" Carmen raises an eyebrow.

"I do trust him," I correct, but it's too late.

Carmen leans back with a frown, pulling a cotton ball apart between her fingertips. "It's one thing for him to check out of the life you two have together, but he's checked out on us too. You realize that, don't you?"

I hold the glue bottle in my hand and blink, processing what she's just said. "What are you talking about?"

"Logan doesn't come to cookouts anymore. He didn't come to our Mardi Gras party this year, and last fall, he bailed on the fantasy football team. Raymond was pissed." She says this more softly so Ella and Anna can't possibly overhear her use that word.

"No, he didn't," I say. "He met Raymond at Farley's every Sunday."

Carmen's expression blanks. "No, he didn't, Del. He always made an excuse to Raymond that he had to work." Her voice has lost the strength it held only seconds before.

I laugh because I can't find anything else to do. "That's ridiculous. Logan was at Farley's religiously every Sunday last fall."

"Is that what he told you?"

Carmen's question hits like a slap. "He wasn't at Farley's?"

"Not once," Carmen says, her usual verve gone. "Raymond was pretty put out."

"Why didn't you say anything?"

"Because I thought you knew," Carmen says, her strength coming back as she nearly hisses the words. "And then after the diner last week, I thought—"

She cuts herself off, but I know what Carmen would say to anyone else. Anyone else but me because I'm probably the only person alive whose feelings she doesn't want to hurt.

"Because I'm too blind to see what's really happening between me and my husband," I finish for her.

"Not blind," she says, setting aside the cotton ball to lean forward and take both of my hands into hers. "Optimistic."

Her grip on my hands forces me to put down my own glue bottle. "Optimism has never gotten me anywhere."

"You and me both," she says. Her brow folds, and for the first time in my life, I'm worried Carmen is going to start crying. "God, Del, I thought you knew."

I try to figure out how I feel about this news, but just like the rest of the evidence I have that suggests my husband is having an affair, it's not concrete. Maybe he was really working and doesn't want me to know. Maybe he was somewhere, just enjoying time alone after a hectic week at work. The fact remains I still don't know. I have no solid evidence with which to confront him, and until I do, my feelings slosh around inside of me like gelatin that won't set.

Carmen squeezes my hands once and lets go.

We're quiet for several minutes then, gluing our respective piles of cotton balls to poster board.

"So what are you going to do about Vicky?" Carmen finally asks.

I sit back in my chair, inspecting what I've covered so far on the blue background. "Well, last week I stopped by the school and had an incredibly uncomfortable conversation with Mr. Wottesley."

"No, you didn't," Carmen breathes, her eyes wide.

"I did." I shudder in memory. "He was indeed with Gabriella Torres the night Vicky died. She didn't leave his place until they both left for school after seven that morning."

"Ew, Mr. Wottesley," Carmen moans.

"My mom says he was a hunk back then." We didn't have him for tech until several years after Vicky's death, and he'd softened a great deal.

"Still. Ew." Carmen mimics my shudder. "So Gabriella Torres has an alibi, and Kevin's alibi checks out."

"Confirmed," I say.

She plucks at a cotton ball. "So that leaves Daryl."

I nod, scanning the poster board for a place that needs more cotton. "And I still don't know how to approach him."

"I could go with you," Carmen offers, but I shake my head.

"No, I don't want to scare him." I spin a cotton ball between my fingers. "I just get this weird sense he didn't do it. You know?"

"Yeah," Carmen says. "Daryl's always been mean and creepy, but I don't think he'd hurt anyone." She pauses before looking straight at me. "Not on purpose anyway."

———

I'm nearly late to the office Friday morning after dropping Henry off at my parents' house for the day. It will be easier for me to swing by and pick him up from there than to drive all the way out of town and back in time to pick up the girls from gymnastics.

It's only because I'm later than normal that I nearly walk into Marty Pruitt as she's coming out of the lodge. Allie is right behind her, and I note the tension in her body before turning to Marty.

"Hello Ms. Pruitt," I say as she clearly tries to get around me without speaking, head down, shoulders hunched, both hands clenched around the purse she has perched on her shoulder. "Is there something we can help you with?"

For a second I think she's not going to answer me, but then she looks at Allie and back to me. "I was speaking with Allie—" Marty hesitates, her lips forming a small *O* like she's sucking on a straw. I wonder if she's uncomfortable. She did ask me to contact her believed-to-be-dead daughter without her husband knowing. But the thing about speaking with the dead is it teaches you how to keep secrets, and I haven't mentioned our little meeting to anyone. She finally goes on, "I was just suggesting to Allie that this year we might make a small change to the Founder's Day program."

It's as though she has just asked the federal government to ban pumpkin spice.

"Change to the program?" I ask.

The sucking expression deepens, and Marty glances at Allie before continuing. I wonder about that glance. Marty has never struck me as the nervous type. She always holds herself so carefully, and I think again about how she must have been brought up, the training she must have received to remain ever poised.

"I was hoping we might do something to recognize Bob," she explains. "Now that he's retired from the school district with a stunning thirty-year career behind him, and—" Her voice catches, and she swallows, her eyes cast downward, and I get the feeling she's going to chastise herself for that slipup for the rest of the day. She looks up and rearranges her hands on her purse strap. "And considering all that is happening to my husband, I thought it would be nice to include him in some way in the Founder's Day program."

Marty's tone suggests this isn't just a thought, but something she very much believed she would make happen by coming here this morning.

I adjust my own backpack strap on my shoulder as I watch Marty's knuckles grow white.

"I'm sorry, Ms. Pruitt, but the Founder's Day program isn't the place for that," I say. Out of the corner of my eye, I see Allie's shoulders drop the smallest of degrees, and I know I've just agreed with her. "Perhaps you should speak with the town council about doing something for Mr.

Reynolds this summer during Old Home Days in the square."

Marty's expression glitches for only a second, but the polite sheen slips away for a moment, her lips curling in distaste, except there's something different in her gaze. Is it fear? It's gone so quickly I can't be sure, and I look to Allie for reassurance I saw it at all, but she's smiling her public smile as she looks longingly at the door behind me.

"I see," Marty says. "Then I guess I'll just be on my way. Good day, ladies," she says, and her grip relaxes on her bag as a soft smile touches her lips.

I step aside to let her through the door, and Allie and I both stand there, watching her through the plate glass as she walks over to her car in the parking lot along the drive.

"Was that strange?" I finally ask when we hear Marty's car start.

Allie gestures to the door. "This is what I'm talking about. I bet this was Bob's idea, and he made Marty come here and ask." She makes a disgusted noise. "Men."

The Mr. Reynolds I know wouldn't ask someone to move if they were stepping on his foot, but there was definitely something strange about the way Marty was acting, and I wonder if Allie is right. Perhaps in my naive teenage years I misjudged quiet Bob Reynolds.

"Mmm," I say, my thoughts churning.

I'm halfway through a lunch at my desk when my phone dings. I usually silence it when I come into work, but after my run-in with Marty, I forgot. So when it chimes I nearly knock my to-go bowl of salad off the table from between my outstretched arms and the keyboard of my laptop.

I unearth my phone from under the proof flyers for Founder's Day to see it's Carmen.

School called. Both girls throwing up. Wedding trip off. Kill me now.

She's inserted both a puking emoji and a crying emoji.

I type back asking her how I'm supposed to tell Henry. She sends a gif of a woman holding up a hand, palm out, shaking her head. I text back to let me know if she needs anything and drop my phone back onto the table.

The final proof for the table tents is open on my laptop, and I need to get it back to the printer this afternoon to have them printed in time for Founder's Day, and now that I don't need to pick up the girls I resolve to get it finished.

The only way I know it's after five is my stomach lets out a terrible noise, and I'm slightly concerned I've turned into John Hurt.

Allie and I are at a table in the main conference space going through the various checklists for Founder's Day, and she looks up from her stack to eye me.

"I think that means we need to stop," she says.

I wave a hand. "I can press on."

"Dude, it's after five, and I have a life. Or I did once." She looks around as if she's lost it somewhere. "Maybe I'll find it again, but I won't find it here."

We gather up our notes and split off to our respective offices. I hear her pack up as I check my phone for messages. There's only one from Carmen. A picture of both girls on the couch, toe to toe, covered in their matching kitten fleece blankets. I text back three heart emojis with a reminder to let me know if she needs anything.

I gather the checklists into my backpack. I'll need to review them again over the weekend. Founder's Day is only two weeks away, and with everything going on with Vicky Gustafson, I'm more distracted than usual. I remind myself this is the historical society's biggest fundraiser of the year, and I need to be on point.

With Kevin and Gabriella both having a verified alibi I'm down to one suspect in the death of Victoria Gustafson, and it's not even someone I believe did it. There was something about Daryl that day in the basement of the Gale Center, a desperation that cannot be faked and an almost fatal sense of loss emanating from him. I could feel it because I carry the same thing inside of me.

I check the lodge before I leave, ensuring everyone's left for the day before I lock up behind me and head home. It's still early, and I decide to give Henry some more time with his grandparents now that his promised sleepover is canceled. I'll pick him up later.

I know something is wrong the moment I step through the back door of the cottage.

My senses open, instincts kicking in, as I search the space around me for paranormal energy. It's because my focus is on the paranormal that I waste precious time, and I'm already in the kitchen when I realize the threat isn't paranormal at all.

My husband stands at the kitchen island, a corkscrew in one hand and a bottle of wine in the other. I've interrupted him in the act of opening it. He freezes when he sees me, the corkscrew held in midair.

Two things occur to me at the same time.

My husband is never home this early, and my brain finally registers what's out of place. It's a scent. A very real, very citrusy perfume.

I look to the open patio doors because somehow I know she's there, and as if summoned by my thoughts, she appears.

Heather Russo steps into my kitchen. Her feet are bare as are the rest of her long, smooth legs running up to the short pencil skirt she's wearing. Her blouse is untucked, flowing around her hips. She's speaking as she comes through the door, but I don't hear her words. Because right there in front of me is the concrete evidence I've been waiting for. It's right there in Heather Russo's white, silk blouse that is unbuttoned a single button too far, so I can clearly see the lace edging of her bra beneath.

One little button too far.

She freezes as my husband did when her eyes fall on me, her lips parted on the words I hadn't heard. She has one delicate foot stopped in front of the other as she stands in my kitchen where she doesn't belong.

It's then my husband says the one thing he shouldn't. "You're not supposed to be home, Del."

I turn to him. I can feel the rage inside of me, deep, deep, deep inside of me, as if it's been waiting, wanting, yearning for a moment just like this one to rip out of me, to finally scream the things it's wanted to scream for years. But there's something stronger than rage inside of me.

There's the unstoppable feeling of injustice.

Words come out of me then. Not the words I should say in this moment. As is typical of me, I say words that should be spoken, but I'm saying them thirteen years too late.

"It wasn't your choice." My voice is firm and steady because the trembling rage is stopped by my sudden need for justice. "I don't care if it saved my life, it wasn't your choice, and you robbed me of that." I take a step forward, not in anger, but in resolution. "I'm the only one who gets to make a decision like that. I'm the only one who gets to decide whether or not I'll ever have the chance to be a mother again." I shake my head, just once to the left and once to the right. "You made that decision for me, and I can't forgive you for it."

I don't look at Heather Russo as I turn and leave the kitchen, walk through the back door and back out to my car.

My car keys are still in my hand, and I go through the motions I've just executed but in reverse. I don't know where I'm going or even truly realize I'm driving until I've reached the main street of the village and must slow for the traffic. The shops in the village are always busy on a Friday night, but even more so tonight as the pleasant weather has everyone yearning for summer and the warm carefree nights that lay ahead. The village is bustling, a cacophony that falls into rhythm with the tumble of my thoughts.

It's only when I've passed Sally's hair salon that I slam on the brakes. I raise a hand in apology to the line of cars behind me as I slip into a parking space at the curb. I backtrack to the glass door of the salon. The sign on the door is turned to closed, but I see Sally through the glass cleaning up.

I knock on the door.

Her head picks up, a frown on her face that melts when she sees me. She sets aside the broom and comes to the door.

"Hey, Del, I—" Her words stop so abruptly I wonder what my face must look like.

I thought when I finally uncovered incontrovertible proof of my husband's infidelity I would come unhinged, wild with hurt and hopelessness. But standing there on the sidewalk in front of Sally, I find the opposite is true. It's like everything inside of me has finally fallen into place, and I no longer need to work just to keep myself together.

"I'm ready," I say to Sally.

She bites her lip, her brow creasing. "Oh, honey. Come here. Let me take care of you."

She pulls me inside the salon with a hand on my shoulder, and the glass door shuts behind me.

It's dark by the time I pull up to my parents' house. My dad is in the kitchen with Henry when I come in.

"Hey, kid—" His words die on his lips, and I don't know if it's from the shock of my short hair or from the expression that must still be on my face. His own expression falls into familiar deep lines, and without any more words, he takes down the box of graham crackers from the cupboard while I bury my face in Henry's fur.

We sit together on the couch, all three of us, and share a

plate of graham crackers with glasses of milk while we watch mindless television.

Mom comes home some time after *Wheel of Fortune*. She calls from the kitchen, but none of us answer, not even Henry.

She walks into the living room. "Did I see Della's car in the drive—"

Just like my father her words stop, but unlike my father's stoic reaction to anything of note, my mother's is always demonstrative.

"Oh, Della," she whispers, pushing the back of one hand to her lips. She kneels in front of me and reaches up, fingering a lock of my shorn hair between her fingers, a smile so loving and pure coming to her lips, I think for the first time that night I might cry. "Oh, Della, you finally said something."

I swallow. "How do you know that?"

Her smile is full now as she says, "A woman always cuts her hair when she decides to change her life."

EIGHTEEN

"2000 called. It wants its shirt back."

I look up from my spot on the floor where I'm sorting boxes of donations on Monday morning to see Carmen standing in the doorway of my office with a Cake & Cookie box in her hands.

"Logan is having an affair with Albany," I say. "I'm staying at the Hopewell Mansion, and this was what was in my old closet." I look down at the forest green henley with the lace tank top under it. "It still fits though, and I'm rather proud of that." I shake my shoulders like a can-can girl, but when I look at Carmen, her face is stricken. I hold up my hands that are still full of the Gerry Insurance Company calendars that were in the boxes. "Oh, come here."

Carmen shuts the door behind her and sets the Cake & Cookie box on my desk before joining me on the floor in the sea of cardboard boxes, their contents strewn about the carpet. I wrap my arms around her, and she holds me back. Again, surprisingly, no tears come.

"You didn't answer any of my texts this weekend, and I

thought you were overworking again." She sits back, crisscross applesauce style, her hands hanging over her knees, and with the shirt I'm wearing, I feel like we're back in high school over-analyzing who might ask us to homecoming.

"I turned off my phone. I didn't want to talk to Logan."

Carmen presses two fingers to the space between her eyebrows, but she doesn't say anything, and that is significant. Carmen can talk her way through a tornado, and when she goes silent, you know her emotions have drowned out her words.

I touch her hand to get her attention. When she looks at me, I say, "I caught them. Friday night. When I was supposed to be at your house."

Carmen's eyebrows lift, but still she doesn't say anything.

"He said I wasn't supposed to be home right then."

It's then I see the reaction I thought I would have had at the realization of my husband's infidelity, and it's somehow satisfying to see it rendered by my best friend.

She mutters a string of expletives she hasn't used since adopting the girls before saying, "Has he ever seen a movie? That's the one thing you don't say."

I nod in agreement. "He was opening a bottle of wine."

Carmen's lips part. "Wine? Logan?" She lets out a puff of air. "All of a sudden he's a wine drinker?" She holds up a hand before I can answer. "Wait a minute. He brought that slut into your home?"

I like how Carmen has already labeled Heather Russo a slut. I nod again. "He did."

I think about my cozy cottage on the lake that I've called home for almost fifteen years. Of the little living room off the kitchen that was once the sunporch, but Logan's great-aunt Marge converted it to a year-round space in the eighties. The walls under the bank of windows facing the lake are still paneling, but I painted over them when we first moved in. A pale green to give the room some light. Heather Russo probably hates paneling.

There's another string of expletives then directed entirely at Logan.

"You can land a plane on that bitch's roots. Can he not see that?" she says, and for the first time in days, I smile. "What are you going to do?" she asks, her voice soft.

I shrug. "I don't know. If I'm being honest"—I pause, gathering myself—"I'm kind of relieved." I shuffle the calendars together in my hands and set them back in the box I just took them out of. "I thought I was going crazy. That I was just imagining the late nights, the distance, the secretive phone calls, the trips to Albany." I shake my head as if it will help rearrange my thoughts. "To finally know the truth, it's a relief."

Carmen lays a hand on my arm. "I guess I can understand that."

"I'll stay with my parents until I figure things out, but right now I need to focus on Founder's Day and Vicky. I think if I distract myself with work it will help me to know what it is I'm feeling."

"I like your hair," Carmen says with a smile then.

I touch it self-consciously. "I don't know how to hold my head. I had a headache all of Saturday."

I laugh, and Carmen laughs too, and it doesn't feel so weird telling my best friend my marriage has fallen apart.

"If your mom tries to talk you into a decoupaging class, you come stay with me and Raymond. I bet the girls will let you have the top bunk."

I laugh again and say, "Thanks. I just might."

Carmen pushes to her feet, using her hands to brush the carpet lint from her black jeans. "You'll talk to me before doing anything crazy now, right? I mean the hair is great, but don't join any cults or anything. Not without me anyway."

"Got it," I say. "No cults without calling you first."

She shakes her head, her lips pursed, and she looks so much like Vanessa, I can't help but smile as she steals a croissant from the Cake & Cookie box on her way out the door.

I take my lunch break at half past one, hoping to avoid some of the lunch rush in the village as I make my way out to the Gale Center.

I find Daryl Walden in the first-floor recreation hall stacking folding chairs. He stills when he sees me, and I watch his mouth tighten, but before he can emit any angry words, I speak.

"I was in a car accident when I was seven months pregnant. It was storming. A tourist was texting while driving and didn't see the red light. She t-boned me on the driver's side." Daryl's hands are wrapped around the folding chair he'd just been about to set on the stack behind him, and his fingers flex against the molded plastic at my words. "By the time they got me to the hospital, there was no fetal heartbeat. My baby was delivered stillborn. I had suffered a uterine rupture, and while I was unconscious, my husband made the decision for me to have a hysterectomy. It saved my life, but I'll never be a mother because of a decision someone else made."

Daryl's face has lost the tension my appearance put there, and the chair in his hands has slowly slid to the floor until one foot is resting on the commercial linoleum. I reach into my bag and pull out my wallet, unsnapping the clasp until the trifold flips open, revealing the only photograph I carry with me.

I extend it to Daryl so he can see. "This was taken during an ultrasound. She was a girl. I named her Audrey."

At first Daryl doesn't move. But then he shifts, and I expect him to turn away from me, but he only sets the chair in his hands on the stack behind him before stepping toward me. He reaches for my wallet, his eyes flashing up to mine as if asking for permission. I nod, and he takes the wallet in both hands, his eyes studying the ultrasound image.

He doesn't speak even then but instead sits down on one of the chairs still arranged on the floor. He studies the photo for several seconds, and I take a chair beside him.

"The woman who hit us was texting the letter *K*." Daryl looks swiftly at me, and I see the pain registered in his eyes. "Not *okay*. Or even *O* and *K*. Just *K*. I wonder sometimes what was so important she needed to text that right at that moment." Daryl watches me now, and I say, "My daughter's life for the letter *K*."

His gaze drops back to the photo of Audrey, his thumbs stroking it on either side of the wallet.

"Vicky and I were going to get married." His words are rough as if he hasn't spoken in a while. He makes a small noise like a laugh as if even now, almost thirty years later, he can't quite believe it himself. "I told her I was going to get sober, and we were going to build a life together." He taps the photo now with one finger. "Probably just like you thought you were going to build a life."

"Vicky agreed to marry you?"

He looks up, his eyes more open than I've seen them before. "You probably heard differently, I'm sure. I don't exactly—" He stops and rubs the back of his neck. "I have a certain reputation in town. It's probably hard to imagine someone would want to marry me."

"I don't actually know anything about you, so who am I to say?"

His eyes move over my face as if weighing my words, and I get the sense I've surprised him again.

"I was in Saratoga, in rehab, the day she was killed. I was going to get clean. Sober up. Marry her. When I heard she was killed, I—" He says the words plainly, devoid of feeling as if he's gone over this again and again in his head, but then his voice stops. I can fill in the blank though. "I wasn't here to stop it." He stops then, and I can almost feel him weighing his words. "You probably heard I was rough with Vicky." His thumb moves back and forth over my daughter's picture. "I have gaps in my memory. Black spots. Things I can't remember because I think my mind doesn't want to remember. I did bad things in those black parts. I know it. The war —" He stops, licks his lips before continuing. "I was going to see one of those doctors up at the VA about it. Start therapy."

I realize he's talking about PTSD. He just probably doesn't have the words to communicate it like that.

His eyes drop to Audrey's photo once more before he looks up, his face cleared of thirty years of doubt, it would seem. "Vicky came to you, didn't she?"

I nod. "She did. I think she was murdered."

He looks away but not before I see him flinch in pain. "Was she—" For the first time, his voice breaks. He puts one hand against his face as if pushing his emotions back in. "Was she in pain?"

"I don't think they feel pain," I say. "I think spirits are the energy that leaves our bodies when we die, and it's only our corporeal forms that can feel pain. Once we've left them behind we no longer hurt like that." I pause as he takes this in before asking, "The last time I was here you said you didn't regret what you had done. Did you mean asking Vicky to marry you?"

He looks sharply at me. "Of course, that's what I meant." He makes a sweeping gesture with one hand. "Vicky's brother didn't like me, and I was sure you were coming to tell me something about it, but asking Vicky to marry me was the only thing I've gotten right."

"So far," I add, and his expression turns quizzical. "It's the only thing you've gotten right so far. You're still alive, so you've still got a chance to make more decisions, right or wrong."

His expression remains puzzled, but I can see curiosity building in his eyes. He glances away, and when he looks back, he asks, "Did Vicky tell you she was murdered?"

"No," I answer. "It doesn't really work like that. Usually spirits only have enough energy to impress a feeling upon me, and Vicky's spirit was projecting negative energy and a sense of injustice. Something isn't right about the way she died."

"And you're going to find out what happened to her?"

It's my turn to drop my eyes. "I'm trying to, but I seem to have reached a dead end. Everyone who had a motive also has an alibi. I'm hoping you can help me find another path to follow."

"Me?" he asks. His tone is filled with such disbelief it hurts.

"You," I say. "Vicky kept repeating two words over and over again in my head, and I think they're important. I was hoping you can help me figure out what she meant."

Daryl looks down for a moment, his fingers kneading my wallet once more before he hands it back to me. I carefully close the wallet on the photo of my daughter before slipping it back into my purse.

"I don't know if I can really help," he says, his tone crestfallen, and I wonder how many times he's been told he's not good enough, not trustworthy, not accountable because of his addiction and the things in his past that haunt him.

"I think you can. You're likely the person who knew her best at the time she died."

This brings his attention back to me. "I suppose I was. What did Vicky say?"

"She kept saying *my heart*. I tried to think of something that could relate to, something she loved that much, but I haven't been able to find anything in her life that she could be referring to."

Daryl's face transforms then, and I think for the first time I'm seeing the man Vicky fell in love with, the man she wanted to marry.

Daryl smiles as he says, "You're not looking for some*thing*, Dr. James. You're looking for some*one*."

NINETEEN

It's almost six o'clock when I knock on the door of the home of Monica Holmes and her son, Jordan. They live in one of the original summer rental detached condos on the north side of the lake that long ago were sold off as individual homes. They had the style of the decade in which they were built with their all-brown exterior and dramatic slanting roofs and a two-car garage that took up the entire front of the house as it faced the road.

Monica herself answers the door, and I'm hit with a wave of nostalgia. Monica's son Jordan was only a year ahead of us at school, but Monica was the high school librarian and a doctor.

She's *that* kind of doctor, the kind that inspired me to become one as well, and I spent every study hall in the library simply to be near her. She radiated elegance and grace and beauty, *and* she was smart. Some kids have superheroes as their idols. I had a librarian called Dr. Holmes.

She's wearing a long, pale blue crocheted cardigan over tan slacks, a lavender blouse, and long strands of beads around her neck. Dr. Holmes had let her short hair go gray long before it was cool, and now it's the kind of silver that only a fairy godmother like her can pull off.

Her smile is slow and knowing as she leans against the door jamb, one hand on the opened door.

"Dr. Della James," she breathes. "I heard a rumor you saw Vicky Gustafson, and I knew it was only a matter of time before you found your way to my door."

I'm not surprised the fact that I saw Vicky Gustafson has made its way around town, and I wonder how long it will take before everyone hears of my husband's affair.

"Well, I hate to disappoint you, but the rumors are true."

Dr. Holmes shakes her head and gives a soft whoop of laughter. "Ah, leave it to Vicky. She isn't done even when she's dead." She gestures behind her. "Come on in then."

While the outside of the home is still nestled in the eighties, the inside is tastefully updated with soft paint somewhere between gray and tan, pastel rugs, and minimalist furniture. The long entry hall ends in a kitchen with white cabinets and warm gold handles and a large center island in snowy quartz. Faintly I hear the sound of a television or a movie playing somewhere in the house.

"I don't suppose I can offer you something to drink." Dr. Holmes walks around to the opposite side of the island and then leans forward, what looks to be the start of dinner on the quartz countertop before her. "I have a feeling you've been talking to a lot of people and drinking a lot of things."

I smile. "Something like that. Am I interrupting?" I ask, pointing to the chopped carrots on a wooden cutting board in front of me.

"Nah." She indicates a stool tucked under the counter. "Have a seat. Jordan still has another thirty minutes on his game timer."

I take the stool she indicates and set my bag on the stool beside me. "I understand you and Vicky were close."

Dr. Holmes nods. "About as close as two peas in a pod. She saved my son. It's my greatest regret that she never lived to know it."

"She saved your son?" Of all the things I had been expecting when Daryl had told me to talk to Monica Holmes, this was not one of them.

I try to think back to high school, but my memories of Dr. Holmes are gilded in adolescent reverence.

"Mhmm," Dr. Holmes says, straightening and pushing the sleeves of her cardigan up as she resumes chopping up the carrots. "Of course she did. I would never have known what was going on with Jordan until she noticed and said something."

"Going on with Jordan? What do you mean?"

Jordan Holmes was always the easygoing one of any group. He was the kid every teacher wanted in class. He always saved a seat at lunch for the new kid, and you could find him every day after school at the arcade before it closed down and was replaced by a workout club.

"I don't know if you remember back then, but there wasn't the awareness there is now of the different learning styles children have. Back then if a child didn't do well in school they were labeled dumb and put in remedial classes. Remember that?"

I nod. "My friend Carmen was put in remedial reading class until they realized she could read just fine. She just needed glasses."

"That's exactly what I'm talking about." She looks up at the ceiling, and I wonder if the distant sounds I hear is her son, Jordan, somewhere in the house. "I was having trouble with Jordan then. This would have been when he was in about sixth grade. It wasn't big at first. Not something where you would point your finger at him and say that's a weird kid." She says this with a derision that suggests plenty of people have called her son weird over the years. "It was little things at first. There was a stretch where he wouldn't eat anything but eggs and toast. Then one day he started crying at the Super Duper. He put his hands over his ears and told me the noise was too bright in there." Her gaze has taken on a distant look as though she's reading her memories. "I got him out of there and took him to Dr. Peters," she goes on, referring to the only pediatrician in Bellegrave back then who has likely listened to the heartbeat of an entire generation of Bellegrave kids. "Thought something was wrong with his ears. Dr. Peters sent us to a specialist in Plattsburgh who did a hearing test, but they couldn't find anything wrong. It was when he got caught reading comic books in class that Vicky called me."

She places the knife down on the cutting board and leans in, her hands on the countertop, settling into her story, and I think of Marty Pruitt without warning. Two mothers with two stories about their children, both different yet the same.

"Vicky told me she had observed Jordan making certain gestures with his hands without seeming to know he was doing it. Now, of course, that has a name, but back then he was just called being a nuisance in class. Couldn't sit still. Couldn't focus. Vicky thought he might be autistic. That was the first time I'd heard that word."

I sit there trying to put the word *autistic* with what I know of Jordan Holmes, and I realize I'm just as guilty as probably so many others of thinking of autism in terms pop culture has presented to me.

"Jordan is autistic?"

"AuDHD is the term they use now." She laughs. "God, all these labels. First it was Asperger's. Then it was Autism I. He's my son. That's the only label I give him."

"So was Vicky going to teach him? Is that why she called you?"

Dr. Holmes shakes her head. "No, nothing formal like

that. Public schools are so quick to mainstream kids, you know? They don't have the budget for special education class-rooms. Not then. Not now. It's just not the priority it should be. Vicky was talking about starting an after-school program for kids like Jordan. She had tried to get the money from the school budget, but she got push back."

Somewhere, deep in the back of my mind, a little bell rings, and I wonder if this is what Vicky was looking for that night at the school board meeting when she got into the alter-cation with Gabriella Torres.

"I don't recall an after-school program. I was only a year behind Jordan, and I was usually always staying after school for music or science club." I couldn't have said *nerd* any louder than I just had, and I only hoped Dr. Holmes didn't remember the days I would loiter in the high school library after school just because I liked the smell and wanted to compulsively check if there were any new Nancy Drew books.

It was slightly less embarrassing than my M.C. Hammer phase.

Slightly.

"She never got it started. She died before she could make it happen." Dr. Holmes's expression is the kind of sorrowful I've only ever seen in dramas. "What an awful waste. I could name six people right now the world would be better off without, so why did someone as good as Vicky have to die?"

"I could add six of my own."

Dr. Holmes smiles in that way she has of making you feel understood. "Vicky had been doing some reading on new methods they were using to help kids like Jordan. She was going to use music as a kind of therapy. She had apparently gotten a student volunteer who was going to help her. I'm not sure how it would have worked with Jordan. He's still over-stimulated by sound, but Vicky was so hopeful. Said music was the way of helping kids like Jordan learn to navigate the world in their own way."

Without warning I see an image of Vicky Gustafson as she'd been in the halls of our school. She always seemed to float between the rows of worn metal lockers, her long flowing dresses trailing behind her. In my memory, she's glowing, but I know I've added that to symbolize how I felt about her. She always brought sunshine with her, and I think Monica Holmes feels the same way.

"I'm sorry Vicky never got to help Jordan."

"Me too," Monica says, straightening. "I think we did all right though. I found him help in Plattsburgh two nights after school, so he could stay in his class during the day. They were able to do a little for him then, but it's not like now. Now he has a therapist in Tupper Lake he sees once a week." Her eyes drift to the ceiling again where I imagine Jordan is on the second floor. "Sometimes I actually think Jordan's happy now." Her expression takes on a sheen then, like triumph after peril, and I envy her that peace. "He's got a regular shift at the Comic Cave, and he has his D&D friends he sees once a month. He said he wanted to join the science fiction book club at the library this summer." Her smile is pure joy.

"Thank you for telling me. None of this is my business, and you're very generous in offering to talk to me about it."

Dr. Holmes brings her gaze back to my face. "I figure it's probably important if Vicky came to you. She fought so hard for Jordan. She used to refer to him as her heart. Did you know that?"

"Daryl Walden told me," I say, which is likely easier to handle than hearing it was Vicky who told me.

Dr. Holmes laughs softly. "God, poor Daryl. He fell in love with a crusader. Vicky didn't like what the school board was telling her about the funding, especially when we all saw how overfunded they were. I don't know what their idea of financial management was, but Vicky wouldn't let them get away with it. She started digging into the budget, and right before she died, she said she thought she found something. Something that gave her hope." Dr. Holmes goes quiet for a second. "She died before it went any further though." She meets my gaze. "Folks are saying you think she was murdered."

"Is that what they're saying?"

"Mhmm," Dr. Holmes says. "Any truth to that?"

"I'm afraid there is."

Dr. Holmes shakes her head. "You'd better get to the bottom of it before Chief Tom finds out. He still hasn't forgiven you for the Brewer disaster."

I cringe. "That wasn't my finest hour, but you will admit when the dress caught on fire after I hosed her, I didn't look so stupid."

"Not so stupid," Dr. Holmes agrees with a smirk.

She walks me to the door, and we chitchat about Founder's Day and the coming summer season. It isn't until I'm at the door that I remember something.

"You said Vicky had gotten a student volunteer who was going to help her with the after-school program. Do remember who it was?"

Dr. Holmes's expression turns sad again, that deep kind of sad that doesn't wash out. "I'm afraid that line of questioning won't do you any good."

"Why's that?"

"Because it was Lisa Reynolds."

TWENTY

As soon as my phone connects after I start my car, I dial Raymond.

"My wife is sitting next to me, so I know you're not calling me to come bail her out," he says when he answers.

"How do I see the school district's budget?" I ignore his attempt at glib.

My heart is rabbiting in my chest, the name Lisa Reynolds echoing in my ears.

Raymond is silent for a beat and then says, "This is about Vicky Gustafson, isn't it?"

It wasn't until Monica Holmes spoke Lisa Reynolds's name that the string that had been tying every interview I'd conducted together had pulled taut so I could finally see it.

The school budget.

Gabriella Torres, Gretchen Gustafson, and even my own parents had said there was a shortfall with the school budget. Why? Where did the money go? And more importantly, what did Vicky Gustafson have to do with it?

For a fleeting moment, I wonder if she'd stolen it. Embezzled from the school. But that just didn't seem like Vicky. The thing that did seem like Vicky though was ferreting out where the money went.

"Why do people commit murder, Raymond?" I pause for emphasis before saying, "For love or money. I'm following the money."

He swears softly under his breath. "Maybe you should talk to Carmen first."

I hear Carmen muffled on the other end, and it sounds like she's trying to get Raymond to give her the phone.

I talk over her. "I just need to see the school budget from the 1996 and 1997 school years. It's a public school. That should be public record, right?"

Raymond says a series of things then too muttered for me to hear. Finally, he says, "It's on the school website. All of it. It's part of the digitization project Dr. Holmes headed up before she retired. You know, that program she did to teach students archiving?"

"Thank you, Raymond."

"Del?" he says before I can hang up. "Don't do anything stupid, okay? You might be able to talk to the dead but don't end up dead, you hear me?"

"I won't. I promise."

"Just don't lose sight of the fact that the information you're searching for probably already got another person killed."

If only that were the extent of it.

I thank him again and hang up before he can think of any more discouraging things to say.

When I get to back to my parents' house, I find them at the kitchen island, cartons of half-eaten Chinese food scattered across the surface, and my mother feeding my father a piece of General Tso's Chicken from her chopsticks.

She turns to look at me and nearly stabs my father in the cheek. "Who did you see now?"

I really must work on schooling my features. "Monica Holmes," I answer, poking through the cartons of food.

"But she's alive," my mom says.

"Sometimes I talk to the living too." I look around. "Where's Henry?"

Dad points over his shoulder to the living room. "We gave him one of those frozen peanut butter things."

I glance toward the living room. "I have some research I need to do, so I'm going to head upstairs." I haul my bag higher onto my shoulder and select a carton of shrimp lo mein and a sleeve of chopsticks. "Send Henry up when he's finished. I don't want to disturb him."

"Does this have to do with Vicky Gustafson or Lisa Reynolds?" my mom asks.

"I think both." I head up the stairs before they can ask anything else.

I perch myself in the nest of stuffed animals that still occupies my childhood bed and open my laptop on my knees.

I navigate to the school district's website and find a photo of the high school/middle school building on the homepage.

It's a chilling photo taken in winter, a fresh blanket of snow coating the entire complex. The high school/middle school building, like many New York State rural schools, was a public works project during the Great Depression and is far more ornate than a public school building might be. The art deco influence is strong in the cornices and large granite blocks used to decorate the edifice of the building, and it feels like something out of time. I suppose it is in some ways.

I click through the menu at the top until I locate the business office page and scroll down until I see a link to audit reports. There are five links on the resulting page listing external audit reports from every school year since 2019. I click a link randomly in the middle of the list.

To be honest, I don't really know what I'm looking at. I've

seen budgets and profit and loss statements aplenty, but a public school audit report is something else. I poke at my shrimp lo mein while I try to decipher what it is I'm seeing.

There's a statement page at the very beginning, listing the name and information of the firm conducting the audit as well as a summary of its findings. Mainly that the school's financial statements as presented are fairly displayed. I'm guessing fairly displayed is a way of saying they didn't find anyone lying in the financial statements.

I keep scrolling until I reach the section about the school district's funds. There's a summary listing the district's net position and bullet points indicating why certain funds have changed, mostly that there was an increase in property tax. I scroll farther until I come to the balance sheet. It's structured like a typical balance sheet with assets at the top and liabilities at the bottom.

I jump to the liabilities section and scan the figures there. I'm nearly to the bottom of the list of numbers before my brain triggers what it has noticed subconsciously and pushes it to the front of my mind. I go back to the top of the list, and I see it now clearly.

Accounts payable dropped by over a million dollars from the previous school year.

I go back to the top of the report, and this time I read every single word of the report. Still there is no indication as to why accounts payable would drop so drastically from one school year to the next.

Thinking it might have been an anomalymaybe the boiler blew that yearI click on the link for the audit report for the previous year. The report for the 2018-2019 school year shows accounts payable hovering at one and a half million. Every year since then it's around three hundred thousand.

I open a new tab and navigate to the *Bellegrave Bulletin*. I type Bob Reynolds and superintendent in the search bar.

Several results about school board meetings pop up, but the article I'm looking for is at the very top.

Bellegrave   Public   Schools   Superintendent   Celebrates Retirement.

I click on it and discover Bob Reynolds retired as superintendent of schools in 2019, the same year as the ballooned accounts payable figure. Knowing I'm making the facts fit the theory that's brewing in my mind, I go back to the school district's website.

I almost navigate away from the page in search of the audit reports Dr. Holmes and her students digitized when I notice there's another link much farther down the page, a chunk of white space separating it from the links for the audit reports.

The link reads *2019 Financial Management Audit Report.*

I click on it.

The resulting document is only fifteen pages long compared to the nearly eighty pages of the school year audit report. But thanks to the report structure, I don't need to scroll far to find exactly what I'm looking for. On page two, there's a list of key findings next to a blurb about the school district's background. I zero in on the key findings, several words already jumping out at me.

Several funds exceeded the statutory limits by nearly a million and a half dollars in several years over a twenty-year period. The school years are noted when the funds were overfunded, and I make a note of them. I quickly scan the rest of the report, which includes the funds mentioned in the key findings as well as actionable items for the school district to take to correct the issue.

There's also a response at the end of the report from the school district thanking the auditors for the report and suggestions, but they will continue to allocate funds as they see fit.

This is what Gabriella Torres had mentioned. The school board was allocating funds to overfunded reserves.

I go back to the school district website, aware my heart is racing now, and my hand is slightly shaky on the mouse pad. I click on the link for libraries and find a section dedicated to library initiatives. It's here that I find Dr. Holmes's archiving project. There's a list of every audit report going back to 1995, and I thank God for Dr. Holmes all over again.

I spend the next hour going through every audit report since 1995, noting how each of the reserve funds are funded, the amount of accounts payable for that year, and the auditors' findings. The years indicated in the audit report in which the funds exceeded statutory limits accounts payable were below half a million dollars. I pay particularly close attention to 1996, the year of the school board meeting altercation between Vicky and Gabriella Torres. Accounts payable that year are over two million.

I then cross reference the audit reports from the years Bob Reynolds was superintendent to the reports of every school year since he retired. Every year since Bob's retirement in 2019, accounts payable have hovered at three hundred thousand, and there is no mention of funds exceeding statutory limits.

I stare at my laptop for several minutes, thinking it can't be this easy. I'm one person with a laptop and an internet connection, and I've uncovered gross negligence on the part of the school board of Bellegrave Public Schools from sometime around 1995 until 2019. Obviously the school district was warned in that financial management report that it might face fines for exceeding statutory limits, but nothing was done about it until Bob Reynolds retired.

Because Bob Reynolds was no longer there to influence the board's funding decisions for his benefit.

That is a leap. I've just decided Bob Reynolds is guilty of embezzlement, and I don't have solid proof of that. All I have is a record of unsound financial management on the part of the Bellegrave school board.

I download everything to my laptop, putting it in a file on my cloud storage just in case. I don't know why. The information is publicly available on the school's website, but I'm suddenly filled with a sense of foreboding.

Raymond is right. Vicky Gustafson is dead, and Lisa Reynolds presumably faked her death and ran.

But why?

Is it because of the information I've already uncovered? I don't think it is. Anyone could find this information.

I think it's because Vicky Gustafson and Lisa Reynolds not only uncovered the mismanagement of funds, but they also discovered where that money went in the years accounts payable was nearly a million and a half dollars or more.

Because that's how embezzlement works. Bob would need to get the money into the system by calling for property taxes to go up, and then he would need to create a fake vendor to pay in order to get the money out of the system and into his pockets.

But he screwed up in a few years. In 1996 he overpaid himself, and in the three years mentioned in the financial review, he underpaid himself, alerting the authorities to the financial mismanagement.

Is that how Vicky got him? The year he overpaid himself?

I snap my laptop shut, knowing one thing.

I need to find where that money went, and I need to find it without getting myself killed in the process.

TWENTY-ONE

I try calling Carmen the next morning at the earliest, reasonable hour, but she doesn't answer.

I text her a simple *call me*, and after my phone call to Raymond the previous night, I thought this would have garnered a response. But by eleven she still hasn't responded, and the need for answers propels me out of the lodge for an early lunch.

I don't know what it is, but something reckless inside of me makes me head straight for the Pruitt camp. I know this is unwise, and maybe even a little dangerous. I have every reason to believe Bob Reynolds is an embezzler and killed someone to keep his secret safe. A secret that drove his daughter to fake her own murder to escape.

I feel my stomach heave as I think of it, but I force myself to concentrate.

I should go to the police. I know that. Show them what I've uncovered and make them dig deeper. But then I remember what Carmen said about the Lisa Reynolds investigation, how Marty had asked for it to stop. Had Bob put her up to it? If Lisa knew about her father's scheme, he wouldn't have wanted her found.

Is that why Marty didn't want Bob to know she'd asked me to contact Lisa?

Maybe Marty didn't know about Bob's embezzlement. She was the innocent one in all of this, and she had lost her only child because of it. Unbidden comes the photo Marty gave Hannah to post on social media. A mother and a daughter with almost the exact same expressions, as if they were simply mirrors of each other.

Marty had lost her, her little girl. What else had Bob made her lose?

I was getting ahead of myself. I still didn't know that Bob was the one siphoning off the overfunded reserves. I was just letting emotion get the better of me. Maybe Bob really wasn't that bad.

I tried to think back to high school, but all I could remember was the way he brushed me off in his advice to join the Navy.

I follow the county highway around to the west end of the lake. It's hard to believe so much has happened since Carmen drove me up here little more than a month ago. The trees have filled in now, their branches full as they shade the long drive up to the main camp. Sunlight cuts through the canopy in disorientating slashes, and it's because of this that I almost hit her.

I slam on my brakes, my heart hurtling into my throat, only for a calmness to sweep over me.

For a split second, I thought it was Marty Pruitt herself standing in the middle of the drive, but I realize it's not.

It's Vicky Gustafson.

She's in the same dress with the daisies along the bodice, long dark hair floating eerily along her shoulders, the back of her head crushed and bloody. I stare at her through the windshield of my car, both of my hands wrapped tightly around the steering wheel as if to hold me there.

Vicky lifts a single arm and points into the trees. I follow her gesture. I was so focused on reaching the main house I hadn't noticed the fact that I'd come upon the track that cuts into the forest here that I saw that first time I came up here with Carmen.

I look back at Vicky. She's dropped her arm now, but I can hear her voice as clearly as if she's in the car with me.

Go.

My arms shake from holding on to the steering wheel, and my stomach is tied into a thousand knots.

"Okay," I say. "Okay. Okay. I'll go."

I want to stay and ask Vicky more questions she likely doesn't have the energy to answer, but I can feel her pushing me in the direction of the track through the forest.

I turn the car, the tires crunching gravel, and I slip into the forest proper. This track is as well maintained as the main road, and I abandon the sudden thought that perhaps Bob Reynolds really did kill his daughter and has disposed of her body somewhere out here. But I dismiss the thought almost immediately. Lisa Reynolds's spirit isn't here. I'd have felt it if she was, but all I can feel is Vicky's energy dissipating behind me.

The trees are closer together here, less groomed than the main drive, and the road turns suddenly away from the lake. Just as I'm wondering what it is I should be looking for, the trees part and a cabin comes into view. Its structure consists of bark-covered logs set into notched corners, the red paint along the eaves, windows, and front door peeling. This must be one of the original cabins that would have made up the compound of the Pruitt camp when it was first built, and I'm seeing the architect's original design for the main lodge before the exterior was replaced with clean planking and gray paint.

I only have a moment to appreciate the cabin before I take in the rest of it. A small sports car and a midsize luxury SUV are parked in front of the cabin. The hatch of the SUV is open, and a pile of grocery bags sits on the porch in front of the open door of the cabin. I pull to a stop and get out before the occupants of the cabin are fully aware I'm there.

I'm not sure what it is I'm expecting, but it's certainly not Marty Pruitt herself, her head coming around the side of the SUV where she's clearly unloading groceries from the back of it.

"Ms. Pruitt," I say, more from shock than anything else.

Her eyes widen the smallest of degrees before something stark flashes across them.

"Dr. James." She says my name curtly, but there's a hint of something breathless behind her tone. Something like fear.

"I was hoping I could speak with you. I—"

"Now is not a good time." She steps from behind the SUV and approaches, filling my vision until I'm forced to take a step back.

Is she forcing me back into my car or shielding what's behind her from my sight? What is she hiding? What doesn't she want me to see?

I don't ask any of these questions, but I don't have to. The answer comes when Bob Reynolds himself steps out onto the porch of the small cabin.

"Marty, what's going on?" It isn't until Bob steps down from the porch into the light that the full force of him hits me.

I take two steps back now, blinking rapidly, but I know it won't change what I'm seeing.

Bob Reynolds is more than seventy now, and it's hard to match up the pale, gray man in front of me with the one I remember from school, striding confidently down the halls in a double-breasted suit and shined shoes. There's a ragged edge to him that would make someone rub their eyes as if not quite seeing him right, but I know it's not my vision that's the problem.

Bob is dying, and his energy has already started to separate itself from his body. That's the ragged light that surrounds him. Soon it will break free of his corporeal form, and he'll discard the human body that has betrayed him. But for now, he's a man stuck in death, and he's coming directly for me.

"Who are you?" His tone is more forceful than Marty's, but I don't back down.

"It's Della James, Mr. Reynolds. From school. Remember? Class of 2002."

"What do you want?"

I glance at Marty, and her eyes seem to speak to me. Is she trying to warn me? Is she telling me to get out of there? I recall suddenly, stupidly, how she didn't want Bob to know about asking me to contact Lisa, and now I understand her fear.

I raise my chin. "I just needed to see Ms. Pruitt. She had some ideas about the Founder's Day programming, and I was on my way to Tupper Lake. Thought I'd stop by and see her to save her a trip into town."

There's just enough of the truth there to make Marty's expression shift, the wariness about her eyes fading.

"That's right," she says, stepping forward. "Now's not really a good time though. Do you mind if we set up something for later?"

Her tone is polite now, almost warm, and I smile along with her.

"Sure. No worries. I'll send you an email with some dates that work for me. How does that sound?"

Marty places her hands together in front of her. "That sounds wonderful. Thank you so much for taking the time to stop by."

"Of course," I say, but I keep my gaze on Bob as I turn for

my car. "Have a good one, Mr. Reynolds," I say as I slam the SUV's door.

They both watch me as I back up and turn around to face the road out of there. I glance at them in the rearview mirror as the SUV lumbers back to the main drive.

They don't move, as if they want to make sure I'm really leaving. But it doesn't matter. I have no need to stay. I've already discovered what they're trying to hide.

That day in the lodge when I'd visited Lisa's room, something had felt odd in the house, an absence I couldn't name by the very essence of it being absent. But I could name it now.

It was electricity.

The electricity wasn't on in the main lodge of Pruitt Camp because Marty Pruitt and her husband, Bob, no longer lived in the lodge. They were squatting in a cabin on the camp's grounds.

And I bet I know why.

TWENTY-TWO

"Why aren't you answering your phone?" I hiss as I plop down in the chair in front of Carmen's desk at the Bellegrave Police Department.

She's typing, her eyes fixed on her computer, and her fingers slow to a tap-tap-tap as her gaze turns to me. "Oh God, you've finally lost it."

"I have not lost it. If you were answering your phone, I wouldn't need to come in here." I'm trying so hard to whisper loudly my throat constricts.

Slowly Carmen removes her hands from the keyboard, her eyes never leaving my face. "So is this a disguise or something?"

She gestures with a single finger. I can only imagine what I look like, but I don't care.

I sit up as straight as I can with one hand holding the rubber tote that usually holds Henry's paraphernalia in the backseat of my SUV on my head. "I don't want what's upstairs trying to get into my head. I'm strong, but I'm not taking any risks with that thing being so close."

Carmen looks over my shoulder and out her office door. I'm sure she's checking to see who saw me come in.

"Why don't I close this?" she says and scoots around me to shut her office door. "Why the tote?" She knocks on it lightly as she scoots back around me to her seat.

"Rubber doesn't conduct electricity, and I have a theory it stops ghosts from pushing their energy into my brain."

"Tin foil hats?"

I shake my head and wrinkle my nose in disgust. "No way. Aluminum is a great conductor of electricity. The obvious way to go is rubber."

Her eyebrows lift. "Of course it is." She stops. "Wait. Why are you here? You don't come in here."

"Marty Pruitt is in danger. You need to save her."

Her lips part, and she blinks as she shakes her head, holding up both hands. "Wait. What. Start over."

"I would have already told you all this if you answered your phone."

"Ella knocked my phone into the toilet while we were practicing her makeup for her dance recital. I haven't had time to get a replacement."

I reach inside my bag I've placed at my feet and pull out the copies I've made of the school audit reports. I place them on Carmen's desk and fan them out.

"Bob Reynolds has been getting the school board to approve overfunding of reserves in order to embezzle for his own gain. I'm guessing by the wild fluctuations in accounts payable liabilities he was doing it through a fake vendor. He's been doing it as far back as 1995, and that's just how far the archive goes back. Maybe he was doing it before then." I put the financial management review report from 2019 on the desk next. "Here is the proof that someone finally caught on, and the overfunding suddenly stopped when Bob retired."

"Whoa. You need to stop," Carmen says, pushing the printouts back toward me. "You can't go around accusing people of embezzlement."

I push the printouts back toward her. "Look at the reports, Carmen. The school board was consistently over-funding every year, and every year accounts payable mysteri-ously had almost a million and half in liabilities. A million and a half. A public school. In the Adirondacks." I sit back and throw up one hand. "Answer me this. If that money wasn't embezzled, then where the heck did they spend it? Because it wasn't on new lockers. It wasn't on renovating the bathrooms. Remember how many times you had to hold the door with a foot while you peed? That's a skill I never should have acquired."

Carmen looks at me, but the shock has melted from her face.

"Look at the reports, Carmen. There's money missing, and we need to find it. Marty Pruitt is in danger, and Dr. Holmes says Vicky uncovered something shortly before her death. Something to do with the school budget." I tap the reports. "This is it, Carmen. I bet you this is what Vicky uncovered." I pause but only for a second because I decide now is not the time to hold back. "And I think Vicky found out Bob was behind the embezzling, and he killed her to stop her from telling anyone, and Lisa saw it happen and ran."

Carmen shakes her head. "Slow down. Okay. Someone—" She stops, her eyes on me as she emphasizes the neutrality of the word. "*Someone* looks to be stealing from the school. Got it. What does this have to do with Marty Pruitt? And why were you talking to Monica Holmes? I thought you weren't helping me with Lisa because Lisa is alive or whatever."

"Remember when we went to see Marty, and we went into Lisa's room. Remember how weird it felt?"

"Yeah, it felt weird. Those are people with money. The kind that doesn't use paper towels as napkins because they can afford not to."

I shake my head. "It felt weird because the electricity was off. Did you notice how quiet it was?"

Carmen leans back in her chair and crosses her arms, making her denim jacket fan out. "The electricity was off. How the heck do you know that?"

I know what I have to say next is going to upset my best friend, but I say it anyway. "I went out to Camp Pruitt this morning to ask Bob about the audit reports."

Carmen closes her eyes very slowly, and when she opens them again, I can see the disappointment there. "You harassed a private citizen?"

"No because what I found there stopped me from doing so," I reply. "Vicky Gustafson showed up, and I nearly hit her with my car."

"Vicky was at Camp Pruitt?" Carmen asks, her voice quiet.

"Yes, she pointed me down—" I stop, hearing my words for what they really mean. "I saw Vicky at Camp Pruitt," I almost whisper, hardly able to believe it. "I saw Vicky at Camp Pruitt," I say more strongly.

"Yeah, I heard you. So what?"

I lean forward so quickly I nearly topple the rubber tote off my head. "A spirit only appears where it's energy's been because—"

"It's an echo. Yeah, I know. You've told me this," Carmen interrupts. "So what does that mean?"

"It means Vicky was at Camp Pruitt. She left an imprint there that allows her to return." I stop, seeing Vicky as she was in the drive. "It's stronger there. Oh God, Carmen, Vicky's echo is stronger at the Pruitt camp than at the river. She—" But I can't bring myself to say it. I can't bring myself to say Vicky was murdered there.

Carmen shakes her head slowly this time, and I know she's

just figured out what I did. "No. Uh uh. Vicky Gustafson was a teacher. I bet a lot of teachers were at Camp Pruitt."

"Maybe," I allow. "But it's still significant. It means Vicky was there."

"All right. So she was at the camp. What were you saying about her today? She was showing you something?"

I try to shake the strange feeling climbing up my arms and say, "There's a track off the main drive that leads to one of the outbuildings. A small cabin tucked back into the forest that was probably used as a guest room when the camp was first built." I lick my lips, trying to slow my words. "There were two cars parked in front of it, and Marty was unloading groceries onto the porch. She was startled when she saw me, but then Bob appeared. He—" I almost say he was starting to separate from his body, but that isn't really relevant. "He was upset I was there. I got the impression he wanted me to leave. Marty seemed scared, so I did. I just left." I'm warming up to my subject now, and it takes all I have to keep my voice steady. "They're not living in the main house anymore, Carmen. They're living in that tiny cabin, and I bet they don't want anyone to know. They don't want anyone to know they've run out of money because Bob retired from his moneymaking scheme, and they are forced to live in an outbuilding on their property."

Carmen leans forward, placing both elbows on her desk, so she can press her forehead into her hands. "Do you hear yourself, Del? You got the *impression* Bob wanted you to leave. Marty *seemed* scared. I know you've got more senses than the rest of us, but police work isn't built on senses. It's built on facts."

I point to the reports. "Those are the facts. Find where the money went, and I bet you'll find Bob Reynolds with it."

"I'm already looking for a backpack, or have you forgotten?" Her expression is nonplussed.

"I thought Tom told you to leave that alone."

Carmen shrugs as she leans back again. "You know me, Del. I can't let it go. You're right. That backpack shows up in every photo with her, and yet it isn't anywhere to be found. If she was really murdered, her murderer would have left it in the car, wouldn't he? But it wasn't there, and it wasn't in Lisa's room. I can't just let that go."

"What have you tried?"

She glances over my shoulder again, and I wonder if she's looking for Tom this time.

"I've done the usual things. Social media searches. Background checks." She moves her head back and forth. "Nothing. Lisa Reynolds isn't out there. She's a ghost. Just not the kind you can sense." Carmen pauses before saying, "Did you say Dr. Holmes?"

I nod, the rubber tote bouncing on my head. "Dr. Holmes told me Vicky recognized autism in her son, Jordan—"

Carmen holds up a hand, cutting me off. "Jordan Holmes? Is autistic?"

It's like I've just told her Santa isn't real.

"He was the only other black kid at school when we first moved here. He was the reason I didn't feel so alone." Carmen's voice has gone soft. "He was so...normal," she says and shakes her head again. "I don't think I'm supposed to say that."

I shrug. "Jordan always seemed so cool to me, but Dr. Holmes says Vicky was trying to start an after-school program for special needs kids using music therapy, only she couldn't get the funding. Apparently she found something right before she died, only Dr. Holmes didn't know what it was. I bet it was this," I say, pointing to the reports. "Dr. Holmes says Lisa Reynolds volunteered to help. They're connected, Carmen." I'm nearly pleading now.

The uneasy feeling that had been crawling up my arms

deepens, and a cold hand closes along my neck. For a second, I think it's the subject matter, but then my eyes drop to Carmen's desk where a blanket of frost creeps along the edge, its icy fingers reaching for the audit reports.

I stand so quickly I nearly knock over the chair I'm sitting in.

"I need to go." I stab the audit reports with one finger, causing them to flinch to the side, revealing that day's edition of the *Bellegrave Bulletin* beneath it. "Find out where the money went. Please. We need to help Marty."

By the time I get out of the door and up the steps leading out of the Opera House basement and the Bellegrave Police Department, my fingers have gone blue with cold. I catapult myself up the steps, my rubber tote swinging from one numb hand as I crumple on the sidewalk outside Papa's Pizza.

I suck in great gulps of yeasty warm air as the feeling slowly returns to my fingers, and although people are staring at me as they walk by to go into Papa's, I can't help but smile.

Because I just figured out how to find Lisa Reynolds.

TWENTY-THREE

I have a headache by the time I get back to my parents'
house.

Henry greets me at the door with a stuffed bear in his
mouth I've never seen before. He wags his tail with such pure
happiness it moves his whole body like he's a merman cutting
through the ocean.

I glance up at where my father stands by the fridge,
pouring water into a glass. He avoids my gaze, his innocent
expression overkill.

"Took Henry to The Dog Shop again, didn't you?" I say.

The Dog Shop sits on Church Street and primarily offers a
wide variety of dog toys. All of them are in bins along the
floor, and dogs are allowed to come in and make their own
selections. This is one of Henry's greatest joys, and I reserve it
for his grandparents, so they can have something special to do
together.

Seeing Henry now lifts some of the pounding pressure
behind my eyes, and I bury my face in his neck.

"Long day?" my dad finally asks.

"Long month," I say, straightening. I pull out my phone

compulsively, but the screen is blank. I blocked Logan's number on Monday after he called me six times in a row. I need my phone for work and life, but I'm not ready to speak to my husband yet.

My dad hands me the glass of water he's just poured before getting another for himself.

"Is it about the living or the dead?" I know my dad is trying to be tactful in his way of asking if I've spoken to Logan, which I haven't.

Now that I've said the thing I should have said thirteen years ago, I don't know what else to say. All those years, my brain was focused on one thing. I never thought to look past it, and now I've found all this space out there I couldn't see because of the things I let stand in the way, and I'm not ready to face that emptiness yet.

"The dead," I say, taking a seat at the kitchen island as Henry scampers off into the living room, tossing his new toy in front of him.

I don't know the rules to this game, but it's one of his favorites, and he doesn't care for it when I try to play too. So I leave him to it.

Dad takes a stool across from me. "Vicky Gustafson again?"

I spin the water glass between my fingers on the countertop. "I think Vicky Gustafson discovered Bob Reynolds was embezzling from the school, and he killed her before she could expose him. And I think Lisa Reynolds knew what her father did, or she witnessed the murder and faked her own abduction and ran."

My dad was about to take a sip of his water, but he stops at my statement, the glass half-raised to his mouth, lips parted. He sets his glass down without drinking.

"Do you have proof of any of this?"

I frown. "You're starting to sound like Carmen."

Dad gives me a goofy smile in response.

I sigh and settle into my story, relaying what I've uncovered so far and my theory of why Bob Reynolds was embezzling.

"You of all people would know how much it costs to keep up an old camp like the Pruitt lodge," Dad says when I finish. "The property taxes alone. The pressure on Bob to provide must have been astronomical."

I think of the way Marty so carefully holds herself, and I wonder if she married Bob because she was simply used to someone else telling her how to behave and look.

"I think that's why they're living in the cabin now. They can't afford the upkeep on the main lodge, and there's no more income stream with Bob retired and—" I stop myself and glance at my father, but he only smiles softly with understanding.

"I know nothing scares you, Delia Ann," my dad says. "Not even the dead."

"Death isn't scary when you can see the other side of it."

"I suppose not." Dad twirls his glass like I had. "But I don't think embezzlement is what's on your mind right now."

I take a sip of water before going on. "When Vicky appeared in front of me on the Pruitt drive, she was nearly solid. Not like she was that day by the river where I could see the bridge through her. I really thought I was going to hit a corporeal body."

"What does that mean?"

I swallow before saying, "I think Vicky was killed at the Pruitt camp."

Dad leans back on his stool, planting both hands on the edge of the counter. "How can you prove that?"

I shake my head. "I can't. What am I supposed to say to Tom? The ghost was more solid here, so that means her energy deposit is strongest here, so that means she died here." I shake my head again. "I can't even make a coherent sentence out of that."

When I meet my dad's gaze, I see his face has fallen into a puzzled expression.

"What is it?" I prompt.

"I get that overfunding and fake vendor theory and the initial evidence you've uncovered that points in that direction." He fixes his glasses as he thinks. "But what I don't understand is the school board would be responsible for the overfunding. They would need to make the decision to over-fund the reserves and risk statutory violations." He meets my gaze. "That would take someone with a lot of influence to get them to do that, and Bob Reynolds just doesn't strike me as the type."

I frown. "I thought the same thing until I saw him at the camp earlier today."

"You saw him?" my dad asks. "Like directly? He's been keeping himself scarce since his diagnosis."

I glance down before remembering I'm speaking to my dad. "He's starting to separate," I say. "I can see the energy leaving him."

My dad shakes his head once and looks away. "Actively dying. What a terrible phrase."

I nod in agreement, but my throat is too tight to say anything. I take a drink of water and push the condensation the glass has left on the countertop with one finger.

"But if Bob wasn't the one to convince the school board to overfund, then who did?"

Instead of answering, my dad folds his arms on the kitchen island and leans forward. "Remember that story I told you about the plane crash in the Everglades?"

"Yeah," I say. "The one where the pilots were focused on a blinking light in the cockpit and were so focused on that blinking light because they didn't know what it meant that they crashed the plane."

"That one," Dad confirms. "I just don't want you to become too focused on the blinking light that you crash the plane."

"Am I the plane in this scenario?"

Dad nods.

"And who is the Everglades?"

Dad blinks. "Aren't you more worried about the passengers on the plane?"

I shrug. "The passengers would be aware of the inherent dangers of flight. They signed up for this. The Everglades were the innocent victim in all of this."

"I think that's Daryl Walden and Gretchen and her son." Dad's voice is quiet with the weight of his words, and I let them sink in.

He's right, of course. They all had their lives altered because of what happened to Vicky. Daryl was robbed of a future he was only on the cusp of realizing. Gretchen lost her daughter, and Kevin lost his confidante and ally.

"I would add Marty Pruitt to the list. She lost her daughter too," I say. "I'm more worried for them. For the Everglades."

"I believe you are. But at the expense of hurting other innocent..." He pauses, and I know he's struggling with the analogy. "Other Everglades?"

"Is Bob an Everglade?"

"He might be."

I shake my head. "No. You didn't see those audit reports. There was definite evidence of negligence, and Bob—"

"Has nothing to directly connect him to it. Not yet." Dad leans forward now, and the shaded light over the kitchen island reflects off his glasses. "You said Carmen was going to look into the reports. Find out who was being paid the most in the accounts payable bucket. Once she finds out who the highest paid vendor was you will have something to work with. Only then can you start walking to someone's door. Not before."

I picture Bob as he was earlier that day, looming out of the dark, his energy oozing from his body, the way he hovered over Marty, his hand on her shoulder.

"I'll try," I say.

But I can't help but think Bob is dying. What does he have left to lose? And how dangerous does that make him?

If he killed Vicky to keep his secret safe, and his own daughter fled for her life, just what is the man capable of?

TWENTY-FOUR

I don't hear from Carmen until Friday.

I'm walking from the library down to Shelly's Diner to pick up a Reuben when my phone buzzes in my pocket. Founder's Day is a week away, and I've been shuttling props from the library to the lodge all week. I still have a few more hours of work today even though it's almost five, and a Reuben from Shelly's sounds like a good dinner on the go.

"You're calling me," I say when I answer.

"Listen." Carmen's voice is all business, and I stop on the sidewalk, scooting over toward the lamppost at the edge to get out of the way of foot traffic and better hear my best friend. "I talked to Shawna's husband."

"Who's Shawna?"

"My nail tech," she says, as if I should know this. "Shawna's husband, Frank, works in the business office at the school. He did me a favor and pulled the accounts payable from 1996 through 2001. I thought that would be enough to give us an idea of where all that money was going and maybe give us enough evidence to open an investigation."

At some point I've wrapped a hand around the lamppost, and now I lean in, as if the lamppost is suddenly a dear friend comforting me as I receive bad news.

"And?"

"There was one vendor who was consistently paid between one and one and a half million over that timeframe. An educational consulting firm called Caledonia Consulting."

I don't know what I was expecting, but it wasn't this.

I grimace. "Caledonia Consulting?"

"Yeah, it's registered in Syracuse, but I can do a check on the company name and see if it's in good standing with the state. I may even be able to find out who is behind it, depending on how the company is set up."

"Okay," I say because I don't know what else to say.

"You sound disappointed," Carmen remarks.

"I was hoping for a big giant *Bob Reynolds did it* sign."

Carmen's sigh is like a blast of air through the phone. "That's not how it works in real life. It's really just a lot of fact checking."

"Yeah, I suppose so. Thanks, Carmen, really," I add. "You didn't need to do that."

There's another sigh, this one less aggrieved. "Well, I kinda did."

I still. "How's that?"

"Tom wants to reopen the Lisa Reynolds case. I told him what you uncovered, and he wants me to review the evidence we have. He said a fresh set of eyes on it might turn up some new leads."

I straighten away from the lamppost. "Tom's reopening the case?"

"Looks like it." I hear papers shuffling on the other end of the phone. "This does not give you carte blanche to go do whatever those ghosties tell you to do. You hear me? Someone died because of this whole thing. Don't go poking the bear that already murdered someone."

"I promise not to poke any bears. Truly." I have no interest in confronting murderers. Uncovering evidence to reveal the truth so souls can pass on? Sure. But that's different than putting myself into a dangerous situation. "What was the name of the consulting firm again?"

"Caledonia Consulting."

When she says it this time, a little bell trips somewhere deep in the back of my mind. I've heard the name Caledonia recently, but I can't place it.

"Thanks, Carmen," I say again and ring off.

Shelly's is busy as always when I get there with people coming in and out, picking up takeout orders, or sitting at the counter. Shelly herself has my Reuben ready, and I take the brown paper bag that's already spotted with grease. My stomach rumbles in response, and Shelly laughs.

"Can't imagine how hard you've been working with Founder's Day only a week away," she says, putting my cash in the register.

I hold up the bag. "Fuel to see me through to the end. Thanks, Shelly."

I'm so preoccupied with the exchange I nearly run straight into Chief Tom Reznick when I turn to the door.

"Whoa," he says, stopping me with a hand on my shoulder.

We shift to the side so others can pick up their takeout orders at the counter, and Tom settles both hands on his belt.

"I suppose you heard I'm reopening the Reynolds case. I'm putting your friend Carmen on it."

Tom is so close to retirement he can probably smell it. He has a solid mustache that's speckled with gray and a thick head of hair to match. He favors Wrangler jeans and work boots, and I'm not sure I've ever seen him in uniform.

"I heard," I say, cradling my Reuben and willing my stomach not to growl. "I appreciate you considering the evidence I've uncovered."

He eyes me, and I wonder if he's thinking about the incident with Becky Brewer's wedding dress. "I don't want you to think you can charge in, guns blazing now, you hear?"

I nod. "I've already been warned. I have no plans of confronting anyone. I assure you."

He crosses his arms over his chest. "That so? I heard you were out at the Pruitt camp only a couple of days ago."

I frown. "Nothing is sacred in this town." I shift the Reuben to one hand. "I went to talk with Marty about a suggestion she had for Founder's Day," I say, sticking to my lie. "That's all. I left as soon as Bob indicated I should." I held up both hands, the paper bag swinging between my fingers. "Promise. I have no intentions of being a hero."

Tom matches my frown, but he shifts to his other foot, and I can feel I've been let off the hook.

"See that you keep those intentions, you hear? Marty and Bob are good people. They've done so much for this town. They don't need anyone poking into their business."

I wonder what Carmen has shared with Tom, and I decide it's best if I don't say anything. I nod. "I agree. Absolutely."

I shift ever so slightly to the door, but it seems Tom's not done.

"Marty was the one to start the volunteer fire department auxiliary. You know when the townspeople turn up at a big disaster to provide water and food? That was Marty's idea. Best thing that's happened to this town."

I nod again, but then something clicks in my mind, and I suddenly picture the photo in the newspaper that started all of this. "Marty started that?"

"Sure did. She was doing it by herself at first. Just showing up with water and baked goods and sandwiches and such. It only got more organized later."

"Was she there the morning you found Vicky Gustafson in the river?"

Tom's eyes shift and harden, and I know I'm stepping on fragile ground. But he answers me. "Of course, she was. That was a terrible day, and she was there to support our crews as they recovered—" He stops himself and considers me.

"I see dead people, Tom. You can talk about death in front of me."

He seems to accept this. "When we recovered Vicky," he finishes.

"I see," I say, but something about this new piece of information bothers me. I can't quite put my finger on it, and Tom has turned away before I can figure it out.

"Hey Chief," I call after him. "How did you know Vicky fell asleep at the wheel?" I ask when he turns back.

His brow wrinkles. "Well, once it was pointed out to us it made perfect sense."

"Who pointed it out?"

"Well, Marty did actually. She's a smart woman. Noticed it right away. Felt awful about how overworked our teachers are."

"I'm sure she does," I say and thank him for the information before heading out the door.

It isn't until I step out onto the sidewalk, the fading spring sun heating the side of my face, that the thoughts that have been circling just out of reach fall into place.

I hadn't heard the name Caledonia. I had *read* it.

Caledonia was the name on the boat in the photograph in the foyer of Pruitt Camp. It would have been Marty's ancestors in that photograph. Marty was the one to suggest Vicky had fallen asleep at the wheel.

Marty.

Not Bob.

I've been so fixated on the blinking light I'm about to crash the plane.

Instead of going back to my office, I find my SUV where I've parked it along the street. Tossing my forgotten Reuben into the passenger seat, I back out as quickly as possible. I head home, my heart thumping in my chest. I drive with an intent I don't usually possess, and the fifteen-minute drive takes me ten.

I don't think about whether or not Logan will be home, and it occurs to me I haven't been back into the house since the night I discovered my husband's infidelity. I wonder if I should feel something about this, but I don't have room inside of me for anything else except the need to get into the house.

I park in the drive and vault from the SUV. The back door is locked, but it doesn't slow me down. The house is silent around me and smells musty as though no one has been here for days. It hits me that now that I know about the affair, Logan might be staying with Heather in Albany. I don't take time to think about that.

I sprint through the kitchen and up the stairs to the bedroom. The bed is made with the same set of sheets I'd put on it last week, another confirmation Logan hasn't been here. He detests making the bed. I go for the headboard, and my finger finds the biometric lock on my gun safe. There's a small click, and the front panel slides open.

My heart slows only when my fingers wrap around my Baretta M9. I let the weight of it sit in my palm before I check the clip and the safety and put it in the back waistband of my jeans, pulling my sweater down over it.

This is not the safest way to carry a loaded firearm, but I'm in a hurry. I need to get to Carmen and tell her what I've missed.

It's not until I step down into the kitchen that I realize I've made a fatal error.

I didn't lock the back door behind me.

I know this because Marty Pruitt is standing in my kitchen, and she's holding a very scary-looking knife.

Twenty-Five

Reflexively I hold up my hands, and too late, I realize I've lost the moment when I could have safely pulled my gun. Now Marty is too close with that knife she's waving in front of her, and her expression does not suggest she's going to play nice.

"We found your little love note in the paper," she hisses at the same moment Bob appears behind her in the door. He's holding a length of rope, and my mind starts tripping through all the possibilities of what's going to happen next. Marty waves the knife. "Tie her up, goddamnit."

She practically yells this at Bob, and I see now his stark expression in the fading light of the kitchen. He stumbles, and the energy around him vibrates precariously. Bob wasn't telling me to get off his property that day at the cabin. He was warning me away.

From his murderous wife.

"There's a switch for the overhead light right there." I gesture with an elbow as Marty yells again.

"Shut up. You don't get to talk anymore."

I ignore this. "You killed Vicky when she uncovered your embezzling scheme."

The knife takes a dangerous thrust forward as my words strike a nerve, and I lurch backward.

"Tie her up," Marty nearly spits out.

Bob switches on the light, and the room is flooded in white light. Marty flinches but keeps the knife steady. Together they back me up to a chair at the table in the dining alcove, and I sit obediently.

The gun in my waistband is cold against my back, and I draw a slow, steadying breath, biding my time.

Bob bends over me, looping the rope through the back of the chair and around my waist, pulling my arms back behind me. It's then I realize he'll find the gun, and I try not to freeze.

Only he does.

Standing behind me, bent over, his hands on my hands as he ties them behind my back, he hesitates, the rope stilling against my wrists. I know in that moment he's seen the bulge of the gun underneath my sweater.

My heart thuds madly, and if I had the ability, I'd probably start shaking. But everything has condensed to that space between me and Bob and the gun in my waistband.

And then he's tying my hands and straightening, the moment blinked into history. I test my hands. They're loose. With a little fiddling, I could be free. I want to meet Bob's gaze, but I don't dare.

"So, Martha Pruitt, how did you kill Vicky Gustafson?" I say loudly and clearly.

Her lips thin angrily before she answers. "I didn't kill Vicky Gustafson. It was an accident. She came to the lodge asking questions she shouldn't have. I just wanted her off my property, and I gave her a little push." The knife tip flickers as if in memory.

Unbidden, I picture the Pruitt Lodge and the row of boulders along the path to the rear entrance. That must be where Vicky died, and that's why her energy is so strong there.

"You pushed her into the boulders at your back door. That's why her head was smashed in like that."

Marty starts. "What are you talking about?"

"I saw her. I saw Vicky. Her head was smashed in like a pumpkin on Halloween. It was you who did that to her."

"It's not my fault she fell," Marty says. "She was clumsy, and she was trespassing. She got what she deserved."

"And that's why Lisa ran away. She knew about the embezzlement, and she knew you murdered Vicky Gustafson." I stop, dread filling me. "She *saw* you kill Vicky."

The knife steadies in Marty's hand. "Lisa is dead. Someone kidnapped her and killed her. Your little ad in the paper was pointless."

That day when I'd stumbled out of the police department it occurred to me Lisa wouldn't have a digital footprint. She grew up before social media and online profiles, and she would have stayed off the internet to keep herself safe. But there was one way she was sure to keep tabs on what was happening back home.

With a subscription to the local newspaper.

I'd put an ad in the help wanted section that simply read *Lisa Reynolds, it's time to come home. You're needed here. See Della James, Bellegrave Historical Society.*

This was before I knew Marty Pruitt was the killer, of course. Otherwise, I might not have been so blatant.

"Lisa is alive."

Marty scoffs. "You're a hoax, you know that? You don't see the dead." But her voice doesn't sound like she believes it.

"I do actually, and your daughter is not dead."

Bob stands on the other side of the island, his hands hanging uselessly at his sides now that he's done the one thing his wife has asked of him. He's wearing a blue, unzipped windbreaker, and it makes him look even more watery than he is. Suddenly I picture him as he was in the halls at Bellegrave High, and I wonder how I ever mistook him for a murderer.

"I was focusing on the blinking light," I murmur, hating myself again.

"What?" Marty sneers.

"Lisa isn't dead?" Bob's voice is weak, almost breathless.

"She's not." I look directly at him, willing my voice to keep him going. "Her energy isn't anywhere around your home, a place she was very much connected to in life. Even if she didn't die there, she would have left an imprint, an echo of her energy that would remain there. But she didn't because she's still alive."

Marty laughs incredulously. "You're making this up. How many movies did you watch to create this make-believe world you enjoy lording over everyone?"

"It's not make-believe. Lisa is alive, and she'll be back as soon as she gets my note. She'll be able to expose you even if you kill me tonight."

Marty stills, considering this. "You're lying. You might believe what you're saying, but it's just not true. Lisa is dead and good riddance. She was just another mouth to feed." She's slowly been inching her way toward me, and now she shakes the tip of the knife almost in my face. "Do you know how expensive it is to keep up a camp like Pruitt? To buy the right clothes? To possess the right cars? To attend the right functions?" She gestures wildly with the knife, swinging it behind her and back, and I lunge as far back in my seat as I can, the rope grating against the bare flesh at my wrists. "And my stupid husband amounted to nothing more than a public school official." This is said with enough vehemence to suggest Bob has committed the worst crime imaginable. "I tried to keep it up. Show I was a good mother, a good wife. I asked you to include Bob in Founder's Day. I asked you to contact Lisa. I did all those things to keep up appearances. What else was I supposed to do?"

"Get a job like a normal person?" I suggest.

Marty's mouth forms a wordless *O*, and I know that despite the fact I have uncovered her greatest secret, it's this remark that will get me killed.

"How dare you!" she screams, lifting the knife high into the air with both hands.

It's at this moment that I know I'm going to die. It's a funny thing staring your own death in the face when you've stared into the death of so many others. Two things trap themselves inside of my spinning thoughts. That I'll be leaving Henry. This thought is easy to reckon with because I know my dad will love him like I do.

The second thought isn't so easy. It's about Logan and all the things we have left unfinished between us.

It's this thought that propels me recklessly forward. "That's why you asked Tom to stop the investigation. If Lisa was found, she could tell everyone what you did. Everyone would know you failed. You weren't the perfect wife. You weren't the perfect citizen of Bellegrave. You weren't perfect." I drop my voice, my gaze steady as I pitch this one straight home, knowing it's the incendiary that will end my own life. "You weren't a good mother."

It's there. The flash of outrage, the spark ignited. It's all reflected right there in her eyes. She lifts the knife higher, the white light of the kitchen flashing along its deadly edge, but I don't close my eyes. I look death straight in the face as I've always done.

"Mom."

The word is soft and calm, coming from the back door of the cottage. I don't need to turn to see that it's Lisa Reynolds because just then Marty turns away from me, the knife loose in her hands, her expression morphing into shocked horror at the sight of her daughter standing there.

It's a reunion I will watch later when I give the police the footage from the home security system I installed after Kevin Gustafson showed up at my house.

But for now, I take the opportunity to tug my hands from their bindings, pull out my gun, and shoot Marty Pruitt.

TWENTY-SIX

I don't shoot to kill. I'm not stupid.

I shoot her in the foot.

She screams and drops the knife as Lisa tackles her. I pry myself loose of the rest of my bindings with one hand, keeping my gun trained on Marty, still screaming as she rolls on the floor, trying to hold her foot as Lisa tries to stem the bleeding with the dish towel she's pulled off the oven door. Bob crumples against the kitchen island, tears streaming down his face as he mutters his daughter's name over and over again. I fish out my phone from my jeans' back pocket and call 911 as I stumble from the house.

I'm standing in the driveway, hands high in the air, my gun at my feet when help arrives. I made dispatch aware that shots had been fired, and I don't want to be shot by arriving law enforcement. A marked Bellegrave police car arrives first, and an officer I don't recognize takes me into custody, handcuffing me and placing me in the back of his car before bagging my gun.

I sit there until Carmen and Chief Tom arrive. The driveway to the small cottage is filled with emergency vehicles by then. I saw Marty brought out on a stretcher minutes earlier, still screaming, a thick bandage wrapped around her foot. Through the window, I see Bob. He sits in the back of another ambulance, blanket around his shoulders as an EMT provides oxygen. His daughter holds him, one arm over the blanket.

It's Chief Tom who wrenches open the squad car door and hauls me out.

"New York is a Castle Doctrine state, and I want to speak to a lawyer," I say before I realize he's unlocking my cuffs.

"Jesus, Della," he says. "I told you not to be a hero."

I point to the cottage. "She came after me. I was defending myself."

"Do you know how much paperwork I'm going to have to do now?"

I've never seen Chief Tom this angry, and I feel bad.

"I'm sorry," I say. "I didn't mean—"

Carmen steps up beside the chief then. "Tom, I've got this. Why don't you go and talk to all those reporters that just showed up?"

I glance down the access road where, sure enough, camera lights swarm in the now inky black like possessed fireflies.

Tom grumbles but disappears down the road.

Carmen tugs on my shoulder. "Come on. EMTs need to check you."

"I'm fine." I pull out of her grasp.

She turns her second-grade-teacher stare on me. "Delia Ann, if you think I'm going to tell your mother you didn't get checked by a medical professional after a near-death experience, you must think I'm crazy."

"You called my mom?"

Carmen nods as I let her lead me away. "Of course, I did. As soon as I heard the call come over dispatch. I checked in with them again when I heard you were okay. I didn't want them to worry." She glances at me, and there's a smirk on her face. "Your dad says he has the bail money ready."

I frown in response and climb into the back of one of the open ambulances. My blood pressure is checked, and I'm prodded for broken bones.

Carmen stands on the ground, looking up at me. "If you had waited just an hour, I could have told you Caledonia Consulting was still registered with the state. It only listed one managing partner. A Martha Pruitt of Bellegrave, New York."

I blink. "That's it?"

Carmen purses her lips as she nods. "She didn't do much to conceal who was behind the company. I think she truly believed she'd never get caught."

"She confessed to Vicky's murder," I say. I nod toward the house. "I can pull the camera footage of her confession from my security system."

Carmen's smile is proud now. "Look at you, Inspector Gadget."

I grin in response, but our little back and forth ends abruptly when Lisa Reynolds steps into the glow of the ambulance's lights.

"Della James is Della Hopewell. I thought that might be you."

I know my lips are parted, and I'm staring, but I'm suddenly back in seventh grade, frozen in awe of the upper-class goddess with the red-gold hair who has deigned to speak to me. Her smile is just like I remember it. Her hair the same golden red with streaks of paler strands now, and there are fine lines around her eyes and mouth. But it's still her. And hanging from one shoulder is a denim backpack gone soft and faded with age.

"Hi, Lisa," I manage. "I'm sorry we had to meet like this but thank you for coming home when you did."

"I'm just glad I got here in time. When I saw your ad in

the *Bulletin*, I searched your name and found your photo with your profile on the historical society's website. I recognized you right away and knew I had to get home."

Carmen has shifted slightly behind Lisa. She looks straight at me now and mouths the words *she recognized you* as her eyes grow wide in amazement.

I smile. "I'm sorry I had to make you come back. This must be hard for you."

She glances behind her to where her father still sits on the edge of the ambulance, an oxygen mask pressed to his face.

"I think it's going to be okay," Lisa says now.

The energy around Bob shivers, and I know for a while it will be. He's not quite ready to go just yet.

Carmen says, "Hey there, Lisa. I'm Carmen Neil." She holds up her badge. "I just have a little question for you." She laughs lightly before going cold, her eyes on Lisa with that second-grade-teacher stare. "Where the hell did you go?"

Lisa flushes and looks at the ground. "New York," she says. "I saw my mother kill Vicky that night, and I was scared. I know what Vicky uncovered. She told me about Caledonia Consulting. She was worried about me. I couldn't trust anyone after she was gone, so I arranged my own escape."

She speaks so calmly, but I try to imagine an eighteen-year-old having the wherewithal to stage their own murder.

"How did you do it?" I ask, not afraid to show my admiration.

"It was easy back then," she says with a shrug, pulling her denim backpack higher on her shoulder. "Remember this was before the internet really took off. I stole a bag of my own blood from the blood drive the last time I donated. I used it to plant the evidence in my car, and then I hiked to the train station in Westport. Bought a ticket with cash and never came back. Once I was in New York, I found a way to get forged documents so I could get a job, and then—" She shrugs away thirty years. "That was it."

"You hiked to Westport?" Carmen asks.

Lisa shrugs again. "It only took two days. I was careful to camp off trail though in case anyone should come looking for me along the trails." She shakes her head. "I know I should have stayed and told someone what I saw, but I just couldn't. Vicky was—" For the first time, Lisa's calm veneer cracks. "Vicky was important to me, and I knew as long as I was safe I would someday have a chance to make it right."

"You hiked to Westport?" Carmen asks again.

"Forty some miles aren't much when you're running for your life," Lisa says.

"I suppose it isn't," Carmen mumbles. Now she turns her glare on me. "What is this I'm hearing about an ad in the paper?"

"That's your fault," I say as the EMT rips the blood pressure cuff off my arm. "That day in your office I figured out how to contact Lisa. She wouldn't have been on the internet. It wasn't safe. But she would have had a subscription to the local paper to see what was going on back home."

Lisa's smile is sure. "Read it every morning on my phone."

"What do you do now?" I ask. "In New York, I mean?"

She smiles harder now, and I can see the girl she used to be. "I'm a music teacher. I worked my way through undergrad. It took a while because I had to work two jobs, but I did it. I've been a teacher for almost fifteen years now." She says this with the kind of pride that's easy to envy. She glances at the badge Carmen has likely forgotten she's holding. "I suppose you'll need to ask me more questions. I'd like a lawyer present when you do."

Carmen shakes her head as if rousing herself from memories. "Don't worry about that right now. Let's go check on your dad, and then we'll do a formal questioning at the station later."

Lisa turns back toward her dad, but Carmen pauses long enough to give me one last look.

"The freaking backpack," she hisses, pointing at Lisa's retreating back. She rolls her eyes and walks away, and I can't help but smile.

The EMT tells me I'm good to go, and I climb down from the ambulance. I'm not sure where I'm supposed to be or if I'm still being arrested, so I make my way toward the cottage, trying to get out of the way of law enforcement and first responders that scurry about the scene like ants on a disturbed anthill.

"Della!"

The shout comes from behind me, and at first, I can't quite believe it's the voice I'm hearing. I turn and see it's him, Logan, my husband, pushing against the restraining arms of a uniformed officer.

"This is my house," Logan is saying. "That's my wife." He pulls an arm free, his finger pointing with such authority directly at me.

Something strange happens inside of me when I hear him call me his wife, when I see him struggling to get to me.

"It's all right," I call to the officer. "He *is* my husband," I confirm.

I speak the words not as a clarification to the officer but as a clarification to myself, and a roiling inside of me settles to a soft boil.

When Logan reaches me, he pulls me into his arms, and for a minute, I want to be there, safe against him, his warmth spreading through me, dispelling the cold and the fear and the dead.

But only for a minute.

I gently push him away.

When he meets my gaze, his brow concerned, I say, "Where have you been?"

His frown is immediate. "I was in Albany. Firing a client."

I study his face, seeing the passage of time in the wrinkles and creases, and wonder at how much of the time mapped on his face we've spent together.

"Firing a client or breaking up with your girlfriend?" I don't say it accusingly. I just ask the question.

"Firing a client," he says again with such conviction I'm forced to meet his gaze.

"Really?" I don't want to hope. I don't want to believe only to be proven wrong once more.

"Oh God, Della," he says. He reaches for me, but I step back out of his grasp. Pain flashes across his face. I know he needs to touch me, to ground himself through physical touch, but I can't give him that right now. "I didn't even know what was happening until I saw that look on your face that night in the kitchen," he goes on.

This pushes through the chaos in my mind, and I'm able to speak. "You didn't *know*?"

He gestures to where the patio is somewhere behind me, his mouth open without words, his eyes a mask of disbelief. "She was wearing shoes when she went *out* to the patio. She took her shoes off *outside*." He drops his arms. "That's not the point. The point is I let myself drift. After our daughter died, I became numb. I couldn't feel anything. And I wanted to feel. I wanted to feel for you, and I—" His voice cuts off, and he turns away but not before I see the tears in his eyes. I touch him then, just a brief hand to his arm, pulling him back to me. He looks over my head as he gathers himself and says, "I wanted to be alive for you, and I couldn't figure out how. I thought it was hopeless, and it got so bad I disappeared." His voice cuts off again, and the pain tightens on his face. "I just disappeared," he repeats, and I think of what Carmen told me about Sundays at Farley's when Logan stopped meeting Raymond there.

I wait, not giving him the comfort of filling the silence.

It's several beats of my heart before he speaks again. "I think on some level I realized Heather was attracted to me. I could feel myself coming back to life, but it didn't feel right. It felt—" He stops, but this time I can tell he's searching for the right word. "Wrong. I knew it was wrong, but I didn't. I just thought if I could come back to life I would be able to finally come back to you." He meets my gaze then, his expression broken and earnest.

The reason why relationships are difficult is because we want them to be black and white. But they're not. They're gray. Humans are too changeable for anything easy. And just like Carmen once said, it's easier when there's someone to blame, and in a relationship, it's too easy to blame the other person. But a relationship by its very definition gives equal opportunity to both parties to screw it up.

"I should have said something." My voice is quieter than I mean it to be, and I know he couldn't hear me over the sound of the emergency scene happening around us. I clear my throat. "I should have said something," I repeat. "I should have told you how I was feeling, and I didn't. I couldn't see past my own pain, and it blinded me to yours." Now I'm the one crying, but my tears are silent, the hurt too old and worn to make a sound. "I wasted so much time."

He reaches for me again but stops himself as if he can sense if he touches me right now, I'll shatter. "Della, I made the choice I did that day in the hospital because I was selfish. I didn't think I could live life alone without our daughter. I needed you there with me." The tears fall gently down his cheeks now, and I watch them fall, knowing the same tears stain my cheeks.

"But I did leave you alone, Logan. I withdrew into myself,

and I left you out there all alone." My voice wobbles, the tears constricting it.

"No, you didn't," he says, reaching for me, his fingers curling into air as the tears come harder. He shakes his head. "You didn't leave, Della. You stayed. Even when I gave you every reason to go, and that means we have a chance now." He pauses, licks his lips, and blinks rapidly as if trying to clear the tears from his eyes. When he meets my gaze again, his expression is determined and true. "I want the chance to know you, Della. And I hope you want the chance to know me too."

His face is a canvas of emergency lights and past hurts, but it's also a mirror in which I see our future, and for the first time, I don't see only despair there.

I take a step toward him. "I don't know," I answer honestly. "I think I need to do some work on myself before I can know. I've already taken so much of your time. Do you think you can give me a little more to figure this out?"

He flinches, and I know he was expecting me to refuse him, to push him away, to tell him we're over, and the relief has made him react physically. But we're not over. We're tied together by something greater than ourselves, and although we'll do our best to test it, it can't be broken.

He swallows, hard, and looks at me. "I'll give you all the time in the world, Della James."

I smile as the tears dry on my cheeks, and my husband returns my smile with one of his own before his expression falters.

"Are you being arrested?" he asks.

I look around us, at the ambulances with their silent lights, EMTs still tending to Bob and Lisa, Chief Tom and Carmen fending off the reporters on the access road, and the officers streaming in and out of our house in their white Tyvek suits and booties.

"I don't know. Maybe. Probably." I look at my husband. "Do you know any good lawyers?"

Twenty-Seven

My phone beeps with a text just as I unload the picnic tote from the back of the SUV. I pause long enough to pull my phone from my pocket and see it's a text from Daryl. It's a selfie, the same one he sends me every day now, standing in front of the Gale Center, thumbs up. It's his way of saying he's attended an AA meeting that day.

I send him back two thumbs-up emojis and put the phone back in my pocket.

Daryl's not only attending AA meetings, he's also started trauma-informed therapy for his PTSD after I gave him the card for Carmen's therapist.

Martha Pruitt has been formally charged with the murder of Victoria Gustafson, thanks to the video footage taken from my security cameras, which captured her confession, one I made incredibly clear with my direct questions stating her name and the name of the victim loud enough for the cameras to pick it up. A team of forensic accountants have descended on the Bellegrave School District business office, and a charge of embezzlement is expected any day now.

Marty's foot only required three stitches, and she is expected to make a full recovery before her trial starts.

Lisa Reynolds is making plans to move home at the end of the school year to take care of her dad who has moved into one of the new apartments out by the supermarket. It has a view of the hills around Bear Lake and no stairs, which Bob likes. Lisa's and Bob's cases with the state are still pending, but Chief Tom says it's unlikely charges will be pressed due to Bob's health and the length of time that has passed since Lisa faked her own murder and the evidence that Martha Pruitt coerced them both to act.

Camp Pruitt has been seized by the state and will likely be sold at some point to recover what can be recovered in the embezzlement case. David Knolls has already started a petition to try to save it from falling into private hands.

I was not arrested the night Marty Pruitt tried to kill me. Chief Tom reviewed the security camera video on my phone, which showed a clear case of Castle Doctrine. The case was given to the district attorney who chose not to press charges in light of such clear evidence, and I thanked the powers that be Kevin Gustafson showed up at my house that day.

I ran into Gretchen Gustafson at the Super Duper on Wednesday, pushing a cart filled with what looked like the fixings for an entire Thanksgiving dinner.

"Kevin's coming home," she said. "And he's bringing Tyler." She said this with a strange glassiness in her eyes that might have been unshed tears on anyone else. I assumed Tyler was Kevin's husband and gave Gretchen a hug.

They're planning a tribute for Vicky this summer. I offered them the use of Lady Josephine Lodge.

Founder's Day is tomorrow. I should be at the lodge right now going through the last-minute checklist, but Allie shooed me away when Logan and Henry arrived to pick me up.

Logan appears around the side of the SUV then, Henry

straining on his leash. He wants nothing more than to be let free, but we're too close to the county highway here. It would be dangerous to let him roam.

We carry the picnic tote up the hill to where I first saw Vicky Gustafson. Logan spreads a blanket on the grass, and we sit. I give Henry a peanut butter enrichment toy, and he settles reluctantly. Logan and I eat the meal I packed in near silence.

Things are awkward between us, but the weight that has been suffocating our marriage for thirteen years is gone. Like a brain that's had a stroke, we're working on repairing the synapses that connect us to each other, and like most things, all it needs is time.

The hillside that afternoon is peaceful, the air composed of the sounds of the wind in the tall grass, water falling along the rocks in the river below, and Henry licking peanut butter off his nose. There's nothing else. Just the sound of the wind and the water and the world, and the rest is at peace.

We sit there until the sun begins to set, and I think of what will come tomorrow, Founder's Day, and the official start of summer in Bellegrave. The tourists will flood in, and the local shops will be overrun by people from Albany, Utica, and even New York. The lodge will see visitors from open to close, and this will be my last chance to sit in peace and quiet for a few months. But that's okay for a time. Those tourists will keep Bellegrave alive through another cold winter. We must only remember that everything has a time.

When the air turns cool, we gather the picnic stuff into the tote. Logan takes Henry's leash and the blanket we sat on as I pull the tote onto my shoulder and head for the car.

Henry thinks he's finally being let loose and jumps on Logan in sheer joy.

Logan laughs and tells him down. He points to the car where I'm waiting and says to Henry, "Follow Mom."

Acknowledgments

As it is with any book, this one was not written alone.

I owe a huge debt of gratitude to New York State Trooper Chad Boyland. Even if modern day law kept getting in the way of a good story. Any mistakes in Della's story are my own and made for the purpose of good storytelling.

Thanks also to Stacey Gordon. I know far more about the New York State School Teachers' Retirement System than I ever wanted to know.

Special thanks to artist Kate Homan. It takes a creative to provide the kind of support a creative needs in the middle of a project. Thank you, my friend.

The internet has given me many wonderful things including my husband, but it's also given me some friendships I could never have imagined. Mel (@sommelierofspice), May (@dissociationbybooks), and Lee (@leeleelovesbooks), you gave me the courage to make this leap. Thank you will never be enough.

And finally, thanks go to my dogs who waited very patiently every time I just needed to finish that chapter before going for a walk. You are the goodest good dogs.

About the Author

Jessica Ann is the author of over 25 novels of historical fiction and fantasy.

A magna cum laude graduate of the University at Albany, Jessica has degrees in history and English with Honors in creative writing.

Jessica lives in New Hampshire where, if she's not at her writing desk, she's probably letting the dog out. Again.

For more, visit her website at authorjessicaann.com.